M000044388

'Teestaji, I do not have words to expr importance in my life. You have immense courage. Your action compel us to bow our heads in respect. We feel proud to be seen with you and our cause has been your cause and the cause of all peace loving individuals. I salute you.'

ZAKIA JAFRI

'तीस्ता हमारी पीढ़ी और आने वाली पीढ़ी के लिए संघर्ष का एक उदाहरण हैं, और यह किताब उस लड़ाई का एक हथियार।'

कन्हैया कुमार

'Teesta's political memoir is her extended statement of happenings – a blow by blow account. This has been necessary to counter the many versions that are afloat. She provides a coherent and well-integrated narrative. Despite the calumny that is sought to be heaped on her in an effort to break her spirit, she will I am sure continue her struggle to reveal what happened. One wishes there were more such citizens.'

ROMILA THAPAR

'I have known the most courageous work of Teesta Setalvad.
The trust of victims is the most crucial test for any human rights defender.
Teesta is a pillar of strength to those who suffered in the Gujarat tragedy.'

ASMA JAHANGIR

'तीस्ता सीतलवाड के होने का मतलब एक बहादुर औरत
का पब्लिक स्फियर में होना है, जिससे देश की सांप्रदायिक ताक़तों और उनके
सबसे बड़े आका को डर लगता है। तीस्ता को बर्बाद करने के लिए सत्ता ने
जितनी ताक़त झोंक रखी है, वही है तीस्ता होने का मतलब। तीस्ता होने का
मतलब राष्ट्र की उस समावेशी परिभाषा में एक नागरिक होना है, जिसकी सबसे
सुचिन्तित परिभाषा बाबा साहेब डॉ भीमराव आंबेडकर ने दी है।'

दिलीप मंडल

'Teesta has annoyed the powers that be and earned the wrath
of powerful forces. She is a committed and determined social and
political activist who belongs to the vanishing tribe of those who take the road
less travelled, and pay the price – physical, financial and emotional –
of their choice and strive for the realization of their ideas.'

CHAMAN LAL, IPS

FOOT SOLDIER
OF THE CONSTITUTION

TEESTA SETALVAD

FOOT SOLDIER
OF THE CONSTITUTION

A MEMOIR

Published in January 2017.
Reprinted, with corrections, in February 2017.
Reprinted May 2017, January 2018.

LeftWord Books
2254/2A Shadi Khampur
New Ranjit Nagar
New Delhi 110008
INDIA

LeftWord Books is the publishing division of
Naya Rasta Publishers Pvt. Ltd.

leftword.com

ISBN 978-93-80118-43-7

Cover photo by Tamara Setalvad-Anand

Printed and bound by Chaman Enterprises, Delhi

To Atul, my father,

whose rock-solid sense of

right, wrong and what is just

energises me still,

strong and sustaining,

even as the next

blow is dealt

To rejuvenated spaces,

neighbourhoods, people and realities,

Juhu, Mumbai, Ahmedabad, Delhi, India,

everywhere that stubbornly still hold out

against the insidious assault on

right, fair, just and equal

To the conviction that we shall,

indeed, one day,

win

CONTENTS

OPENING

The work in Gujarat for which people know me, Teesta Setalvad, did not just begin overnight. It did not begin out of nowhere. It grew from a lifetime of public interventions for accountability and justice. What has driven me is a much larger conviction – the need for India and our institutions to be just.

I was brought up with the fierce belief that all Indians are born equal and should be able to experience that equality. My first year as a journalist at Russi Karanjia's *The Daily* in 1983 allowed me to bear witness to the sheer viciousness and waste of communal violence. My work pushed me to search, in both writing and action, for recompense towards the victims for the wrongs inflicted upon them.

Born the elder child in a privileged home that breathed the law and constitutional values, this recompense for me was instinctively to be sought from the courts. But, as I grew politically, I realized that more was needed than the courts alone. The legal approach had to be backed and supported by a wider consciousness that legitimized the legal interventions within the portals of justice. Nonetheless, romantic and naïve as I sound, I believed – and continue to believe – that the Court is a mechanism to right the wrongs inflicted by the government, the executive arm of the State. The Rule of Law must be premised on a philosophy. In the Indian scheme of things, this philosophy, this template, can only be the vision that is encapsulated in the Indian Constitution. The Court, I feel, should be the honest arbiter to provide recompense for the lives, dignity and properties cruelly and hatefully snatched away from the victims of violence.

A basic question should be asked of every citizen: in the case of targeted and vicious violence, should the victims not get justice – both in seeing the guilty perpetrators punished as also in being given reparation, with dignity for the losses suffered?

Russi Karanjia, the editor of *The Daily*, was a fair employer of journalists – not only as far as salaries and bonuses were concerned, but also in how he encouraged us reporters. Each month, we would get food coupons that could be encashed in a few of the restaurants around Cowasjee Patel Street: Moti for earthy dhaba fare, Mocambo for the fancier stuff (going here would have eaten substantially more into the monthly ration of coupons!). Down the road was our *paqnwalla* where on one occasion – defied by my colleagues at work – I dared to, straight-faced, ask for a *palangtod paan*! (a *paan* that is supposed to also have sprinklings of an aphrodisiac!). Those were heady times, stepping into a profession and being allowed to flower! At the time the News Editor for *The Daily* was P. N. V. Nair. I had just finished my Bachelor of Arts Philosophy Honours paper in June 1983 when Karanjia hired me. Covering the communal violence in my city, Bombay, in 1984 shaped me. It was my first direct experience of communal violence. *1984*, the title of George Orwell's horrifying and dystopian novel depicting a grim anti-life or anti-utopia came to life across India. Several catastrophic upheavals, that have become markers of public memory, took place in 1984 across the country.

Many of these events find resonance in the country even today. In June 1984, the government sent the Indian army to flush out Jarnail Singh Bhindranwale and his supporters out of the Harminder Singh Complex within Amritsar's Golden Temple. This was Operation Blue Star. In a gory form of retaliation, possibly for this act, two of her Sikh bodyguards assassinated Indira Gandhi in her own home. The anti-Sikh pogrom that followed in Delhi – and elsewhere – ran from 1 November to 3 November, leaving a death toll of over three thousand Sikhs (the figure from all over India was higher). It was a monumental event. Justice for the victims is as elusive now as it was on 3 November. A month later – in December 1984 – the Bhopal Gas Leak from the Union Carbide factory led to the death of at least ten thousand people. These events remain in the public memory.

What has receded from our public understanding is the Bhiwandi (Bombay) rounds of communal violence in May 1984. Few outside Bombay remember these events, and young people are utterly unfamiliar with them. For me, the Bhiwandi conflict had a tremendous impact: shaping me professionally and allowing me to properly prioritize my concerns.

It was during the Bhiwandi conflict that I grew close to my colleague Javed Anand, a special correspondent at *The Daily*. Javed was covering the Bhiwandi violence. I was in other parts of Mumbai – at Jogeshwari and Cheetah Camp (Gowandi). These riots – I remember writing – had an East-West divide (this was different in the 1992-93 post-Babri Masjid demolition pogrom in Bombay when the class backgrounds of those who were targeted did not seem to matter; even rich Muslims faced the wrath of well armed mobs in the latter pogrom). In 1984, the fault line in Bombay ran along the Bombay Western railway line, which goes from South Bombay (Churchgate) to Virar. The western side of Bombay escaped the wrath of the killers in 1984, which is why the people who lived there could, conveniently, look the other way. This was not the case between December 1992 and January 1993, when the attackers rampaged across the city.

One incident at Cheetah Camp (Gowandi) stays with me. It showcases the partisan brutality of the Bombay police – until then much acclaimed as the most professional force in the country. The

Cheetah Camp was a hutment colony set up during the Emergency in 1976. The people who lived here had previously made their homes in the Janata Colony, a large area whose residents had been relocated when the Bhabha Atomic Research Centre expanded. Most of the fifty-five thousand residents came from South India – from places such as Kerala and Tamil Nadu. Almost all were Christians and Muslims. This was also an area where rival criminal gangs operated. The police, who had an antagonistic relationship with this Camp swooped in suddenly and violently, killing eight people. I was present when the arm of a poor Muslim man was chopped off; the vision of it dangling is a bruised – if faded – memory. I remember setting aside all squeamishness to rush him – with others – to the Sion Hospital. One young (23 year old) zari worker from Cheetah Camp named Abdullah was writing a letter to a friend in Kuwait, telling him about the birth of his child. He died as he wrote. The police burst into his room and dragged him out. Two policemen held him while a third shot at him. He tried to crawl back into his hut, but the police prevented him by locking the door of his hut. They left him in a drain where Abdullah died.

Javed had been covering the Bhiwandi violence. He was shaken by the brutal killing – the burning to death of some twenty-six or twenty-seven people who had sought refuge inside a barn in Ansari Bagh. Neither the Police Chiefs of Bhiwandi nor Bombay were able to respond to the magnitude of the violence nor could they correct the gross failures even by their own men. Every evening, after being bruised and battered while on this coverage and submitting our 'copy', Javed and I would meet to exchange notes and share the burden of this personally witnessed brutality. Those moments of sharing our experiences produced not only healing, but as importantly, a bond that has endured till now – thirty-two years later. We were startled by the increasingly visible partisan behaviour of the police and other agencies responsible for law and order. The issue of the partisan police would become central to our work after 1992-93 and it would come into even starker focus after the Gujarat genocidal pogrom of 2002. In the 1992-1993 round of violence in Bombay, after the demolition of the Babri Masjid, evidence of communal bias reflected in police behaviour finds detailed mention not just in media reports but in the testimony of the then additional commissioner of police V. N. Deshmukh before the Srikrishna·Commission.

Bal Thackeray and his band of violent rabble-rousers of the inappropriately named Shiv Sena had been found guilty of stoking communal violence in the Bhiwandi-Mahad Jalgaon riots of May 1970.[1] Rabid anti-Muslim rhetoric had foregrounded the massacre. In the Shiv Sena's mobilization techniques *against the outsiders*, Bombay's South Indians and Gujaratis bore the brunt of the violence. Nevertheless, from its inception, the Shiv Sena's founding and legitimising principle rested on its anti-Muslim rhetoric – a point established by the Justice Madon Commission report. Many members of the Rashtriya Swayamsevak Sangh (RSS) joined the Shiv Sena after 1970. It was, however, not until the 1984 Bhiwandi bloodletting that the Shiv Sena made its public allegiance to the politics of Hindutva and to the establishment of the Hindu Rashtra.

The 1980s saw a sharp surge in communal violence. Mid-way through the decade, the fangs of Hindutva politics became more and more visible on the Indian political scene. Central government figures showed an increase in the bouts of communal violence: In the year 1980 there were 427 recorded incidents (official figures); in 1981, 319; in 1982, 474; in 1983, 500. The number of lives lost was also sharply increasing from 196 in 1981 to 238 in 1982 and 1,143 in 1983.

[1] Justice D. P. Madon, Report of the Commission of Inquiry into the Communal Disturbances at Bhiwandi, Jalgaon and Mahad in May 1970, excerpted in Sabrang, *Damning Verdict* (Mumbai: Sabrang Communications, 1998).

Hidden away from these figures was the Nellie massacre in Assam that took place in February 1983. The six hundred page Tewary Commission Report showed that the death toll in that massacre was 2072 (although Appendix F of the report suggests that the actual number was 3023). It has always bothered me that the RSS-BJP reflexively respond to every accusation about the 2002 Gujarat pogrom by pointing their fingers at the Congress Party for its role in the 1984 anti-Sikh violence. This comparison, of course, always puts the Congress on the defensive – for the Congress' responsibility is unquestionable.[2] The RSS-BJP, however, never raises the question of the Nellie massacre. Perhaps this is because of their Hindutva worldview – since the vast majority of lives lost in Assam were Muslims.

Media persons, especially the shrill and savvy television anchors (but increasingly also our newspapers as well) fail to puncture the RSS-BJP paradigm: doing so would require a thorough exploration into the historiography of communal violence, a course that I believe should become compulsory for students and practitioners of mass communications. However, as the hold of the extreme right on power and authority has grown, media colleges and colleges of journalism that had begun – tentatively – explorations of such a course designed by us, halted the practice in their tracks.

*   *   *   *   *

I was born in a family of Gujaratis, of Gujarati lawyers to be precise. Gujarat was always a part of me, though we were proud migrants to Bombay. My great grandfather left his government job in Ahmedabad within four days of taking his post to study law in Bombay. My mother, who was related to my father prior to

[2] PUCL-PUDR, *Who are the Guilty? Report of a joint inquiry into the causes and impact of the riots in Delhi from 31 October to 10 November 1984*, Delhi: PUCL-PUDR, 1984.

their marriage, had a paternal uncle in Ahmedabad, who was the Advocate General of Gujarat for twenty-six years. Once or twice a year, we would visit Ma's mama and mami. Lawyers surrounded me during my childhood. My father – Atul – was also a lawyer. He would sometimes visit Gujarat for work at the High Court, flying down while we took the overnight Gujarat Mail train from Bombay Central to Ahmedabad. My mother would take us (my sister Amili and me) to the wholesale garment bazaar – Dhalgarwaad – within the old city. But my father would not ignore the delights of Ahmedabad while he was with us. A keen and committed non-vegetarian would never return home to Juhu without a few dozen *kuccha* samosas from *Famous* in the old city. They are mutton mince samosas with minutely chopped green chillies, onions and mint leaves – delicious and memorable.

That Gujarat – of lawyers, garment bazaars and samosas – seemed distant when I came back to report for *The Daily* and later *Indian Express* and *Business India*. In July 1991, I did a statewide report on the surge of entrenched communal conflict in Gujarat. The BJP had, at that time, taken out the *Rath Yatra* – the chariot of L. K. Advani that threatened violence and desired votes. I visited six or seven cities within the state, taking the intra-city trains. One conversation on one of these train journeys has remained with me. It was with a Gujarati Hindu businessman. He was gleeful at the growing popularity of the aggressive and violent organizations that owed their allegiance to the ideology of Hindutva and the Hindu Rashtra. 'They have removed the fear within the Gujarati to fight and kill, to take to violence. That is good', he said. He was referring to the unashamed espousal and use of arms and violence against the imputed 'minority enemy', the Other of Gujarat.

An incident from 1991, while reporting for *Business India*, remains sharply etched in my mind. Following my father Atul's lead, I wanted to return to Bombay from my harrowing ten-day sojourn with some of Ahmedabad's famous mutton samosas. I had a final interview with Rauf Waliullah in the old city. We talked at length about the challenges before the Muslim community, whose rich role included contributions to business, economic exchanges, artisan trades and other professions that had been crudely stereotyped as 'criminal'. For instance, Raufsaab explained how, despite the fact that there were Muslims among professionals, artists and academics in Gujarat, the fact that some political parties patronized the infamous smuggler-lord Abdul Latif (who won elections even while in prison) became an easy way to stigmatize an entire community. He was passionate about the need for a questioning, rational leadership among Muslims who would demand their space as a matter of right, not patronage. It was a long and valuable conversation that helped me understand the details of life in urban Gujarat. As I was leaving, I said that I wanted to get some of the famous *Bera* samosas. Raufsaab was thrilled: I had to be a real Ahmadavadi if I knew and loved those samosas, he said. He had an interview scheduled with the BBC just after mine. I left the old city and drove to the airport. It is merely a forty-minute flight to Bombay. I landed and reached home, just 20 minutes away. In the hour and twenty minutes that it took me to get from Ahmedabad to Bombay, from the interview with Raufsaab to my house in Juhu – a life ended. The phone rang and I was told that Raufsaab had been shot dead. It seemed as though a sane and moderate voice who challenged the way things operated and who defied stereotypes could not be tolerated. This wider understanding of what was happening in that state and its society, came from what Raufsaab told me and other experiences and conversations that focused my mind on the issues within Gujarat.

Between the businessman's words and Raufsaab's death, I detected a strong undercurrent of anti-Muslim sentiment in Gujarat. It was far cruder in the state than anywhere else in the country at that time. Gujarat is my heritage. And yet, because of our migratory history, my family was unashamedly Bombayite. A popular family narrative speaks of how the Setalvads preferred the cosmopolitanism of Bombay to the parochialism of 'Amdavad'. I speak better Marathi than Gujarati, though thanks to my paternal grandmother, Vimla Setalvad – also a writer of short stories — I am familiar with the Gujarati script. This familiarity came in handy as I ploughed through First Information Reports (FIRs) and Charge Sheets related to the investigations into the massacres of 2002.

Part of the explanation for the palpable anti-Muslim sentiment in the 1990s can be found in the methodical work of the RSS and the Vishwa Hindu Parishad (VHP) from the 1980s onwards. The RSS and the VHP build on all kinds of false resentments to generate an anger of the Hindu middle-class and sections of the Hindu working-class. One of the issues they played on was the obvious business *savoir-faire* of the Bohras and the Khojas – only a fraction of the ten per cent-odd of the state's Muslim population – because they had a visible presence in the commercial world. Their success made them objects of social and political envy. Such an explanation though is not sufficient to fully describe the growth in anti-Muslim sentiment. In April 2000, I had published a story in *Communalism Combat* – the journal Javed and I began in 1993 – to offer a richer explanation for this cultural turn. We called that cover story – *Face to Face with Fascism*. The details of the abuse of state power and the linkage between the RSS-VHP thugs and elected officials tell the story. Here is an extract from my article:

The Ahmedabad Municipal Corporation (AMC) has cancelled most non-Hindu holidays. It was forced to restore the Good Friday holiday last year after an outcry from the Christian community. Muslim children studying in several schools in Ahmedabad city, (Vishwabharati, Naujeevan, Karmasheela, J. P. High, B. R. Somani and Prakash High schools are some examples) have to routinely give examinations on the day of Ramzan Id or Bakri Id; Muslim teachers, too, are compelled to remain present for invigilation! At the Hindu-managed V. R. Somani and Bhakta Vallabh schools, where 95 per cent of students are Muslim but teachers are Hindu, the teachers have adopted a unique technique of getting at their students: they just do not teach.

Bakri Id on March 17 this year was used, as it has been over the past couple of years, by the BJP-RSS-VHP squads to provoke the Muslim minority by deliberate emphasis on the Cow Protection Act. The commissioner of police and the municipal commissioner issued a joint appeal to all citizens asking them to be mindful of the provisions of the act. The VHP and Bajrang Dal members decided to act as informants of the police.

Despite a clear message from the state government that the question of dealing with any violation of the law should be left entirely to the police, VHP men in Ahmedabad forced nakabandis on Muslims taking animals for slaughter. In one such incident on the night of March 15, a young Muslim narrowly escaped the swords and lathis of the VHP. But another Muslim boy, Yasin Mohammad, was attacked by the VHP team with knives and swords, simply because his domestic servant, the pillion rider on the scooter, was carrying a bundle of grass. Yasin Mohammad collapsed on the spot. Policemen present did nothing to prevent the murder. It resulted in a Muslim and Hindu mob gathering at Dariapur and communal tension growing. Rajendra Vyas, a VHP worker, was present when the murder took place.[3]

Now – since 2014 – we have entered the age of the Gau Rakshaks or Cow Taliban. What is happening across India was pioneered in

[3] Teesta Setalvad, 'Face-to-Face with Fascism', *Communalism Combat*, April 2000.

Gujarat sixteen years ago. It is where the Cow Taliban mastered its acts of targeted violence. The increasingly commercialized and corporate sponsored media has today, however little time for in-depth, background checks. When we were trained by the best minds in the field, Beat Journalism meant that you did your research, looked back and forth of the issue, and interrogated the present with insights drawn through the experience and patterns of the past. If the media today were doing just that, we would begin to see where the mind-sets that so easily lynch and humiliate – be it Dadri, Latehar or Una — first experimented with their feats: in Gujarat. The culture of impunity bred there has now spread its vice like grip through the length and breadth of the country.

Gujarat had been and remains critical to the RSS-VHP project of building a Hindu Rashtra. This project is laid out clearly in 'Guru' M. S. Golwalkar's *Bunch of Thoughts*, published in 1966 (and now widely available as a free download from the RSS website). Golwalkar addresses the members of the Constituent Assembly, who wrote the Constitution that is the law of the land,

> They forgot that here was already a full-fledged ancient nation of the Hindus and the various communities, which were living in the country, were here either as guests, the Jews and Paris, or as invaders, the Muslim and Christians. They never faced the question how all such heterogeneous groups could be called as children of the soil merely because, by an accident, they happened to reside in a common territory under the rule of a common enemy.

The RSS leader wrote of being 'sufficiently fooled until now by their exhortation that we Hindus, who are having a great philosophy of human brotherhood, catholicity of spirit and so on, should not narrow ourselves by the talk of Hindu Nationalism and all such "communal," "medieval" and "reactionary" ideas!' He said that those who believed in Hindutva 'must be able to see through the game and revert to the truth of our nationalism as an ancient fact and the Hindus being the national society of Bharat, so clearly restated by our revered founder when he decided the word "Rashtriya" for our organization. We must once again stand up in our true and full stature and boldly assert that we shall elevate the Hindu National Life in Bharat to the peak of glory and honour which has been its birth right since hoary time.'

The Indian Constitution poses a serious problem for the aspirants of the Hindu Rashtra. Since the 1980s, especially since the RSS-backed BJP came to power in Gujarat in 1995, the Hindu Right has subverted in a crude and brazen manner the institutions of the state and society to its agenda. They have produced borders within cities, by cleansing religious communities from neighbourhoods and segregating spaces that had been – at least – convivial. Even the Courts became places of bitter contestations. The Gujarati Muslims – ten per cent of the population of the state – live a peculiarly constrained existence, in ghettos of place and mind. This has not shaken up us Indians as I believe it should have. We have been numb to this produced reality. Slowly, creepingly, ghettoization is becoming a rigid reality in western India. A 'siege mentality' is settling into sections of the Indian Muslim population. The ghetto existence has become the favoured choice for existence. For many, though, thankfully this is not the case.

While I was with *Business India*, I covered two incidents that revealed the depth of this new reality. In the area of Narangpura in Ahmedabad, a Muslim family was an eyesore. How could they have moved from the old city to such an upwardly mobile area? At the height of the 1991 violence, some Gujarati Hindu women pushed one Mr. Shaikh (an employee with ONGC) of one such family off a second floor balcony to his death. 'Muslims not wanted here', said his crushed body. In July 2016, as the editors to this memoir despaired of my finalising the transcript, I narrated this incident to a packed audience in Nagpur. At the end of the public lecture, the correspondent of *The Times of India* (Shishir Arya), visibly shaken, asked to have a word with me. As we snatched a few minutes away from the crowd, he said that he was sixteen years old, in Standard X, when the incident I had narrated at Narangpura had taken place. He added a footnote to the anecdote that caused a chill in the bones: he said that year, after Shaikh had been so brutally killed, the women who 'did it' had been publicly felicitated during the annual 'Navratri/Garba' celebrations before Dussehra. The brutalization of the Hindu faith had begun with slow and steady steps in Gujarat.

In Ahmedabad, the VHP used to distribute a map of the city that depicted their utopia. They coloured one part of the city – the old part – green and they coloured the new part of the city *bhagwa* (saffron). The point was for the saffron part to overwhelm the green part, for Hindus to overrun Muslims. Hindu-Muslim and inter-caste marriages also became targets for the brutality of the fascists. They imposed their code on who could live where, and how they must live. Quite a few young couples – who had been in inter-caste and inter-communal marriages – moved into the safe Muslim ghetto.

Today, the old city of Ahmedabad has become premium real estate. Gujaratis being Gujaratis, business opportunities have been seized: old havelis are now spruced up as tradition and heritage becomes chic. Even the Crime Branch Office at Gaekwad Haveli has been cleaned up, with a much more breezy look. Never mind that in the dark chambers, behind the light of the external architecture, terrible things happen. I have by now spent quite a few hours in that building undergoing 'interrogations'.

By August 1993, Javed and I became disillusioned with the mainstream media. It did not give us room to do in-depth coverage *before* and *after* the violent conflicts, such as communal violence. Its spaces seemed circumscribed by and limited to coverage of the sensational violence during the conflict. No context was allowed – nothing that would explain how communal violence erupted and what was its fallout: little space for investigations into the pursuit of justice. Javed quit his job as Deputy Editor at *Sunday Observer* and I left my job as Senior Correspondent with *Business India.* We launched Sabrang Communications and its well-remembered magazine – *Communalism Combat.* Yet, even after the launch of *Combat,* our role in complementing the existing media was not insignificant. One key cover interview, of February 1995 with a serving police officer, 'No Riot Can Last For More Than 24 Hours Unless the State Wants it to Continue' was picked up in an abbreviated form by thirty-four Indian publications, including *The Times of India.* The officer was Vibuthi Narain Rai. Constitutional expert, H. M. Seervai's scathing legal opinion written exclusively for us on the shameful verdict of the Bombay High Court in exonerating Thackeray and *Saamna* for the hate speech against Indian Muslims also received wide coverage ('Crime and Punishment', January 1995). There are several more such examples.

After the launch of *Combat* in 1992-93, my visits and work in Gujarat became more intense. At *Communalism Combat* we did five cover stories on the communal politics of Gujarat long before the 2002 massacres. I authored all these. It was through this intense investigative reporting and analysis that a statewide base of sources – even from within the Gujarat police – developed and eventually contributed to the quality and genuine inputs received by the magazine once the tragedy at Godhra happened on 27 February 2002. Titles of the five cover stories provide a window into the kind of work we were doing at *Communalism Combat,*

Welcome to Hindu Rashtra (August 1998).
Conversions (January 1999).
How Textbooks Teach Prejudice (October 1999).
Face to Face with Fascism (April 2000).
Split Wide Open (February 2001).

The last story (before 2002) was on the aftermath of the Bhuj earthquake. It documented how the state authorities discriminated along caste and religious lines when distributing earthquake relief. Here is an example of the kind of reporting I was doing in those days,

> Hajaram is an upstart *ajrak* painter whose natural inclination for colour and blocks led him to acquire the technique of the famous *ajrak* printing from the local Khatris of the famed Dhamadka, 54 kilometres from Bhuj. Even before the devastation wrought by the earthquake, his village, like scores of others in Kutch, had been reeling under a two–year–old drought, forcing people to buy food from the market, a practice alien to them.
>
> Today, Hajaram is a survivor of the quake that has left him bereft of five close family members. His workshop and home are badly damaged. Dazed and disoriented with the loss of family, home and workplace, he is busy trying to rebuild his own life and that of 150 other similarly affected families.
>
> Everything is under rubble. No heavy machinery has been brought to clear the debris. Dhamadka is on the international map thanks to the *ajrak* printers. But, today, no attention is being paid to the vibrant *karigars* who have brought the region fame and richness.[4]

In 1999, through my work with school education and textbooks, KHOJ, we had done a detailed study on the Social Study textbooks

---

[4] Teesta Setalvad, 'Split Wide Open', *Communalism Combat*, February 2001.

of Gujarat. This was published in *Communalism Combat* – 'How Textbooks Teach Prejudice', October 1999. Appalling passages that were not simply historically incorrect but were exclusionist caused the Parliament to appoint a Committee of Parliamentarians to review the texts and the passages that were found to be problematic. Needless to say these textbooks continued to be used for over fifteen years. In a paper I read at SAHMAT's Communalization of Education seminar not long after, I drew a cause and effect relationship between the content of teaching within the class and the creation of an ever ready, partisan group of persons that could be called to action, like a mob, whenever the need arose. Now, while those texts are no longer used, Dinanath Batra's Compulsory Reading in 42,000 state schools is several degrees worse. Batra's readings became part of the curriculum after 2014, with Modi in power in Delhi.

The journeys made to report these stories were intense and challenging. One question hung over me as I formulated my ideas and thoughts: *why Gujarat*? Many insights surrounded me – did this have to do with the Hindu Rashtra's project of burying the legacy of Gandhi? They killed Gandhi on 30 January 1948 after four previous attempts on his life. What were they trying to kill? Perhaps his philosophy of non-violence, weaned during his early years in Gujarat? Carriers of the brutal and violent ideology of Hindutva had often talked openly of the need to discredit and demolish Constitutional governance. Perhaps they wanted to do so first in the land of Gandhi's birth and childhood? How did modern India accept and live with this brazen subversion of the Constitution and refuse to see the dangerous signals coming from Ahmedabad and all of Gujarat?

❖   ❖   ❖   ❖   ❖

The phone did not stop ringing that Wednesday. From about 9 a.m. on 27 February 2002 till months afterwards, the ringing was relentless and ceaseless. Gujarat has twenty-five districts. I had travelled across many of these before 2002 and many of the reports and exposes in *Communalism Combat* and elsewhere had resulted in some administrative action for the victims and survivors of previous communal events. Perhaps it was because of this history and the trust that built up as a consequence that the people across Gujarat connected with me immediately when things fell apart so tragically in 2002.

This was the day of the Godhra incident.

My mobile phone number was the same as it is today. It was being shared as a response number among many survivors and apprehensive citizens in many districts in Gujarat. The calls were frantic. Panicked voices hoped that help would come, particularly protection from the police. Cold and unresponsive, the police had not moved – assuredly with external pressure on their officers. Many knew I was the Editor of *Communalism Combat* and it would not take me too long to understand what had happened in Gujarat and to envisage what was in store. The cost of one call on the mobile phone was expensive – Rs. 21-22 per minute. But the mobile phone was to become a boon for the victims and survivors as well as human rights activists and journalists. It also became a tool to track the operations of the perpetrators as the mobile phone records of all those in power were submitted in a CD as evidence before the Nanavati-Shah Commission (five lakh phone call records) by a serving police officer, Rahul Sharma (August 2004).

These phone calls to me were the first source of information. Even before the news came on television I received absolutely distraught calls. Both Muslims and Hindus were fearful of what might follow. Some were actual witnesses of the train burning. They said that a terrible incident had happened in Godhra and everyone's concern and fear was that there would be huge repercussions. They were palpably seeing and feeling the atmosphere building up all around.

These were very worried calls. Eighty-five to ninety per cent were from persons who belong to the minority community. They came from far corners of the state, from Dahod, Rajpimpla, Ahmedabad, Vadodara, Himmatnagar, Sabarkantha, and Panchmahal District (of which Godhra is the district headquarters). People were watching the events in Godhra through incessant television coverage. The burning of the S-6 Sabarmati Coach had taken place between 7:50 and 8:20 a.m., and since then, thanks to the internet and television, the news – however digested – had spread like wildfire. My notepad from 27-28 February is still with me. It tells a story by itself.

I was frantic, obsessed. These calls continued the next day and the next. Ahmedabad was specially targeted on 28 February. The bodies of many of the dead Godhra victims were brought in a motor cavalcade to Ahmedabad – an act that has never been sufficiently interrogated. The decision to take the charred and maimed bodies of Godhra victims in a motor cavalcade to Ahmedabad was made at the highest political level in the state. The decision was taken at the Collectorate at Godhra where Jaideep Patel (Gujarat state General Secretary for the VHP) had been allowed to be present. Before this, post mortems of those burned in the Coach took place out in the open – at the railway yard – as Health Minister, Ashok Bhatt and later even the chief minister were present. There are strict procedures for holding post mortems and each and all of these – including allowing photographs to be taken – were violated that day. The VHP's Jaideep Patel officially took charge of the bodies at Godhra. This and other acts were revelatory of the government/VHP nexus. These burned unidentified corpses were paraded in two parallel funeral processions as mobs of frenzied RSS men and women got inspired or instigated into going on the rampage in Ahmedabad the next day, February 28. 'Acharya' Giriraj Kishore was given a special police escort to reach the spot of these processions. The government could spare the police for Kishore but not for the victims. They said that there were not sufficient police to defend the people of Naroda Patiya and Gulberg. Smaller cities and district centres (even villages) such as Sardarpura, Mehsana, Vishnagar, Eral, Vadodara, Sesan, Patan, Randhikpur, Sanjeli, Kidiad, Panchmahals, Vadodara came under fire on 1 March.

My next step was to act like a mini control room. I had done similar work in Bombay during the riots in 1992-93 along with other colleagues like Nikhil Wagle, Sajid Rashid, P. Sainath and Javed. I spoke to several senior police officers who I knew from my reporting in Gujarat as well as a few whom I did not know. I had many simultaneous purposes for making these calls.

First, I urged the police to give immediate protection to areas that were being mobbed. There were no less than four or five dozen locations in Ahmedabad city where the mobs operated on 28 February. The next day, 1 March, the armed groups traversed a frighteningly large number of far-flung villages in fourteen to nineteen districts of the state. Like a woman possessed, I spoke to virtually every senior level officer in Ahmedabad, Vadodara and even SPs of districts in the first three days. It was as if planned and vicious mayhem had been unleashed. Areas of Ahmedabad not prone to communal violence, where Muslims lived in a relative minority, were the specific targets.

The officials I called were mere names then: K. Chakravarthi (DGP, Gujarat), P. C. Pande (Commissioner, Ahmedabad), P. B. Gondia (DCP, Zone IV Ahmedabad), D. D. Tuteja (Commissioner, Vadodara), K. K. Mysorewala (PI Naroda), Raju Bhargava (SP

Godhra), Subha Rao (Chief Secretary), and Ashok Narayan (Home Secretary). Little did I realize then that years later these men were to assume a sharper focus as their specific roles in a wider conspiracy played out. That conspiracy emerged when we unearthed documentation in our investigations and later in the documentary evidence accessed by us in the Zakia Jafri case. I called up Commissioner P. C. Pande, the senior most police officer responsible for maintenance of law and order in Ahmedabad. At that time I called him because of the immense responsibility of his post. Later, as evidence unfolded, he would emerge as one of the villains of the piece. People called him and other senior officers because of the expectation that they should uphold the police's Constitutional oath: to protect lives and provide help in areas of targeted violence.

The second reason to call the police officers was to try and get relief to the same areas, to nudge and push the Delhi political class (mainly the opposition) to intervene, to acknowledge the violence, to flag the orchestration of the violence. I called the media, political leaders, the Army helpline – everyone and anyone who I thought could help the victims. I called the police again and again. There was little social media then. But there was television. Godhra and Gujarat 2002, were in a sense, the first full-fledged televized bout of communal frenzy and violence.

In the heat of a frantic emergency response, it takes a few hours for a pattern to sink in. Even now I remember calls coming from Naroda, Chamanpura, Gomtipur and different parts of Ahmedabad. I recall how even the office of the Muslim-owned *Gujarat Today* was targeted in the old city. I called a police officer friend stationed at a nearby rural district and yelled and wept about the fate of the assistant editor and his family who lived in the building – in fear for their lives. Finally, due to the merciful intervention at a higher level, the assistant editor and his family were saved. Each tip-off led to another round of phone calls. The violence spread with great rapidity and with little resistance. The tone of the calls was fearful, apprehensive and frantic. In villages and districts, the people who called witnessed – first hand – the orchestrated mobilization of RSS-VHP-Bajrang Dal and BJP cadres immediately after Godhra. My phone records carry in them the geography of the attacks – the route of the violence from one end of Gujarat to another.

These early phone calls already told us that the attacks were widespread and they came through a planned mobilization. Years later, between 2010-13, in the evidence gathering during the Zakia Jafri case, and after a hard fought legal battle (where we were opposed by the Special Investigation Team – SIT), we received twenty-three thousand pages of documentary evidence in sixty-four box files. These documents clearly show the planned nature of the attacks. Each day I received seven to eight hundred phone calls. These calls came from across the state. Those first-hand testimonies can now be substantiated by state information bureau (SIB) reports and police control room (PCR) logs on the careful, organized, virulent mobilization of perpetrators in every district. The mobilization was ostensibly based on revenge for what had happened at Godhra. Evidence gathered by us subsequently re-established what *Communalism Combat* courageously reported in its seminal issue on the *Gujarat Genocide* in March-April 2002. The sustained and intense communal mobilization had produced the conditions for a communal holocaust in the state. We showed that the tragic deaths of the fifty-nine people in the S-6 Sabarmati Express at Godhra on 27 February 2002 was only the much-needed trigger for that violence. Retaliation for Godhra had been planned weeks and months before the actual event. It was not a spontaneous outpouring of anger as much as a pretext for violence that had become – in a sense – necessary for the forces of the

Hindu Right. Five years later, in 2007, *Tehelka*'s Operation Kalank, led by Ashish Khetan, added further evidence of how bombs, guns and other weaponry had been brought to Gujarat from Punjab, Rajasthan and other states months before the mass killings.[5] This evidence is part of the criminal revision application in the Gujarat High Court – the famed *Zakia Jafri vs. SIT* case, which seeks to establish a chain of command responsibility for the violence and assign criminal culpability to men politically and administratively responsible for acts of commission and omission.

The killings in Godhra took place on 27 February – a Wednesday. The next day, organized groups with close ties to the RSS attacked Naroda Patiya, Chamanpura – where the Gulberg Society is located, Gomtipur and other parts of Ahmedabad. The village massacres took place on 1 March – a Friday – soon after the *Jumma Namaaz*, the Friday prayers. In broad daylight, the attackers went after Muslims in villages in the districts of Pandharwada, Sabarkantha, Banaskantha, Mehsana, Anand, Dahod, Patan, Ahmedabad rural, Vadodara rural and targeted villages such as Odh, Sesan, Kidiad, Randhikpur, Prantij, Dardarpura, Eral, Fatehpur, Sanjeli, and Dairol. The patterns were similar – large mobs seemed to be under the direction of men on motorcycles, with the local police unwilling or unable to act because of orders from the local political class. The mobs came well armed with weapons and chemicals. They also used gas cylinders, which make ferocious bombs. Those villages and districts that defied this pattern were sent 'bangles' as spoof gifts – the archetypical patriarchal motif that labels men as 'sissies'.

My obsession was not only to get the media to cover the crimes, but also to get a parliamentary delegation to Gujarat. This delegation was essential, because by the afternoon of 27 February

[5] 'Gujarat 2002: The Truth in the Words of the Men Who Did It', *Tehelka*, 7 November 2007 and Ashish Khetan, 'The Sting in the Story', *Tehelka*, 8 September 2012.

and certainly by the evening of 28 February it appeared as if there was complete complicity in the violence by the state apparatus. The state was just not responding in a positive way. We sensed it in all the conversations with journalists in Gujarat and with other very seasoned people on the ground. Gujarat is not new to communal problems. There have been communal incidents in Gujarat before, but in each case the police responded. They picked up the phone. They talked. They sent the forces to vulnerable areas. In 2002, things looked and felt different. Either the police was not responding or was seen going to another destination – sometimes in the opposite direction from where the distress calls were coming. This was the state of affairs in at least eleven districts. We were repeatedly calling the police but they were not helping. It cannot be a mere coincidence when a similar chilling pattern repeats itself over eleven to twelve districts.

On Friday – March 1 – there was an aborted visit by a parliamentary delegation to Gujarat. Then on Sunday – March 3 – I remember addressing a press conference in the old SAHMAT office in Delhi. The idea was to communicate to the country the sheer spread of the violence and depth of subversion by the state. The National Democratic Alliance (NDA) government, led by the BJP, ruled at the centre. It was not at all receptive to the kind of intervention we were making at that time. Nonetheless, I decided to approach the government as a citizen and an activist. Veteran Gandhian social activist Nirmala Deshpande got me in touch with the President of India's secretariat as well as senior officials in Gandhinagar and Delhi. I was constantly feeding information to the President's secretariat. The President of India at that time was K. R. Narayanan. He would later say that as President, 'Gujarat was a major example of helplessness.'[6] He would also say, 'I feel there

---

[6] 'I felt helpless during Gujarat riots: Narayanan', *Times of India*, 13 August 2002.

was a conspiracy involving the state and central governments behind the Gujarat riots'.[7] I returned to Gujarat on 4 March.

* * * * *

On 4 March, I was at a relief camp – the Shah Alam Camp – in Ahmedabad. I remember meeting women from Naroda Patiya there. They described how they had reached the Dargah. They came with no clothes on when they were rescued, a humiliation easy to recount but difficult to comprehend. This meant that they had been stripped off clothes and dignity, apart from being physically abused for the better part of twelve to thirteen hours. They sat in that state at the police station. They had been brought back bloodied, bruised and naked to the camp.

The holy war of the RSS-VHP-BJP had been unleashed at the Gangotri and Gomti housing societies. These residential barracks carried the names of Mai Ganga, the holy river of Sanatani Hindus. They were not spared. On 28 February, the attackers unleashed their violence on the daily wage earning women and their daughters and mothers. Women and men from the entire neighbourhood watched the 'spectacle' of iron rods and worse being used to sever young, innocent Muslim girls and women. A chillingly cruel, militarized and dastardly face of Hindu dharma was being manifested; a thousand times worse than what I had witnessed on Bombay's streets in 1992-93. With each such multiplication of organized horror, humiliation and crime, the shape of the Hindu Rashtra was being drawn with more and more sharpness.

I had my spiral diary with an orange cover and a tape recorder with me. Never one to fully trust the technology demon, I have always relied on my copious notes and collaborative memory. I

---

[7] George Iype, 'The Rediff Interview/Former President K. R. Narayanan', *Rediff*, 7 March 2005.

remember meeting this shopkeeper who had seen his wife raped. She was one of those rare survivors of the gendered violence. Most of the others were killed after being brutalized. He remained by her side even as she testified in Court. I met this woman who had seen young girls getting raped. It was horrible – the words, the accounts, the monotony of detail. What does it take for a survivor to recount the story again and again and again?

We met in groups. Many of the survivors by now had become very close to me. I met the Gulberg survivors in Dariyakan Ghumbat camp. Ironically the man who was running this camp was always seen by survivors as a BJP-supporting Muslim, yet he still ran the camp very well.

It is chilling that for seven to eight hours a whole locality was actually enjoying a massacre. When you have women and men celebrating the persistent hounding and killing, including the daylight rapes of the young girls and women, it is reflective of the public space *before and after the macabre violence.* Such violence also qualitatively affects the space in that area. For Rupabehn Mody and Sairabehn, the loss of a loved son each was and is as bruising as the fact that their precious society – 'Gulberg' - had, for several hours on 28 February been host to bloodletting and daylight rapes. It is too painful even to speak or write about. At Naroda Patiya, one hundred and twenty-six people were killed on 28 February, although the official charge sheet says ninety-six. A well in a nearby field became their grave for months.

The sheer viciousness of the attacks - at least in Ahmedabad – had even paralysed activist friends within the city. In Vadodara a dogged citizen's effort with Trupti Shah and Rohit Prajapati held the fort, but they were unable to visit the outlying districts. Several times each day we would speak and exchange notes. The extent of culpability and partisanship revealed by the mainstream Gujarati media has been documented in the Editor's Guild Report of 2002 (*Rights and Wrongs*).[8] *Jansatta, Kutch Mitra* and *Gujarat Today*, a Muslim-owned Gujarati paper, did the only responsible reporting in the vernacular. *Sandesh* and *Gujarat Samachar* beat the government's drum with the worst form of propaganda. It was quite frightening in the way perceptions had been built up about what had happened in Godhra, since seventy per cent of Gujaratis got their news from these partisan publications.

Dozens of young men and women would come to me in the camps – embittered and angry. I thought: how do we redeem their faith in the country, in the people, in their neighbourhoods? I gave a particularly bitter young man a small tape recorder and asked him to tell the story of what happened. It was from such documentation that justice would have to come.

A fortnight after the Central Bureau of Investigation (CBI), instigated by the Modi government, raided my home in 2015, I re-visited the Shah-e-Alam Dargah. I hadn't been there for many years. The Zakia Jafri case hearings in the Gujarat High Court had concluded for the day. It was twilight. My driver – Aiyyub – recalled how he had spent weeks at the Dargah as a refugee. There was something magical that evening in 2015 – the light, the lit candles, the sparkling water within the Dargah, the vast expanse of space. I remember looking around and taking it all in, with a deep, deep breath. It seemed so vast then. In 2002, with twelve thousand five hundred people crammed together, the Dargah had shrunk. It had been crowded and stifling, with the cries of women and children and a bare-boned silence from the men. There was nothing magical then. The memory of that time interrupted my reverie.

* * * * *

[8] Aakar Patel, Dileep Padgaonkar, B. G. Verghese, *Rights and Wrongs: Ordeal by Fire in the Killing Fields of Gujarat: Editors Guild Fact-Finding Mission Report*, New Delhi: Editors Guild of India, 2002.

From the night of 4 March till early April, I travelled across the districts of Gujarat. I would travel all day and return late at night to Father Cedric Prakash's centre in Ahmedabad – *Prashant*, which is the Jesuit Centre for Human Rights, Justice and Peace. Dog-tired, I would write and send out 'News Alerts', which became the primary source of information all over the country. The media – even if it did a good job – covered only bits and pieces of events, not the entire story. It could not make sense of the fact that an orchestrated mob had been used by the government in power. The experience I had from the earlier riots as well as from my work in *Communalism Combat* allowed me to have a fuller understanding of the events. This is what we tried to convey in the 'News Alerts'. We sent these alerts to the President of India, to the Chief Justice of India, to Prime Minister Atal Bihari Vajpayee, to the leader of the opposition, to heads of every political party and to human rights organizations. The old *sabrang.com* website became our outlet to the world. I reported and wrote the alerts myself; then, Father Cedric and my friend Sushobha Barve would read and correct them. Wilfred D'Costa of Insaaf was also a signatory to many of them. All of us signed off on them before we sent them out into the world. Sushobha and I had worked together during the Bombay riots of the 1990s. She had come with me to Gujarat. Now Sushobha heads the Delhi-based Centre for Dialogue and Reconciliation. She has done a lot of work in Kashmir and India's North-East.

Here is a taste from one of the 'New Alerts' – this one from March 2002,

Around 6 p.m. this evening, the Vatwa police turned on a group of Muslims who had emerged after a plastic godown was burned down by aggressors living in the buildings across the relief camps. Two persons were killed, including a woman and a child and five others are injured, three of them seriously. Another person belonging to the minority community was stabbed in Ahmedabad this afternoon.

In nearby Himmatnagar district a mob of 5,000 set ablaze the Takiawala Masjid and a *dargah* before gutting down a hotel and a dozen shops also owned by the minority. Modassa, that had witnessed severe tensions yesterday, when eighty trucks owned by Muslims were torched, was not spared today either. The main market, Naushtakht bazar and Borwar were burned and destroyed. The local Muslims were terrorized as a mob attacking from all four sides was unchecked by the police even as it kept them terror-struck within. Proof if any were needed that the situation in Gujarat is *not under control;* in fact, it is a simmering pot of premeditated violence.[9]

By now, to us, the pattern was crystal clear. It is best described in this irate conversation I had with Major General Zameeruddin Shah, who was in charge of Army Operations in early March of 2002. His was one of the emergency response numbers given to me by Nirmaladidi. Since I had called him quite often he knew my voice and recognized my number. 'Why are the areas that you indicate in your calls where help is required at a different spot from where the local police are asking us (the Army) to go?' he challenged. I was silent for a few seconds and then I dared to query back, 'Sir which ones turn out to be correct: the ones I indicate or which the police do?' His utter silence gave me the answer and a bitter satisfaction.

Once the killings and displacement stopped, we began to closely observe the discriminatory distribution of the relief material across Gujarat. We had experienced this in Bombay in 1992-93. Between 10 and 18 January 1993, with the help of some Muslim youngsters, I taped the police wireless messages, where

---

[9] Teesta Setalvad, Fr. Cedric Prakash and Wilfred D'Costa, 'The Violence is Relentless', *Sabrang*, 20 March 2002.

the police abuse Muslims and 'instruct' relief teams not to go to the Muslim areas. This investigative exposure had been telecast on international channels, CNN and BBC, and on Indian news videos such as *Newstrack* and *Eyewitness*. That work began my journey into researching, investigating and tracking the issue of communal bias within our police, intelligence and security forces, a journey that continues to date.

Bias and State hostility towards a section of the people of Gujarat was unprecedented. The calculated and coordinated abdication of responsibility gave it direction, emanating as it did from the State's leadership. The instructions not to act and save lives, it was felt palpably, were coming from the very top. This had become clear to the Muslim survivors at least by the late afternoon of 28 February.

I remember a meeting at Jamalpur, attended by a wide section of the Muslim community. Jamalpur – in Ahmedabad district – is an interesting area, 'mixed' in religious composition. In earlier times the annual Rath Yatra celebration sparked communal violence. An elderly gentleman, tears brimming in his eyes as he recounted the horror of the days of the riots, was apprehensive of my adamant resolve to travel across the districts. One non-negotiable aspect of reporting on communal violence is to report only first-hand information – rumours and exaggerations play a diabolical and so misleading role. *Mathe par tilak aur bhagwa dupatta odhna beta*, he told me (put a bindi on your forehead and wear a saffron covering, he said – meaning to dress like a Hindu Gujarati). *Yeh log insaan nahi hain. Jiska khud khandaan nahi ho woh khandaan ko bacha ke rakhna, mehfooz rakhna kya jaane?* (These people are not human. He who does not have a family, what does he know about keeping families secure). The man without a family was a reference to Narendra Modi.

I went to Sardarpura, Godhra, Himmatnagar, and Ghodasar. I

would leave in a car early in the morning. There was no question of protection. That would come much later. Three drivers left me in villages saying that I would get killed and their own fate would not be any different if they continued to drive me around. For months, the highways belonged to the RSS and their storm troopers of the Bajrang Dal and the VHP. It was a sight to behold, and a sight to fear.

Along the highway, I saw gutted hotels – almost eleven hundred had been destroyed in this way. The Chiliya Muslim community owned many of these hotels. At the time I remember that the major industrial and business lobbies – FICCI, CII and Assocham – had put the approximate figure of Rs. 4,000 crore as damages to Muslim property. It could have been more than that. We reproduced these figures in our alerts.

I worked around the clock to complete our massive March-April 2002 issue of *Communalism Combat*. Its cover said 'Genocide. Gujarat 2002'. It could not have been more straightforward. The issue sought to and succeeded in ensuring an all-encompassing look at the victims and survivors of the Godhra arson and the post-Godhra killings. I had painstakingly reported from all districts of the state. The information collection was a mammoth task – conducted virtually single-handedly. Javed, my sister Amou, Rashmi, Uma and of course the indomitable team at our office who had seen us through thick and thin worked to put this issue together. We decided, after careful journalistic consideration, to reproduce photographs depicting the depth of violence perpetrated on human bodies, post-Godhra. We felt it was important to print and document the images depicting the depth of bestiality that had been allowed in the fervent hope that the exercise itself could initiate shame, acknowledgment and correction. In the Editor's Note, I wrote, 'Dead bodies no longer resembled human beings: they were reduced – whenever they had not been burned to ashes

– to a grotesque and pathetic sight that were a haunting reminder of the depth of hatred and the intense dehumanization that the politics of inherent superiority and exclusiveness generates.'

Flashes of images remain with me from my first visit to Naroda Patiya and Gulberg Society, two sites of the worst massacres on the first day of the carnage. The Society is on a one-acre plot in which Ehsan Jafrisaab lovingly constructed a society that now lay in ruins – strewn with thousands of broken glass bottles, crushed. Rubber stoppers used to shut these bottles were strewn all over. The smell of burned remains was overpowering. The homes of Sairabehn, Rupabehn, Firozbhai and Ehsansaab were so thoroughly burned that the cement in the walls had been seared down to where the internal electricity lines ran. Fans resembled gnarled witch-fingers. The homes in Vatva – just outside Ahmedabad – looked the same. Never have I seen such complete destruction by arson. On the human body it left no flesh. On inanimate objects, their bare skeleton. *Hamare log jal kar kabaab ban gaye* (Our people were reduced to grilled meat), Amina Aapa – who lived in Hussain Nagar, Naroda Patiya – said to me in the relief camps. *Chhat se sab kaam hua* (It was all over in a flash).[10] We saw remains of a white chemical powder, which we later learned had been used by the assailants. I collected several packets: they bore the name of Laxmi Industries, Hyderabad. Though this evidence was given to the Special Investigation Team (SIT), it has not been investigated. Nor has there been an investigation into the fact that areas of Ahmedabad that experienced the worst of the targeted violence on 28 February had all had a fortnight long 'LPG Gas shortage'. Gas cylinders were the weapon of choice for the attackers at Naroda and Gulberg.

Neither have the rapes that took place in the midst of the

[10] 'Naroda Gaon and Naroda Patiya', *Communalism Combat*, March-April 2002.

carnage received proper scrutiny. Women's organizations put the number at between three hundred and four hundred. The Gujarat's government admitted to only two hundred rapes. In only three cases – of Bilkis, Eral and Naroda Patiya case – there had been a judicial acknowledgment of the gendered violence. Though evidence of villages and towns being subject to targeted gender violence was documented, this has been swept away or buried from public memory. While the patterns of the violence were clearly meant to send a message of humiliation and subjugation to an entire community, the calculated erasure made that subjugation appear complete.

On 2 and 3 March, the mass cremation of one hundred and thirty three dismembered bits of bodies – the remains of the victims of the Naroda and Gulberg massacres – took place at a *kabrasthan*. Young Muslim men, themselves eye witness survivors, angry tears flowing, performed the last rites. It is yet another image that has been shrouded away from public memory. There was no Indian television coverage of this heart-rending burial. The camera teams of CNN recorded it, however.

* * * * *

One of the most disturbing aspects of the large scale anti-Muslim violence that convulsed Gujarat after February 27 was the brazen manner in which the state's police force wilfully abandoned its citizens to the depredations of homicidal mobs. Gujarat 2002 provides cold and horrific proof of the systematic hate in the minds of a substantial section of the state's police. They acted on principles hostile to the rule of law.

Police brutality was on full display in 2002, from 28 February to mid-May. Several instances of police firing at point blank range on Muslims, including minors, had been recounted by the survivors. Those among the police who remained true to their legal and constitutional duty and defended Muslim citizens were transferred (or punished). In mid-March 2002, twenty-seven such inappropriate transfers had taken place, including that of Rahul Sharma who as SP of Bhavnagar had risked his own life to keep the city and district safe. Rahul Sharma had even initiated action against communal leaders. The brazen transfer of honest and honourable officials sent a message from the state executive and the Home Minister (who was also the Chief Minister, namely Narendra Modi) down to the level of the police constable. Only a handful of officers now remain firm in their resolve not to bend before political pressure. Most do so. It has become the way things work.

Right after the Godhra tragedy, senior officers of the state had issued instructions for the prevention of escalation of violence. P. C. Pande (then Commissioner of Police, Ahmedabad) had even advised against bringing the bodies of those who died in Godhra to Ahmedabad. It would be a provocation for violence. Slowly, but surely, after the first meeting at the collectorate in Godhra, and then later at meetings at the Chief Minister's residence, a subtle and contrary message went out – standard operating procedures were suspended.

Official statistics gathered by me for *Communalism Combat* revealed this deliberately lax behaviour by the police. On 27 February 2002, only two men – Mohammed Islamil Jajluddin and Fareh Mohammed – were arrested under preventive detention laws for shouting slogans at Astodia (in Ahmedabad). These two men were Muslims. They were the only people to be arrested despite the fact that attacks against Muslims had broken out in many cities, including Ahmedabad, by the afternoon of 27 February. The police was consistent in its general inaction – except when it came to these two Muslim men. Evidence gathered by us in the Zakia Jafri case now shows how the state intelligence services had documented violent mobs attacking the minority community after they arrived from Godhra on the Sabarmati express (minus the burned coach) by the afternoon of 27 February. Sixteen FIRs registered by the Ahmedabad police on that day are documentary testimony to the fact that attacks had well and truly started. Yet the first signs of any preventive action in Ahmedabad were on the late night of 28 February after the macabre deeds were completed.

Commissioner of Police P. C. Pande's initial warnings were not implemented. They had been overturned by later orders. By 3 a.m. on 28 February, the bodies of the Godhra victims were brought to the Sola Civil hospital. RSS men and women had already gathered there, agitating an angry crowd. The police did not try to disperse them. The funeral procession was permitted. A Judge's car was attacked near Sola hospital. The police watched as the well armed and angry crowd went to attack Muslims and their homes. There was no attempt to stop them. On the other hand, the police did fire – but mainly at Muslim crowds. On February 28, in Ahmedabad, the police killed forty people – all Muslims – in police firing at Morarji Chowk and Charodia Chowk. By the third week of May 2002, of the one hundred and five people killed by police firing, seventy-five were Muslims.[11] Law Minister Arun Jaitley in the NDA-I government obfuscated on this issue in Parliament – refusing to provide the religion of those who had been killed by police fire.

On 1 March, Pande went on STAR TV, where he revealed the brazen attitude of the senior echelons of officers toward the violence. 'These people,' he said, 'they somehow get carried

---

[11] Vinay Menon, 'Cops admit killing more Muslims', *Hindustan Times*, 3 May 2002. As Raveen Thukral reported, 'The real numbers are probably likely to be far larger: major manipulations are alleged to have been done at the stage of carrying out autopsies.' 'The missing are dead, Gujarat toll may go up.' *Hindustan Times*, 24 May 2002.

away by the overall general sentiment. That's the whole trouble.' His constitutional conscience and duty had been set aside. This justification for criminal acts by policemen sent a strong message down the chain of command.

Police control rooms became places where ministers in the Modi government established themselves. BJP leader Ashok Bhatt, now dead, sat with Pande in the Ahmedabad control room for over three hours on 28 February. Bhatt had faced charges for murdering a police head constable in 1985 in Khadia, his Ahmedabad constituency. The stain of that allegation did not seem to bother Pande or the other senior officers. The ministers were most concerned when news came that Bhushan Bhatt, son of the BJP leader Ashok Bhatt, had been mobbed. Police personnel rushed out to rescue him. No such alacrity for the Muslims. In the Gandhinagar control room, the chief minister's right-hand man – I. K. Jadeja – stationed himself.

Victim survivors told me about an incident that involves Police Inspector K. K. Mysorewale of the Naroda Patiya police station. They said that not only did he burst tear gas shells at them – the victims – but that when they ran to him for protection, he said, *Jao, mere to upar se order hain* (Go away, my orders have come from above). For seventy-two hours, the mob was to be given free reign. Mysorewala escaped punitive action and instead has enjoyed promotions.[12]

At Gulberg Society, joint commissioner of police M. K. Tandon led a fully armed police vehicle away from the tense spot instead of leaving it on stand-by for the protection of the residents. When the violence started in Gulberg, former parliamentarian Ehsan Jafri made over several dozen-phone calls to the police and

---

[12] In August 2012, Judge Jyotsna Yagnik sharply criticized Mysorewala. 'While people were flocking the streets, Shri K. K. Mysorewala reported to the Control Room that "every is okay" (*khairiyat hai*). It was like, When Rome was burning, Nero was fiddling.'

to his fellow politicians. These went unanswered. Jafri was killed that day. In Vadodara, the police simply drove past as the Best Bakery was torched. In Sardarpura, SP A. Gehlot did his best to help the victims even as his junior officers staunchly refused to provide them protection. In Odh (Anand district), the fire brigade that could assist the victims was deliberately turned away by a mob as the local police watched. These stories are a few of a long list.

I had tracked and reported how positions within the police, especially the home guards, were filled with persons from the RSS-VHP, resulting in a complete infiltration of the force by persons owing allegiance to an ideology that does not subscribe to democracy and equality since at least year 2000. Any study or resolution within Gujarat will need to tackle seriously the issue of infiltration into the criminal justice system – police, home guards, and public prosecutors – persons owing allegiance to the RSS, an organization that publicly mocks India's Constitutional vision. Police conduct throughout the state simply refused to inspire confidence. In the fourteen years since the genocidal carnage, little has been done to restore confidence. In fact, the opposite has taken place as good police officers are punished while those charged with serious crimes are reinstated and promoted.

The police did not or could not respond to the plea of one retired and one sitting judge of the Gujarat High Court – Justices Akbar Divecha and M. H. Kadri – to send in the army for their safety. Then Chief Justice of Gujarat – D. M. Dharmadhikari – actually told the judges not to rely on the police! The army had been on 'stand by' on 28 February till 1 March. The troops could easily have entered the cities and stopped the carnage. But they were deliberately not given autonomy or magisterial orders to act until the marauding RSS-VHP mobs had completed their tasks. The nine hours that the army was deliberately delayed made a difference to at least one hundred, if not four hundred lives.

It is not possible to write about Gujarat 2002 without recourse to the outstanding and restorative reports of the National Human Rights Commission (NHRC) – both the preliminary and final reports (April and July 2002). These documents are all the more substantive and historic because in its twenty-five year existence, the NHRC has only on a couple of occasions justified its statutory existence. This was one of them. The Chief Justice of India Justice J. S. Verma's *suo moto* cognisance of the killings in Gujarat brought him and his team to the state on 21-22 March. He was accompanied by the highly-regarded IPS officer, Chaman Lal. Chief Justice Verma was attacked by RSS-VHP hoodlums at the Shahibaug Circuit House. His team requested me to be present at the Shah-e-Alam camp to help record testimonies on 21 March. Justice Verma was an eyewitness to the first physical attack on my vehicle, as we drove behind his motorcade on the highway toward Godhra city on 22 March.

There were a total of one-lakh sixty eight thousand internally displaced people in the camps. What was awful was that along with rape, humiliation and murder, there was a concerted effort to deny acknowledgment of the crimes and suffering. There was a cruel deliberation in the attempt to wipe out the facts and history of the perpetrated mob violence. From the camps onward went the chant to 'move on' – let the past be the past. This was made sharper after the 2007 state assembly elections, when the chief of the macabre orchestra won a second victory at the polls. Forgive and forget was the call. This forgetting was not to be for the families of those who had died at Godhra – but only for the Muslim survivors and for those who wanted justice for the dead. The political class of Gujarat has tried to create a narrative that the massacre did not actually happen. They have tried to paint those of us who campaign for justice as the villains of the piece. It is therefore essential to keep the memory of what happened in Gujarat alive – not only for justice in the past, but to prevent a repeat of it in the present, and the future.

*   *   *   *   *

Images of the train at Godhra were flashed across the television screens, repeatedly. Images of charred bodies lying in a single file in the Godhra rail yard are now imprinted in the collective memory. Groups affiliated to the Sangh have circulated and re-circulated them. The memories of charred bits of bodies of children, women, men, old and young of the post Godhra retaliatory violence remains are today blurred and erased. Though charred to a cruel nothingness –and the figure totalling close to 2,000 – these images have just not had the same impact.

What is often not interrogated any more is what provoked that ghastly incident. The Sabarmati Express was scheduled to reach Godhra at 2am each day. On 27 September, the train arrived five hours late at 7:50 a.m. Why was the train delayed? This same train left for Faizabad-Ayodhya on 24 February and returned on 27 February. This was a train that had large numbers of highly motivated BJP-RSS cadres, who went to Ayodhya as part of the anti-Muslim Ramjanamabhoomi campaign. On the train, the leaders of the RSS-VHP-Bajrang Dal riled up the passengers with their violently communal rhetoric. Sheetla Singh of *Jan Morcha* (Faizabad) reported that the boisterous band of *karsevaks* provoked Muslims on the train. They even attacked some Muslims at the station. This evidence is widely available. Through the court cases (particularly the Zakia Jafri case), we got evidence that the UP Police and the Gujarat Police sent warnings about the tension on the train. These dispatches suggested that the *karsevaks* were behaving in a very communal fashion. On 27 February at 4 p.m., Prime Minister Atal Bihari Vajpayee said that there was no evidence of any conspiracy at Godhra, only an accident. This would be forgotten once the carnage began. Journalists at that time did not confirm anything other than the facts, which were that there had been an altercation and a fire. There was no question of terrorism or any conspiracy.

The Gujarat government made the tragedy at Godhra a rallying point. Chief Minister Modi received a fax from the District Collector Jayanti Ravi, around 9 a.m., a communication that laid out the bare facts about the Godhra incident. Modi's first call – on his Personal Assistant A. P. Patel's mobile – was to VHP leader Jaideep Patel, not to the police or to other administrators. A senior minister in Modi's cabinet, Suresh Mehta (who has been chief minister of Gujarat for a year) testified to the fact that Modi, seated next to him in the Gujarat state assembly when the Godhra train burning was discussed, had a look of satisfaction on his face. 'Now the Hindus will awake', was the remark made by him. The post-mortem of the Godhra dead took place in the open as angry crowds of RSS and VHP men were allowed to watch. The Chief Minister and the Health Minister sanctioned this. What became clear to long-time observers of the situation in Gujarat was that the government used every moment to instigate its cadres, who had already been prepared by the RSS and VHP propaganda, to begin what they called 'retaliatory killings'. How could a state have decided on its own that there was a terror attack *before investigations have even begun* and then sanction attacks against its own innocent citizens as a form of retaliation?

The images of the Coach S-6 and the burned corpses remain firmly entrenched in the public memory. But the maimed, bruised, burnt and cut up corpses of two thousand Muslims – many babies — escaped the public gaze. The maimed images of Gulberg, Naroda, Sardarpura victims did not pierce the public consciousness that had been already successfully and emotionally blocked by the anger generated by the images of the Godhra train burning.

Communal violence forces a selective response and selective mourning in a deeply prejudicial context. History tells us that often an incident, a violent incident, even an accident or a deliberate attack can be very cleverly used by those in power. From what we know now that is what happened. A very tragic incident – for which a set of persons present in the mob was in all likelihood responsible – was very cleverly used to justify and actually orchestrate violence against an entire community. That is the story of the Gujarat genocidal carnage. It transformed Gujarat. It also transformed me. As I said to a journalist interviewing me some years later, 'it is not easy to be normal again.'

ROOTS

We had a good childhood. Always in Bombay, living by the sea in Juhu.

I was born in Purandare Hospital on Chowpatty in 1962. My mother had gone to her parent's home for my birth. My maternal grandparents had a small flat in Girgaon. My sister and I were both born in the same place – she after me. My parents were second cousins. My mother's side of the family was clearly middle class. My maternal grandfather worked in an insurance company and I spent many weekends with my maternal grandparents at Temple View, often donning a cap to watch the races at Mahalaxmi where Bakukaka – as my maternal grandfather was called by all of us – took me. My sister and I were both father's pets. My relationship with my mother was turbulent, but I nonetheless always carried some sound values, my grounding, from her. For instance, that the value of money can and should never be taken for granted.

My parents lived at our present home at Juhu Tara Road in Mumbai before I was born. The bungalow where my father and I were born was next to the one we now live in, where we moved in 1965. It was where my grandfather M. C. Setalvad, the eldest son of Sir Chimanlal Setalvad, had moved in 1933. My grandfather was the eldest son of ten siblings! He preferred the wide-open spaces of Juhu with a view of the sea. It was better for him than the family home, which also had a sea view, at Napean Sea Road – the home of his father – in South Bombay. The road on which the house sits is now called Setalvad Lane. At the time of the Setalvad shift to

Juhu, the British government was offering incentives for moves of residents, northwards!

My grandfather – M. C. Setalvad or Dada – was India's first Attorney General, having served from 1950 to 1963. He was the first chairman of the Bar Council of India, founded in 1961. He was also the voice of the government in the United Nations (vociferously making the case on Kashmir, for instance, after Pakistan's invasion in October 1948). He was a stoic man who loved children and had a piquant sense of humour. Dada was a great lover of the outdoors and chose his homes around that passion – by the sea or up in the Ootacamund hills. He would come away to Bombay and Ooty from Delhi for four or five months of the year. My mother made us write regular letters and cards to our grandparents. We would always receive replies. Dada was very disciplined. One memory I retain of him is his regular evening walks across our lawn. It always felt very special to walk along with him on these strolls. I took my first steps (just past 3 years old) in the Ooty home. He had this habit of walking with his hands behind him and I would imitate him. There is a photograph in the family album where he and I are walking together, and I, a sixth of his height (he was a tall man), have my hands crossed behind my back in careful mimicry. I was 12 when he died on 1 August 1974. He was afflicted with fever for just a few days. As we were on our way home from school, someone came rushing to hurry us home. We knew there was a crisis. We were ushered into my grandfather's bedroom where he was lying back in a chair, our heads bowed as he weakly stroked ours. He died within a few minutes. The rest of that evening is a blur but I recall being silent witness to sobs racking my father, Atul, that night, as he wept with my mother, hidden away in their bathroom. I had never seen or heard him cry before that. The twelve days of *Geeta* recitation at home in the afternoon organized by my grandmother Vimla were the first experiences of ritual we had experienced. Before that it was the odd trip to the *kul devi* mandir at Gamdevi that my mother sometimes went to.

There were many stories about Dada and Chimanlalkaka that we heard about as we grew up. Chimanlal Setalvad, Dada's father, was a contemporary of Motilal Nehru. He was one of the eminent Indians on the Hunter Commission, which investigated the Jallianwallah Bagh massacre. His role in cross-examining General Dyer was a favourite anecdote in the family. Here is an extract of the exchange:

CHIMANLAL SETALVAD: You took two armoured cars with you?

DYER: Yes.

CHIMANLAL SETALVAD: Those cars had machine guns?

DYER: Yes.

CHIMANLAL SETALVAD: And when you took them you meant to use the machine guns against the crowd, did you?

DYER: If necessary. If the necessity arose, and I was attacked, or anything else like that, I presume I would have used them.

CHIMANLAL SETALVAD: When you arrived there you were not able to take the armoured cars in because the passage was too narrow?

DYER: Yes.

CHIMANLAL SETALVAD: Supposing the passage was sufficient to allow the armoured cars to go in, would you have opened fire with the machine guns?

DYER: I think, probably, yes.

CHIMANLAL SETALVAD: In that case the casualties would have been very much higher?

DYER: Yes.

CHIMANLAL SETALVAD: And you did not open fire with the machine guns simply by the accident of the armoured cars not being able to get in?

DYER: I have answered you. I have said that if they had been there the probability is that I would have opened fire with them.

CHIMANLAL SETALVAD: With the machine-guns straight?

DYER: With the machine-guns.

CHIMANLAL SETALVAD: I take it that your idea in taking that action was to strike terror?

DYER: Call it what you like. I was going to punish them. My idea from the military point of view was to make a wide impression.

CHIMANLAL SETALVAD: To strike terror not only in the city of Amritsar, but throughout the Punjab?

DYER: Yes, throughout the Punjab. I wanted to reduce their morale; the morale of the rebels.

CHIMANLAL SETALVAD: Did it occur to you that by adopting this method of 'frightfulness' – excuse the term – you were really doing a great disservice to the British Raj by driving discontent deep?

DYER: I did not like the idea of doing it, but I also realized that it was the only means of saving life and that any reasonable man with justice in his mind would realize that I had done the right thing; it was a merciful though horrible act and they ought to be thankful to me for doing it. I thought I would be doing a jolly lot of good and they would realize that they were not to be wicked.[1]

History has adjudged that it was Chimanlal's cross-examination that actually pinned Dyer down. When the British on the Hunter Commission would not go along with the facts, the Indians on the Commission filed a separate report (it was drafted by Chimanlal Setalvad).

Dada had an abiding interest in historical studies, and in the history of law in particular. The values of parity and non-discrimination – basic constitutional values – were very important

---

[1] Teesta Setalvad, 'Bloodbath on Baisakhi: The Jallianwallah Bagh Massacre, April 13, 1919' *Communalism Combat*, 12 April 2016.

to him. Even more important, however, was faith in the law itself. He believed that the fundamental rights granted by the law would or should become reality at some point. Dada occupied many important posts in post-Independent India and each post he held became a place for him to enact his values.

As a child I remember meeting Sheikh Abdullah when we had gone to Kashmir. He had been a close colleague of my grandfather and had lived with us when he was underground. The betrayal of Sheikh Abdullah's cause by Nehru framed how we saw the Kashmir problem. I remember when we went to Kashmir for a holiday and we asked for an audience with the Abdullahs. We were invited and had tea on this enormous lawn with them. Then there was the visit and audience with the Dalai Lama when we went to Dharamsala as ordinary tourists; the evening when we had tea together was special. These visits were a benchmark for me – showing me where we came from and what we had to fight to get. It was awe-inspiring and also humbling as we sat in the presence of these people, awkwardly squirming.

My father – Atul Setalvad – was the younger of two siblings. My sister and I always called him 'Atul' – not Papa or Daddy. This was at his insistence. He was an innately egalitarian man who rejected hierarchy in all things. As we grew older, we would rile him by calling him 'Paaaapa' with an exaggerated Gujju accent. He hated it. Atul's sister Usha, thirteen years older than him, died relatively early in 1983. She lost her husband nine years before her death. She had been active in the freedom movement, organising girls and women in Tara village as part of the satyagraha campaign. My father had gone to prison for a day at that time.

On 25 October 1983 – when I was in my first job – I remember well how we together organized my father's 50th birthday party. It was a surprise party with all his close cronies. We grilled kebabs and dished out delicious food out in the open. Atul was in his heyday, with his favourite people around him. It was a wonder to see him hold forth! While the Setalvad name and heritage had been so much a part of our growing up, we did not have much contact with our extended family. Family for us comprised of our grandparents, paternal aunt Usha and her husband Sundar, as well as a large number of family friends – who always were and remain our real family.

Among them is Priti Desai. Her story influenced me as a child and as a woman. The Desai family came from Gamdevi, a street dividing my mother's family home and their home. Priti and my mother went together to the New Era School, steeped in the traditions and values of the national movement. There were four sisters and one brother in the Desai family. None of the sisters married because the dowry in their mid-level Gujarati caste was too high. So, in what must have been a radical and painful choice after much deliberation, the sisters decided never to get married. The brother, Asit, was the only one to marry amongst the siblings.

I have been deeply influenced by the Desai family. They are a middle-class, Gujarati family from Baroda, so utterly and thoroughly cosmopolitan in their outlook. They epitomized for me the move from Vadodara to Bombay, a Bombay that then opened horizons, choices and worldviews whether for a Chimanlal Setalvad or a Priti Desai. Bindu, the youngest sister, sent me a lovely note after Priti's demise that came with a bag that Priti always used. The note said 'You are her own: her first daughter.' For the Desais, the world was vast and challenging, not inward looking: they looked at the world from Palestine to Ireland with shared human concerns. I would receive long notes from Priti and Bindu, with newspaper clippings from difficult to get Left foreign publications, on the struggle in Ireland, Palestine, and various African countries. I had a vibrant childhood that spanned the five thousand-book library that my father built at home to this wider mentoring and education from family friends. I still recall the books that Navroz Seervai would send me to read as I matured into womanhood. One, in particular, *The Scalpel, The Sword*, on the journey of the communist doctor Norman Bethune through conflict-ridden China and Spain, marked me.

Ma has always been fond of classical music, especially stalwarts like Kesarbhai Kelkar. This was a passion she shared with Priti. My mother – Sita – and Priti continued to be close friends after my parents married. They would often go to music concerts together. My father was the Desai's best friend. The Desais became part of our childhood – Priti's three sisters, Sita, Jyoti and Bindu as well as their brother Asit and his wife Penny. There were many holidays together. Jyoti and Priti left us in quick succession – the loss has been immeasurable. Bindu, the youngest Desai sister, is a neurologist in America. She is a comrade in arms, personally and professionally. She was one of the first contributors towards the Gulberg Memorial.

My mother and father got married on 27 April 1959 through a civil marriage, another radical first in those days. Atul was an unashamed atheist and self-proclaimed beef eater. He would taunt my mother on issues of religion, saying that they should marry on *Amavasya* – the moonless first day of the lunar month. A marriage on that day would have been a clarion call, a tempting of the fates as it were. Ma put her foot down though quietly agreeing to the civil ceremony. For her, ritual and religion is part of a whole, never entirely wished away, even if her commitment to it is far from all consuming. She did manage to ensure that my father bowed to her wishes to the extent of visiting the Hanuman *mandir* at Santacruz for a quick round every Saturday morning. He would leave early morning in the car, step out, and barely offer the flowers demanded of the ritual and return. On every return he would bring fruits for both households, especially for the children.

My father and mother had both been sent to Gujarati medium schools in the best traditions of the national movement. Atul went to Pupil's Own, a school started during the Independence movement in a small abode in Ville Parle, which then moved to Khar. His friends from school included Dileep Purohit, Dilip Dalal, and Hamir Doshi. They made up a jolly foursome who stayed close to the end. My father had this unique and rare capacity to keep and stay in touch with all his friends, even if their paths had diverged. Friday morning before Court at the Neo Coffee House is where they would often gather.

My father's friends would include his colleagues from the bar – including his juniors. Sam Bharucha – Samkaka or Sammy to us – joined the Bench at the Bombay High Court and rose to become the Chief Justice of India. The moment Bharucha was elevated to the Bench my father simply stopped appearing before him; those were the ethics by which we were born and bred. H. M. Seervai was India's constitutional expert. He was also a wonderful humourist and conversationalist. Seervaikaka would sit with us children and have us in wonderment at his antics. He had the unique ability of performing a weird kind of act, maintaining a poker straight face even as his ears twitched and trembled. It was awe-inspiring. Sammy and Perin Bharucha, Rusi and Arnoo Sethna, the Desais, Seervaikaka, Pheroza Aunty and the family – especially Navroz – were prominent figures in our lives: people with whom we went on holiday. There were the Shroffs, Rusi and Polly, and their three wonderful daughters: Havoo was a year older, Anahita (Ana) was a year younger and Zenobia (Zen) was the youngest. Zen and I, though so utterly different, have been very close. I remember always feeling that of all communities, Parsis have played a huge role in our life, especially the growing up years. It is not surprising then, that in public life, when people are unable to place me through the name that bears no label of community or caste – I am often dubbed a Parsi!

Atul's young colleagues also became part of our family. The list is long. Mohan Korde, Kasim Master, Rafique Dada, and Darius Shroff. One person – Ravi Kulkarni – stands out, as he has remained the most special. His romance and marriage to the middle of three vivacious sisters, Shakuntala, was a great source of excitement and thrill for us onlookers at the budding romance. My sister and I are deeply influenced by the way Atul related to women colleagues. He was extremely egalitarian in the way he engaged with women in the family, with women friends socially and also women in the legal profession. Some of his close women associates would come home and have long conversations with him on our lawn. We would never know what they were discussing. He was a mentor to many lawyers – both women and men. Indira Jaisingh, who is now a friend, and my father would sit in the quadrangle of our lawn and have intense discussions. We never got to know what they were talking about. Though Indu and he were diametrically opposite in ideology, they had a lot of mutual respect. Javed has a similar ease and dignity with the way he deals with women friends and colleagues that is extremely endearing and draws respect. It is also similar to how Atul related to women of all ages.

It was not all law and the courts, though. I remember the excitement when a distant family acquaintance by marriage (Mayur Madhwani) married the actor Mumtaz, and we actually got to attend the reception at the Sun-n-Sand hotel in Juhu! We were watching and counting the celebrities: I remember Dimple and Kaka Rajesh Khanna, Dimple had just then starred in *Bobby* (1973). Once I was with my friend Vinita Vaid at Carter Road, Bandra, on our morning walk, when we encountered the flamboyant poet Harendranath Chattopadhyay. Vilayat Khan –

the sitar maestro – was part of our lives, as was his family. I flirted with learning the sitar though never very seriously, I must admit.

Family holidays and family time were sacrosanct for us. We would take holidays once a year and we would also spend every alternate holiday with my paternal grandparents at their house in Ooty. The Diwali and December holidays were in Delhi as my grandfather – Dada – was a Member of Parliament after his long tenure as India's Attorney General. Shorter sojourns were with my mother's maternal uncle in Ahmedabad. The idea of a family holiday remained with me and despite the pressures on Javed and myself we have always tried to do this for our kids and ourselves. We would try to take a two to four week holiday every year. The only complaint our children have is that we took them repeatedly to the Himalayas and not to other heritage spots of India. With our love for the hills, we have done the *parikrama* from one end of the hills to the other. This time together with family has grounded us and kept us replenished to face endless challenges.

The law, public ethics, and family: these are the influences on me. Examples of commitment and integrity from my larger family have stood me in good stead, as the challenges life has thrown at me have demanded that I dig deep into these reserves.

The sea and its tides outside our house in Bombay have been a close companion and abiding friend. When tumultuous questions, great anger and resentment bubbles within me, I turn to the sea. It somehow reflects my moods: the lashing, forceful waves on a moonlit night at high tide or the serene low tide spectacle of the beach with the sea ready to come in or else the light of the moon reflecting on the water. In calm anticipation.

*   *   *   *   *

I grew up around the law. My great-grandfather Chinmanlal Setalvad was an eminent lawyer. His son was the Attorney General of India. My father was also a lawyer. I had a sense until about Class VII that I too would take to the law as a profession.

But I had other interests. I was obsessed with cricket and the news. I would listen to BBC World Service and All India Radio. I would read the three newspapers that came home, from cover to cover, every day. During the 1973, England-India Test series, I remember Gundappa Vishwanath and Faroukh Engineer scoring centuries in the Bombay test. They, and Patuadi, were our heroes! I remember weeping when India got all out for 42 runs against England in 1974. I was a fanatic watcher of the game – a loyal Indian. My sister enjoyed it more for the fun of it, which is why she liked Tony Grieg!

Listening to the news on the radio and then discussing and debating all events with the family were regular features of the dinners at home. Heated arguments would follow, Atul gently stoking the discussion further. On the couple of nights a week that my mother and he were out visiting friends, I would jot down copious notes from the news feeds that day, leave the note on the dining table for him to read, so as not to miss out on the arguments around the subjects raised on the next night at dinner!

When I was barely twelve, in standard VII, in 1974, my father came home one day with the paperback edition of *All the President's Men*. He had bought it at the Strand Book Stall. The Watergate scandal had broken out in the United States. Reading the book, my world tilted on its axis, never to be the same again. I read and re-read the book seeing in the effort of these journalists the mission behind what journalism should or ought to be: exposing wrong-doing, help setting things right. Haltingly at first, but then, again and again and again, I spoke my mind with my father: journalism is where I want to be, not the law, although the law will and shall be an abiding ally. Not once did Atul try and dissuade me. Through his discussions he only helped my resolve to be clearer and sharper. The ultimate democrat, Atul was not interested in a formal continuance of the legal lineage. That was Atul. When I published a letter to the editor in *India Today* at age 14, I wore that as a badge. My future seemed to unfold from that letter.

Our school was the Maneckji Copper School, a neighbourhood school, small and homey, barely a walk away. 1977 was the year of the board examinations and also the year India was passing through a heady, rebellious time. Bombay had opposed the horrors of the Emergency both on the streets and even within its institutions. Its citizens came forward in an unprecedented show of strength – asking us to choose between democracy and dictatorship. All our homes had been seats of hectic parleying and meetings. I remember Atul telling me not to worry about studies but to campaign against the Emergency and the Congress party. The home of Ramdas Bhatkal (of Popular Prakashan) became the hub to gather materials and to strategize for the campaign. You had law students and solicitors stepping out of their offices and joining in the campaigning. In 1977, Bombay returned all six parliamentary seats to the Janata combine. Today as India is faced with an undeclared Emergency, where majoritarianism and parochialism tarnish seven decades of nation-building, syncretism and pluralism, does that spirit of Bombay still survive? What is this Bombay spirit? It is the spirit to come together, against all odds to right the wrongs of state repression and curtailment of basic freedoms.

My younger sister's name is Amili, but she has always been Amou (and Mau – a short form for *Mausi* - to my children). She was born in 1964. My mother had two miscarriages after Amou was born. I never ever sensed that my father Atul regretted not having a son. My mother perhaps wanted one. But for Atul, his two daughters were his all. Bringing us up with a strong sense of right and wrong, he also felt that we could do little wrong! Amou is and has been a best friend, a second and more hands on mother to our children, a person with a huge heart and wonderful sense of humour, something she shared with Dada, Motilal Setalvad. Her PJs (poor jokes) were part and parcel of our childhood and home even now. We are lucky to inhabit the same glorious space of the sea at *Nirant*.

Always conscious of the law, rights and freedoms, justice and the Constitution, I recall a game that Amou and I used to play as children, to challenge any moments of boredom. We would chant, 'Atul, Motilal, Chimanlal, Ambashankar, Har-rai, Brijrai Setalvad' – counting playfully and proudly the paternal lineage associated with the law. This was chanted by us without musical ability – unlike my mother, both us sisters have inherited our father's toneless voice, though we adore music, which he did not. We would intone this mantra for years as we drove for picnics and holidays with family and friends. This was how we, as sisters, celebrated the fact that we were part of one of India's pre-eminent legal families. The patriarchal essence of the chant of course hit home soon enough as did the sombre and humble realization that we were and are, here speaking of the seventh generation of higher learning that reflects entrenched privilege. On the flip side, the fact that we are third generation post-graduates (even my maternal grandmother had completed her MA in Sociology) is another mark of this. It is this realization that has grounded me to be always conscious of my entitlement and my rights: the privilege that class, birth and – in the Indian context – caste inevitably gives you. Shouldn't one then use that entitlement to further and deepen rights and democracy as well as the sense and quality of justice?

I have often found the conversations among the upper echelon of the elite about privilege and reservations, caste and exclusion to be arid. I prefer to answer questions with more questions. Someone asks: What do you have to say about reservations? Do they not deny merit? I answer: 'Take my family for example, seventh generation learners, third generation women learners: Can we in any real sense have the arrogance to ask for a level-playing field that puts our children with this history of privilege on par with the child of a working-class and peasant Dalit or Adivasi or Muslim, who is a first generation entrant into the education system?' Put like this the person raising the shrill query lowers their eyes – in acceptance or embarrassment. Chimanlal Setalvad was a close colleague of the inspirational Dr Bhimrao Ambedkar and together they had formed the Bahishkrit Hitakarini Sabha. It was rare then for a person born to privilege to accept the historical discriminations caused to us by the inhuman existence of caste.

*　*　*　*　*

In 1978, I joined Elphinstone College. My father, grandfather and great-grandfather were all alumni of the college, which was founded in 1856. My horizons – both personal and political – had widened and deepened. I was ready to grow as fast as college would allow. I was drawn into full-time active student politics. I was part of the protests against fee rise, active in the debating and film societies, and I contested elections. It was a heady period. The college was my home till I graduated in 1983.

During College Day, I was rappelling down the stonewalls of the college. Something in the harness slipped and I remember dangling face down, my breath caught in fear. The people in the College Quadrangle seemed to let out a collective gasp. The safety latch was used and I was gingerly lowered down. My sweatshirt that I wore over my jeans had slipped, allowing the rope to cut into my skin. The rope had sliced a one and a half inch gash into my waist (which was then a neat 24 inches, making me sport an envious figure!). Determined and cavalier, I dabbed some toilet paper on the wound and carried on painting posters, participating in and organising the contests. Late that evening, I caught a local train home, hopped off at the Khar station and went to the family doctor, Dr. Vaidya, to get the wound cleaned. It was a mess, more painful as some pus had gathered. But the euphoria of College Day and the bravado of all the activities – the sheer joy of being part of all that – was balm for the wound. Attendance in classes was never the priority, but excelling at the literature and philosophy assignments and tutorials was!

I loved the hills and enjoyed trekking. It was a love born out of a deep friendship. A young lawyer colleague of my father – Firdauz Taleyarkhan – became a close friend through our hikes. An intrepid mountaineer with advanced skills, Firdauz like me, was an asthmatic and taught me how to overcome this debility, strengthening my lungs through arduous exercise. Youth Hostel Association (YHA) treks became part of a life choice, as the valleys of the Himalayas were traversed for two or three week long treks. The sense of vastness and relative insignificance of the human endeavour was another grounding and humbling experience that remains with me.

I grew in so many ways during college. I made many more friends from the different circles that enfolded me. Often, my friend Amrita and I would drive down with Atul in his car to college, which was near the High Court. Navroz Seervai, who was already a family friend, became a personal friend in this period, as did Aspi Chinoy, Jimmy Avasya and others. The list would be longer, but – for obvious reasons – discretion is important. Friends from college have endured. Many of them drew me out of the limited circle of my upbringing. Farhad Sorabjee and I had been together in school. Amrita Shah, Gautam Khandelwal, Aroop Mukherjee,

Niloufer, Viswanath Ramachandran, Janaki Nair, Karun – these were the Elphinstone friends' circle. Sanjoy Ghosh, Arundhati and others with whom we contested elections became tight friends. Sanjoy became a rural development activist in Gujarat and then later at Majuli Island on the Brahmaputra River. He was abducted and killed by ULFA militants in 1997. I republished his editorial that he had written for *The Elphinstonian* in *Communalism Combat*. His wife – Sumita Ghosh – also a fellow Elphinstonian requested the original issues of the magazine, which I gladly sent her.

College was a beehive of challenging and creative activities. It was a heady period. We sharpened our thoughts and political choices, always ready to challenge the status quo. At the Elphie canteen – filthy and dimly lit – the double special chai and the oily samosas sustained us. It was the place where we had many of our intense conversations, which included discussions with challenging political stalwarts from the far left. We would go watch five or six films a week. Some well-chosen classic films, some mainstream – each one broadening our horizons even further. I once caught the 123 bus to the House of Soviet Culture to a screening of *Battleship Potemkin* with the seniors in tow. The Film Society, headed by the indomitable Kala Rao, showed us Ingmar Bergman and Fellini films. The professors of English and Philosophy, while gently chiding us for our nonchalance towards attending classes, were appreciative and supportive of the concerted efforts to make the college the pivot of the university's intellectual and cultural experience. The relationship between professors and students, though edgy at times, was incredibly special. It is also a relationship that has endured.

Thanks to my mother Sita's belief in a frugal and disciplined existence, we were given fixed amounts as pocket money from which all daily expenses had to be met. Exact extra amounts for the three-month pass on the local train were given; but otherwise food, non-textbook book purchases, theatre, films and everything else had to be managed within the monthly sum. We would actually think and scrimp and save to buy books out of that pocket money. It was made quite clear to both of us sisters that though we might be privileged as a family, living in a beautiful home, the norms we lived by would be governed by a firm sense of reality: public transport and budgeted existence. We did manage a fair amount of both fun and frolic even within those limited means.

At Elphinstone, my friends and I were active both politically and socially, but we also did our share of non-serious college stuff. Our bungalow in Mumbai is by the Arabian Sea. It has a beautiful lawn and a terrace overseeing the sea. My friends loved hanging out here especially when our parents were out of town; budgeted celebrations, shared company, levity as much as politics and debate. Our home, *Nirant*, was an extension of the college quadrangle and pigeon-shit infested classrooms; life seemed to have opened up vast challenges in ideas and relationships.

*   *   *   *   *

At college I got involved with its magazine – *The Elphinstonian*. For a brief while I edited it as part of a team. Armed with that experience, the day after I submitted my last paper in Philosophy in June 1982, I did my rounds of the city offices of *The Times of India*, *Indian Express* and *The Daily*. I left my resume in each office. *The Daily*'s chief reporter Maneck Davar offered me a job on the spot. I was to be a cub reporter for Rs. 500 per month as a stipend. I gleefully accepted. Throwing myself into work I was thrilled when I got my first by-line within a week!

These first few weeks of journalism were heady and inspiring. We had a great team at *The Daily*. There was a sharp News Editor – P. N. V. Nair – who could cut you down to size in seconds by flinging away a story that he felt was not newsworthy into the dustbin across his table. If you stood your ground and could effectively counter his assessment rationally, point out that it was a story worth carrying in the paper, he would not only retract his position but grudgingly respect you for not cowering, and standing up. Not for him the servile and the meek. There were many occasions when we had it out – me, this slight and oh so slim thing of 48 kilos and the seasoned P. N. V. Nair! I would stand there unmoved and relentlessly point out the worth of what I thought was my contribution. Victory or defeat was not as important as putting the principle on the table.

I had many mentors in journalism. One of them was Dinkar Raikar, our chief reporter at *Indian Express* and a seasoned political correspondent. He might have been dismayed at first that so many young women had been assigned crucial beats – University and Mantralaya among others. But he had a modern and reasoned outlook, gently teaching us the way around the bureaucracy and archaic institutions. I believe I was among the last generation of reporters to benefit from training on the beat – the loss of this structured framework has seminally reduced the quality and standards of the profession. We honed our skills as observers and critics of the system by talking to people in the university, in the municipal corporation (the BMC beat), in the Mantralaya (the seat of the state government), or in the courts. We listened to court proceedings and debates in the assembly. To cover the courts – to understand and report on the issues being contested – meant ploughing through court records, petitions, and affidavit annexures. It was not only about flippant oral comments made in the courtroom. Each encounter allowed us to understand better the way these structures worked in our democracy. Mundane beat reporting allowed us to pour through the agenda of the Standing Committee meetings of the Municipal Council or to sense the pulse behind the assembly sessions. Our exclusives, our front pages had to be built on long hours of hectic consultations, learning and questioning. The office space, the reporter's room, the space belonging to the Bombay Union of Journalists where we held our meetings were also spaces where bonds took root and grew. By the mid to late 1980s – as the neo-liberal economic agenda took root, the labour beat began to be dropped, abandoned even. We built enduring friendships through conversations around shared ideals and differences. The collapse of beat journalism has also contributed to non-serious reporting. If beat journalism had remained the norm and if say, an agricultural beat, a rural beat, an environmental beat, a human rights beat were added to the traditional contours, how vastly would the expanse of journalism have spread?

It was also the time that we had formed the Women and Media Committee and were battling for the rights and dignity of women reporters as also the representation of women in the media. One of our demands was for women reporters to have the right to night duty assignments. A fire broke on the second night that I was assigned night duty as part of this struggle. The western railway had just started all night trains for the first time and to reach the spot of a fire at the airport I left the *The Daily* at Cowasjee Patel street after 9.30 p.m. Dhiren Bhagat, a young and intrepid journalist, who tragically died very young, had become a close friend and we went on this assignment together (he actually accompanied me to and from the assignment). I returned in the early hours and filed my report. Those were heady and trusting times, which now seem a lifetime away. That night as we travelled by train I recall Dhiren's account of his family, Partition refugees, his sister brutally affected. Yet there was no rancour or hatred, just a sad realization of what hate and violence can do.

Apart from city coverage and coverage on civic accountability,

I was given the opportunity to cover the courts, an assignment that I loved. I poured through legal submissions, affidavits and wrote legal analyses late into the night. My coverage of the courts at *The Daily* gave me the chance to report on legal issues, past and present. I was given the chance to cover the on-going Antulay trial that the media had zealously covered for several years. I recoil with horror at the kind of court reporting we see presently, except in rare cases. As a rule, the substance of the legal challenge is rarely understood and reported. Later, as we became a victim of this selective reporter's lens, we saw how news feeds by influential men and women in power dictated headlines not the voluminous records filed by us in court.

In 1981, Arun Shourie had rocked the journalistic world with his expose of the five trusts set up by the blue-eyed boy of Mrs. Indira Gandhi – A. R. Antulay, then chief minister of Maharashtra. These ostensible charitable trusts that collected crores of rupees in contributions from people and companies doing business with the government, were shown by Shourie, with documentary evidence, to be actually foundations that were fully and perpetually controlled by Antulay and his wife. *Indian Express* broke the story. It rocked Parliament. Mrs. Gandhi was one of the trustees. Antulay's own Finance Secretary wrote to Mrs. Gandhi that coercion had in fact been used to solicit contributions for the fund. Antulay himself acknowledged that he had levied a surcharge on each bag of cement allocated to contractors. He added, however, that the money was not intended to make him rich but was meant for the Congress Party and for the poor. Mrs. Gandhi's name had to be removed from the trust fund, and Antulay had to resign. For a cub reporter to be given the chance to cover the proceedings of this sensational case was a dream that only could be dreamed. Soon I was given a double spread each day to document the legal happenings and analyse the implications and consequences.

As my coverage was appreciated and recognized, my editor (Russi Karanjia) gave me the chance to author a weekly spread on historic trials. I researched and wrote on my grandfather, M. C. Setalvad's role as the Attorney General during the hearings of the Mundhra Commission. I learned that in that period – the late 1950s – people in the institutions lived by their fierce independence, their autonomy from powerful interests, and their integrity (values that were integral and ingrained). Today, when institutions are being eroded by a corrosive anti-Constitutional worldview, we have lost the ability to appreciate the value of autonomy of institutions. The role of the Attorney General of India, the highest law officer in the country is a unique one. My grandfather occupied it and the position was tested during the hearings of the Mundhra Commission (headed by the Bombay High Court's former Chief Justice M. C. Chagla) that was set up to investigate the first scandal of independent India. As Attorney General, speaking truth to executive power, M. C. Setalvad was expected to defend the State – not necessarily the government. It is a constitutional position. M. C. Setalvad understood the need to balance the Attorney General's duties towards the Client (Government of India), the Court, and the Constitution. As the first Attorney General, he led by example when he appeared before the Chagla Commission inquiring into the Mundhra scandal. His tough comments on the conduct of then Finance Minister, T.T. Krishnamachari, and Chagla's report itself led to TTK's resignation. When the Commission's report was released, one Member of Parliament criticised Dada's independence, 'The Attorney-General whom we sent to defend our case, became the prosecutor of the Finance Minister and, incidentally, of the Government.' While the hearings of the Mundhra Commission were on at the Old Town Hall (opposite Regal Cinema), the Prime Minister even held a public meeting expressing displeasure at the independent behaviour of the Attorney General.

I also wrote about the Sardar Pratap Singh Kairon scandal in Punjab in which a former chief justice of India S. R. Das had investigated charges.

Through this the conviction and understanding of constitutional principles and institutional autonomy, critical to deepening our democracy, took further and further root, now grappling with not mere ideals and stories but real life's experiences.

We need very high standards of ethics in the legal world and within our institutions. We, as Indians, need to have an abiding sense of building-up institutions because in that exercise is the investment in the long term, a commitment to non-discrimination, equity and a sense of fair play. We revere individuals or rather we either revile them or revere them (we don't seem to be seeing anything in between), but it is institutions made up of men and women in positions of power, wedded to non-negotiable principles of constitutional values, that actually produce democracy.

Today we speak about Indian democracy, while glorifying our existence in a very stratified, casteist and communal society. This democracy cannot work without strong institutions that adhere to constitutional principles. Individuals may make institutions but the integrity of institutions can also be compromised if we don't believe in the principles of the institution itself. It is the principle that needs to be the abiding foundation of the institution.

There was a whole period right after Independence when ethics were considered extremely important. It was not only in the legal field, but also in the arts, in culture, in science and in public administration. I have been lucky to have been born into my family, and have been mentored by not just the examples of my father, grandfather, H. M. Seervai in different ways, but also by others such as Justice Hosbet Suresh, Justice P. B. Sawant, Justice Verma and Justice V. R. Krishna Iyer (who would summon me to take him from one airport to the next in Mumbai). They tested public life with grit, frugality and principle. Not for them the flashy BMWs that lawyers now sport, forget the Mercedes Benz. Not for them the flashy and questionable arbitrations that have become the means for retired judges. The voices that boomed within the courtroom, between Bar and Bench – often in heated exchange – echoed with the strength of uncompromising principle. That tenor of voice did not allow false affidavits to be filed even if a wily client wanted them to; that strength of character did not allow a falsehood to be uttered within the Court. It was a time when India still stood proud and strong, if battered, after winning Independence and weathering Partition. More than anything else, it allowed for decency and exchanges within the courtroom, even between adversaries.

I worked hard between the demands of being part of the Women and Media Committee, as an officer bearer of the Bombay Union of Journalists, and also covering elections and drought in southern Rajasthan for *Indian Express*. Journalism, for me, was about stretching the boundaries of the looking glass, searching into where the establishment does not want you to see, raising questions that are awkward. Coverage and analysis was always about deepening democracy and accountability, pushing for access to justice. Why don't papers have a labour beat, I remember asking Arun Shourie – the iconic editor of *Indian Express* and vocal member of the People's Union for Civil Liberties (PUCL), of which I had been a life-member from my school days. Shourie simply said that *Indian Express* did not cover labour. The union at *Indian Express* had been on strike around that time. Reporters at that time had an interest in labour, perhaps because they saw themselves as workers. The neoliberal economic policies of the 1990s brought higher wages for journalists. But it changed the culture of journalism. Journalists in the new period do not have security of tenure – many work on contract. This is the *Times of India* model. Some of us – the archaic and committed few – refused to succumb to the market. As wages increased, and security of position vanished, the quality of courageous, investigative journalism also diminished. Issues of wider democratic concern that affected the largest number of Indians did not make it into the press.

Between 1987 and 1989, I extensively covered the drought in southern Rajasthan – in Udaipur district. That work began a long association with Kishore Saint, who has spent his life trying to change the public understanding of water conservation. One day Alyque Padamsee, the marketing whiz and then chief of Lintas, invited me to the 22nd floor of the Express Towers. This was after the *Express* ran my story of starvation deaths in Udaipur district (including one gruesome incident, a father killing his two children and himself after he left his wife at her maternal home). I went up to his office after work, in awe of the invitation that came on a small chit. Alyque and his team began a public interest ad campaign (for which Lintas had become famous) to raise aid for drought stricken Rajasthan and raised substantial assistance. A death row convict wrote to me from his cell. In the epochal *Express* style that always encouraged the reporter, the editors ran the story on the front page. It made a difference to the life of the young man who suddenly saw some doors open for his case where there had been no headway before.

Journalism not only allowed me to build a professional life, but it also enhanced my personal life. It was, after all, in the field of reporting that I met Javed. We bonded at levels that few could hope for in a personal relationship. Friends and family were very anxious when Javed and I took the decision to live together, in sin as it were. Conversations with senior colleagues in the profession come back time and again, as they grappled with me, a 21 year old who had chosen to shift out of her home, and was then living in Antop Hill with her partner. This was 1983. My choices bespoke independence, autonomy and even rebellion. I will never forget Raikarsaab's reaction when Javed and I invited him to our wedding, a civil ceremony, three years later. We had a hand-written invitation on the hand-made Chimanlal paper letterheads, in *haldi kumkum* colour and on this invite we told our brief story! He has kept this as a memento.

*   *   *   *   *

The Bhiwandi conflagration of 1984 drew me – as a journalist first – into the world of communal riots. Bombay started to fall prey to communal mobilization from 1984, when Bal Thackeray, the Shiv Sena supremo, had – for the first time – used *Hindutva* as an overt plank. His annual speeches on Vijayadashami Day had become strident, incendiary and indicting, carefully aping and sharpening what the Rashtriya Swayamsevak Sangh (RSS) and Vishwa Hindu Parishad (VHP) were saying. His Shiv Sena was to proudly claim credit for tearing down the three domes of the Babri Mosque on 6 December 1992, eight years later.

From 1986, there was a countrywide mobilization around the Ramjanmabhoomi movement, which had less to do with building a temple for Lord Ram and more to do with ostracising the Muslim community. *Babar ki Aulad*, a slogan popularized by Sadhvi Rithambara, came to epitomize the venom spouted from that year onwards against India's Muslims (Rithambara, who had a long invisible spell, rushed to tie a *rakhee* on Modi for Raksha Bandhan after he won the Lok Sabha elections in 2014). The Ramjanmabhoomi campaign was a sustained and skilful demonising of a large section of the Indian population. It justified hatred and violence that thereafter was perpetrated against

Muslims. In 1983, the VHP and leaders of eighty-five sects of Hinduism conducted an Ekatmata Yagna (integration rite), which projected a picture of Bharatmata (Mother India) and the *kalash* (brass vessels) of 'holy water' from different rivers. Religion was being made totally political. In October 1984, the VHP tried to make the mosque-temple question a national issue with its Sri Rama Janma Bhoomi Mukti Yajna Samiti. The Samiti was formed on 27 July 1984 with the sole aim of 'liberating' the disputed site. A 130-kilometre march was started on 8 October 1984 from Ayodhya to Lucknow, the State capital. The *yatra* (march) participants reached Lucknow on 14 October, organized a public meeting, and called on the Chief Minister 'to fulfil the long outstanding demand of the Hindus.' The next day, a Sri Rama Janaki Ratha (Ram-Sita chariot) began to tour major UP towns so as to mobilize public opinion and to administer a Janmasthan Mukti Pledge to the public. Although the ratha reached Delhi on 31 October to join a Hindu Convention on 2 November, Indira Gandhi's assassination forced the cancellation of the programme.

The Shah Bano verdict by the Supreme Court in 1985 led to a marked polarization in Bombay – especially in the iconic Mohammedalli Road areas, near the Minara masjid where huge meetings were held. Dominated by Muslim male clergy, the meetings were large, attended by strident men (and a few women). The Supreme Court had granted a paltry Rs. 125 in civil maintenance to an elderly deserted and divorced woman, Shah Bano. It had taken her years to get this result. 'We will not allow any interference in our personal laws', said the leadership of these demonstrations – standing for a Muslim community against people like Shah Bano. On the one side there was the seriously vicious anti-Muslim rhetoric epitomized in the notorious Bal Thackeray speech of October-November 1986 where he exhorted 'Hindus to arm themselves'; on the other side was the blind and immature Muslim leadership that walked straight into the paradigm set by the Hindutvawaadis. Majority and minority communalism fuelled each other. Rajiv Gandhi's Congress played dangerously with this terrain. He succumbed to pressures to pass the Muslim Women (Protection of Rights on Divorce) Act, 1986, on the one hand, and on the other hand, took the decision to unlock the gates of the Babri Masjid and allowed priests to enter the mosque's compound in February 1986. After attempts made to install an idol illegally soon after Independence, an administrative bar had, in a sense, closed the dispute since 1949. Secularism took a beating as these incidents began to define the situation.

Bombay was turning onto itself, defying the very spirit of inclusiveness and cosmopolitanism that has been its guiding principle. By 1984, I had shifted to the *Indian Express* – offered the job for my coverage of the Antulay trial – and by 1989 had joined *Business India*. I remained at *Business India* till both Javed and I quit our professions in mainstream journalism to start *Communalism Combat*. But even before this formal move, we had both become drawn, as journalists, to mobilize media persons against the systemic hate speech and hate writing emanating from the *Saamna* and often – when it came to Bal Thackeray's speeches — being reflected even in mainstream newspapers. In 1986 Thackeray said, 'Hindus should arm themselves', which *Maharashtra Times*, a much respected Marathi daily, had splashed across banner headlines. We ran a campaign to register an FIR against Thackeray. Several hundred journalists had signed. We met the Chief Minister S. B. Chavan on this issue.

Bombay and India appeared to be at a frightening cusp – would it collapse into hatred? In our own small way we tried our best to stem the tide, mobilize public opinion, raise a dissenting voice through meetings, the writing and distribution of pamphlets, and the creation of campaigns. Bal Thackeray cast a pall over Bombay in those days. In *The Sunday Observer*, Javed wrote a strong piece, espousing an unusual viewpoint. In it, Javed argued against the stridency of the Muslim leadership under the Babri Masjid Action Committee (BMAC), urging that the issue should be left to the Constitutional authorities and not to those determined to break the law. Making the question of the Babri Masjid an identity-driven conflict, he argued, would inevitably impact adversely on society. It was a strong argument, even if it seemed idealistic at that time. Javed was, surely, proved to be correct as events unfolded in the decades ahead.

In 1989, a friend and colleague Sajid Rashid – a bold and courageous journalist for the Urdu and Hindi press – decided to run for Assembly from the Kurla seat on the Janata Party ticket. He indomitably stood for secularism and always defied his community's archaic and self-serving leadership. Sajjid lived in the belly of the Muslim ghetto. During the campaign, a young Muslim boy went to eat *paan* days before the election. He was killed. It was a nasty, pre-emptive move to generate terror and prevent Muslims from coming out to vote. Sabrang – our informal platform at that time – decided to act. Founder members included Javed and myself, of course, but also CITU leader and communist Vivek Monteiro and journalist Sudheendra Kulkarni (before he crossed over to the other side). We held a public meeting outside Kurla station, where over nine thousand people gathered. Ahilyatai Rangnekar (CPI-M), Ramdas Athawale, leaders of the Dalit Panthers and film-star Amol Palekar addressed the gathering. Pamphlets and posters were distributed as we re-claimed the streets. We were being drawn more and more into interventions that were not only journalistic.

The 1992-93 violence that rocked Bombay altered the direction of our lives. A decade-long experience of covering, researching and understanding communal violence prepared me to understand what was to come between 6 December 1992 and late January 1993. I was out in the field from that first afternoon – Sunday 6 December. I visited Dharavi, where the first 'victory' procession – a cycle rally of two to three hundred Shiv Sena activists – was allowed by Inspector Gharghe. In Pydhonie, the local Shiv Sena and others organized a 'temple bell ringing ceremony' to celebrate the demolition.

The RSS and the Shiv Sena worked cleverly together. The streets were theirs. A few of us correspondents, confounded by the sheer extent of the violence and the organization behind it, scoured the streets to record testimonies, shared insights with each other and tried our level best to get the police and authorities to act. At the time I developed a thesis – *Who Cast the First Stone* – that made the case that the assailants would conduct brute bouts of violence and then craft a shrill narrative that made the aggressor the victim and the victim the aggressor. It was clear that after the demolition in Ayodhya, the first acts that violated the law were 'celebrations' organized by the RSS and the Shiv Sena in Dharavi and Pydhonie. Yet, the BJP-Shiv Sena successfully flipped the story. Dharamsingh Choradia of the BJP said that 'mad, enraged Muslims attacked buses and public property', adding that the violence came from areas that housed Bangladeshi migrants. Certainly, enraged and upset Muslims did protest in disbelief and anger on 7 December, but nothing can take away the fact of the senseless and brazen provocations on 6 December both in Ayodhya and in Bombay. Worse, the police fired to kill on 7 December – eighty per cent of those who died were Muslims. This alienated and angered the Muslims of Bombay even more. The Bombay police showed an ugly face in this period, something that additional commissioner V. N. Deshmukh testified to before the Justice B. N. Srikrishna

Commission. Deshmukh's testimony should be widely read.

I have always felt that the dynamic of communal violence is a dynamic of revenge. It is true of any ethnic killing in the world. The narrative is to justify violence because you have experienced it once before or supposedly experienced it once before.

Naresh Fernandes, correspondent, and Darryl D'Monte, residential editor, of *The Times of India*, Nikhil Wagle at *Mahanagar*, P. Sainath, Sajid Rashid at *Urdu Times*, and Javed at *Sunday Observer* – all of us were working individually and together to make sense of the complete destruction and mayhem. The BJP-RSS-SS combine began their Machiavellian programme of *maha aartis* on 22 December with a press release announcing the event. Between then and early January when organized intimidation and stray attacks on Muslims took place (and in parts of Mumbai Muslims retaliated), Bombay simmered. These were acts from the BJP-RSS-Shiv Sena. Yet, it was the Radhabai chawl incident on 8 January that was taken as a justified provocation by Thackeray and the Sena to unleash terror on Bombay's Muslims. Between December 1992 and January 1993 the stabbing of Hindu Mathawadi workers in south and central Bombay had also kept the pot boiling as a communalized underworld got into the fray. The blasts orchestrated by the Bombay underworld took place on 12 March 1993. On 22 February, weeks beforehand, some of us journalists had met the commissioner of police S. K. Bapat to warn him of worrisome developments. He – like many among the top police and intelligence – deliberately or otherwise, turned the other way. To this day, powerful men in the BJP, SS and RSS like to flip the storyline. For them it was the blasts that led to the riots. Lazy, uninterested television anchors rarely square the tale, leaving it to us to continue painstakingly to put the record straight. This Goebbelsian desire to change the narrative lay at the heart of the Sangh Parivar strategy: Who cast the first stone? For them every act of violence of the majority Hindu is an act of retaliation of the perennially and permanently barbaric Mussalmaan.

In the context of the reporting that I was doing at this time, I broke a sensational news story that was featured on BBC, CNN, on *Newstrack* and *Eyewitness*. As I combed the streets gathering details for two cover stories I wrote for *Business India,* we (some persons from the victim community and I) tapped into police wireless messages between police control room and mobile police vans. We managed to capture the frequency and taped the conversations. They were as frightening as they were sensational. The policemen on the PCR-wireless exhibited a strong, sharp and abusive anti-Muslim bias. These revelations created a sensation. The issue of communal bias in the police force has been a deep concern that I have persistently tracked in my journalistic and activist career.

Through activism and writing – journalistic and academic – the issue of an increasing incursion of communal, majoritarian biases within the Indian law enforcement agencies, intelligence gathering structures, in fact several institutions of governance has been a consistent matter of research and investigation. The eight reports of the National Police Commission (1979-81) flag this bias and yet there is an overall reluctance to acknowledge this openly. In this journey, we have been fortunate to gather knowledge and experience of the best among our senior officers—K. F. Rustomji, tasked with raising the Border Security Force (also chief security officer to India's first Prime Minister, Jawaharlal Nehru), Padam Rosha, a former DGP, Satish Sahney, former Commissioner of Police, Mumbai and Julio Ribeiro, not only former DGP Punjab but so much more. Chaman Lal, a senior IPS officer – former DGP Nagaland – spends his retirement days working among the most deprived even as he urges the young entrants into his profession with a call to conscience. As he so aptly puts it, 'the job of the police is to maintain peace, order, security, stability and be the building blocks of a harmonious society. We must ensure not just the political rights of our people in terms of equality and non-discrimination but strive for the realization of economic rights as well. All those marginalized, Dalits and minorities must feel safe and secure in India. Then we will have a secure and stable India.'[2]

Each episode of such a deep conflict makes a sharp imprint on the witness, including the journalist. The most important and crucial thing is to be able to see a pattern, not to get lost in each detail – which could be seen without context. Senior journalists mentored me to understand the larger patterns. S. B. Kolpe and Madhu Shetye had seen me in those wretched weeks of 1992-93. Kolpe recounted his own experience from 1961, while covering the first post-Partition riot in Jabalpur for the *Free Press Journal*. Sent to Jabalpur ten days after the breakout of violence, his editor asked him to test and explore the narrative of 'Hindu girl abducted by a Muslim boy' that led to the riot. The first person he met there was the SP, a man of principle, a Kashmiri Pandit. He advised him to go to the area, speak to the neighbours – which is what Kolpe did. The story was much more complex. The Muslim man was a 'bidi worker' and his relationship with a Hindu woman from the middle caste and class had irked sentiments at various levels. Though the relationship and marriage was one of consent, it had led to these divisions and a distorted narrative. Kolpe wrote three pieces for *FPJ* on the incident. These opened the eyes of many all over the country and also got him a letter from Prime Minister Nehru. He told me this story – then wrote it later in *Afternoon Dispatch* and *Courier*.

Five or six journalists tried determinedly to fix the narrative of 1992-93 – to be more accurate in our coverage. Choradia, the BJP president for Maharashtra, held a press conference at BJP

---

[2] 'Policemen speak out', *Sabrang*, 3 December 2015 (https://sabrangindia.in/article/policemen-speak-out).

headquarters, which is behind the Mantralaya at Nariman Point. He kept saying that the violence began from areas dominated by Bangladeshi migrants. As soon as his spiel ended, I raised my hand and asked, 'If this is indeed true, it is worrisome. Can you help us journalists with empirical facts as to where in your estimation the violence first broke out so that we can tally and compare these with what the police is saying and facts on the ground?' He dodged. I persisted after a few minutes. Finally, in exasperation he asked, 'Are you conducting the press conference or am I?'

Then there was the L. K. Advani press conference at the Indian Merchants' Chamber where Javéd asked, 'You say that the BJP does not stand for a theocratic state. Similarly Mohammed Ali Jinnah had said that he did not wish for a theocratic Pakistan. But just as the logic of a theocratic state was written into what Jinnah stood for, can it not be said that a theocratic state is written into the movement that you, BJP and Hindutva are spearheading?' That morning Advani had visited Jogeshwari where the Radhabai chawl is located. As he alighted from the car, Arifa, a social activist, stopped him. *Advaniji yahan Mussalmanon ka bhi jaan aur maal ka nuksaan hua hai; aap hamare taraf kyon nahin aate?* (Advaniji even we Muslims have lost lives and property. Why do you not visit our side also?).

Finally, Prime Minister P. V. Narasimha Rao of the Congress came to Bombay. The state was then ruled by the Congress, led by Sudhakarrao Naik. Maseeh Rahman of *India Today,* Javed and myself asked him about the abdication of the state government and the immunity shown towards Shiv Sainiks as well as the overtly communal role of the Bombay police. Back then, these interventions helped – to some extent – to shape the national discourse. That was then. Today, we find the media abdicating its seminal non-partisan, rational and courageous role.

I began a journey to study the history of communal violence.

I poured through riot commission reports and academic work – towards preparing courses on the issue for journalist students. It would be valuable if colleges across the country taught the history and sociology of riots to all our students – as part of our corrective action. A society that continues to absorb this level of hatred – whether from Thackeray, Togadia or Modi – at some point becomes not just immune but an active partaker in the hatred. This is what appears to have happened to us in urban India even as an elite and middle class, lured by the shine and gloss offered by a neo-liberal lifestyle, appears to have not abdicated but seceded from the rest of India. So, long before Modi was feted by industrialists at the Vibrant Gujarat affaire in 2007, Bombay saw the foul-mouthed tigerman Thackeray be felicitated by the Rotary Club at the Taj Mahal Hotel even as the Amitabh-Jaya Bachchan duo went into the business of video manufacturing with him. It is this middle class and this elite that even today sits comfortably with the politics of hate.

Soon after the fires that lit Bombay were doused, but even as the embers burned, a citizen's effort began to book the perpetrators of hate speech. The official Shiv Sena mouthpiece – *Saamna* – showed a pattern of incendiary and provocative writing from July 1991. My father Atul drafted a public interest litigation (PIL), asking for an FIR to be lodged against Thackeray. J. B. D'Souza, former Chief Secretary of Maharashtra, and Dilip Thakore, a senior journalist, became petitioners in the case. The court was reluctant. In June 1993, Thackeray appeared to cross all limits, when he wrote (and *Saanj Jansatta* published), *Hum Adalaton Ke Faisle Par Laghoo Shanka Karte Hain* (I piss on the judgments of the courts). Finally a division bench of the Bombay High Court passed a judgment (30 September 1994) that justified the editorials in *Saamna* saying that they only referred to 'anti-national Muslims.' By then *Communalism Combat* was in its second year. When even the

Supreme Court dismissed – without a hearing – the Special Leave Petition, constitutional experts H. M. Seervai, Nani Palkhiwala, Fali Nariman, Soli Sorabjee, and Justice Suresh condemned the dismissal urging the Supreme Court to recall its order. Seervai's was a five thousand word exclusive legal opinion authored for *Combat*. (This was our cover story, *Crime and Punishment*, January 1995.) A countrywide signature campaign was launched in which trade unions and the Fishworkers' Union led by Thomas Kochery also joined. However, we were not successful in getting Thackeray's hate speeches scrutinized by the higher courts. This failure has affected Indian jurisprudence on hate speech.

*   *   *   *   *

The events of 1992-93 in Bombay pushed me into a major shift – from journalist to activist. It was not the Gujarat pogrom of 2002 that moved me in that direction. By 2002 I was already an activist. We started Sabrang and *Communalism Combat* in August 1993.

The riot in the mind simmers for months before it spills onto the streets, leaving no space for dialogue. The *raison d'etre* of starting *Communalism Combat* was to somehow use our skills, as journalists, to prevent this riot from spilling onto the streets. We wanted to deconstruct hate politics and encourage voices of peace and hope. We believed always that there are many paths and not a single narrative to show us the way. One of the reasons why we started *Communalism Combat* was that we wanted to look at the shadows and silences of the mainstream media. We wanted to look at why the media doesn't report on what should be obvious stories. Mainstream journalism's increasing impatience with tracking the build-up to conflict and tracing its fallout was another reason behind our move to create our magazine. In *Combat*, we have believed in trying to set the agenda for larger publications – in a sense edging and nudging the media to do what it ought to do. The decreased interest of the news curve and short memories makes one thing 'topical' today and forgotten the next. But *Communalism Combat* and Sabrang have tried hard not to fall prey to this short-term thinking, while at the same time trying to remain relevant.

Vijay Tendulkar, Admiral Ramdas, Rajiv Dhawan, J. N. Dixit (former foreign secretary) and jurists of consequence wrote for us. We wanted critical minds to write for us. We had a disproportionately high influence given our small numbers. The magazine reached people who made policy and who framed the news. Our interview with IPS officer Vibhuti Narayan Rai ('No Riot can Continue for more than 24 hours unless the state wants it to continue') was reproduced by thirty-four Indian newspapers. Tendulkar's *Muslims and I*, which was also published in *Combat*, was widely read.[3]

In our cover story on Mani Ratnam's *Bombay*, we de-constructed the film. Much tension was generated over the release and the Bombay police had organized special shows. I watched the film with the wife of the advocate Yusuf Muchhala by my side. As the closing credits rolled she turned to me and said, 'What is with you all? It is such a beautiful Hindu-Muslim romance; I loved it!' We were disappointed in Mani Ratnam's mainstream effort to 'balance' the Hindu don with a Muslim bad man. For us, who had lived through the horrors of Bombay 1992-1993, the incursions of the Bombay underworld notwithstanding, the aggression was overwhelmingly one way.

Communalism Combat won many international and national awards. There was pressure on us to start a Hindi edition. Our close and lasting relationship with Tapan Bose opened us up to the world of the Pak-India People's Forum for Peace and Democracy (PIPFPD). At the first core group meeting in Lahore in 1994, we

---

[3] sabrangindia.in/article/muslims-and-i-vijay-tendulkar.

met with Asma Jahangir and I. A. Rehman, both of whom remain comrades in arms. We understood that there needed to be a South Asian perspective on communalism and minority rights. It has remained a focus area for *Communalism Combat*. In 1997 on my first ever visit to Sri Lanka – after which I authored the cover story for *Combat* — the reality of disenfranchisement and alienation giving birth to communalism deepened. I went to Colombo as a romantic secularist, believing that Buddhism had been driven out from the land of its birth. It had, of course. There was another twist in the narrative, however. Even Buddhism, when it came into positions of power and authority, became crudely majoritarian and oppressive.

Javed and I grew a great deal during our work with *Combat*. The magazine reflected our collective concerns. Javed strained to get the Muslim community to address the sticky questions of secularism, gender justice and democracy. Five years after launching *Combat*, I began to further and more thoroughly understand the relationship between caste and communalism. My great grandfather had set up the Bahishkrit Hitakarini Sabha with Dr Babasaheb Ambedkar.[4] The implications of caste for communalism set in during the late 1990s. Javed and I had intense editorial discussions about the need to interrogate caste. We invited many Dalit writers to write for us, which enriched our content. This inclusion and editorial consciousness hugely deepened our understanding. Today, the democratic secular discourse whether on issues of deepening democracy, rule of law or understanding of the social sciences

---

[4] Dr. Babasaheb Ambedkar convened a meeting on 9 March 1924 at Bombay's Damodar Hall to launch a social movement for the uplift of the Untouchables. At the meeting the participants considered the desirability of establishing a central institution for removing difficulties of the untouchables and placing their grievances before government. After much discussion and debate, it was resolved that an institution be established. It was founded on 20 July 1924 under the title Bahishkrit Hitakarini Sabha, and was registered under Act XXI of 1860. Chimanlal Setalvad was its first President.

needs to factor in this historical omission. Issues that are related to Dalit exclusion, Bahujan history and the Adivasi narrative need to not just be mainstreamed but be reflected in our representation of reality (and in the authors represented in our magazines and newspapers).

In September 2001, I was in Ahmedabad on a three-day training of Dalit and Muslim women. The training was on how to approach the law and order machinery, register complaints, and spot signals of any build up of conflict. As we interacted over three days, ominous portents began to emerge. Dalit women spoke of the RSS-Bajrang Dal luring their sons at Rs 3,000-4,000 per month to attend camps where they were taught how to wield lathis and arms. Muslim women spoke of how their children were not allowed to carry eggs in their tiffins to school. Abuses against the community had become sharper and shriller. 'Laandya, Miyaon' were words recorded and thrown about. My children were with me on that trip to Ahmedabad. At the end of the training, I took them to the home of my mother's maternal uncle. That was my last visit to a home I had visited often through my childhood.

Our work with *Communalism Combat* taught us that something terrible was on the horizon.

Minority and majority communalism is and has always been on our radar. In November 1998, *Communalism Combat* was the first South Asian magazine to publish a cover story on the horrific role of the Taliban years before the Bamiyan Buddha destruction put them on the headlines. The *Communalism Combat* cover story read, 'Hell on Earth: Afghanistan'. 'How Green Is My Valley' dissected the Islamization of the Kashmiri movement, as did our cover stories on the plight of Bangladeshi Hindus: 'Living With Terror – Minorities in Bangladesh', September 2004. Javed's sharp critique of the Jamaat-e-Islami in *Communalism Combat* (July 2012, 'Reluctant Democrats') is testimony to the stand we have taken against theocracy and its threat to democratic ideals.

Our focus on Gujarat and Bombay did not abate. We published our first cover story on Gujarat in *Communalism Combat* in October 1998. The cover of that issue had an illustration by my sister. It said 'Welcome to Hindu Rashtra'. The cover report was on Randhikpur and Sanjeli in the Panchmahals – the headquarters of Godhra. This was later to become the spot of the horrific gang rape of Bilquees Bano on 1 March 2002 and the killing of fourteen others including her three-year old daughter, Saleha.

For four days in 1998, around Independence Day in August, Muslim villagers had been forced to live outside their village because of the concerted attack by the RSS and VHP on their lives and property. Hateful pamphlets had been distributed in the thousands. The RSS had also given a call to economically and socially boycott the minorities. We had published the report by Shanti Abhiyan and PUCL. I interviewed the DGP of Gujarat, C. P. Singh, who denied the charges made by the rabid supremacists that 'conversion of Hindu girls was happening through marriage'. The dominant narrative used to financially and socially isolate the minorities in these areas was that of inter-community marriages. The VHP and RSS would say that Hindu-Muslim marriages were social crimes, especially if the man was a Muslim.

In January 1999, our cover on Gujarat was on *Conversions*. It interrogated the Hindutva discourse around Christian missionaries allegedly converting people from Hinduism. This story was relevant after sixteen churches had been brutally attacked around Christmas Day in 1998. On 23 January 1999, three days before Republic Day, Graham Staines – an Australian Christian missionary – and his three sons were burned alive in Orissa.

Later that year, in October, *Combat* looked at prejudice being fostered through Gujarat's Social Studies textbooks and in 2000, the creeping stranglehold of fascism. There was no sign of Modi at that time. Modi came to Gujarat only in September-October 2001. He was brought in quite consciously because in September that year, the BJP had lost a series of by-elections after many years in the state. Long before Modi's arrival, the ground had been prepared and the field set for what was to follow. As part of this cover story, I had accessed an anonymous pamphlet widely circulated in Gujarat that had a Hindutva and Om symbol. It was a detailed instruction manual for the cadres on how to file false complaints and mislead the police after leading violent attacks. A senior Gujarat serving police officer had used this circular widely in trainings to warn cadres of the Gujarat police on the dangers posed by such supremacist organizations.

In the same year, I was part of a collective fact-finding mission to look into how Praveen Togadia's hate speech had wreaked havoc on Muslim property totalling Rs. 15 crores in several districts of the state. To investigate this I had travelled from Surat upwards ending up in Ahmedabad after looking at damages as far as Limbadiya. Terrorists had set upon Amarnath pilgrims killing 99 persons, pilgrims and jawans included. At a press conference, Togadia said, *Wahan ka jawaab yahan denge* (We will give an answer for that right here). That call was enough to bring the trained mob out to loot and burn. Six people died.

Our campaign to 'Punish the Guilty' for the Bombay pogrom of 1992-93 did not stop. We held meetings and public hearings to shame the Congress while it remained in power. This we pursued in the months that followed especially after the Shiv Sena-BJP government disbanded the Commission after coming to power in 1995. A spontaneous day-long dharna by Bombay's citizens at Hutatma Chowk on 30 January 1996 brought in a vast array of persons in support of an investigation. The Bombay violence had shaken us all: Nani Palkhivala stepped down from Bombay House, Shashi Kapoor and Sanjna Kapoor joined in and the indomitable

K. G. Kannabiran, then vice president of the People's Union of Civil Liberties, also participated. It was one of the moments of resistance, rare and special, that are impossible to forget. In 1998, while the SS-BJP combine ruled Maharashtra, Justice B. N. Srikrishna had submitted his report to the government. The government refused to accept it and filed an adversarial Action Taken Report. Sabrang Communications accessed copies and printed the entire report along with excerpts from the Madon Commission (1970) in two editions. We sold the first black and white cover edition for Rs. 60 and the second for Rs. 90. Our aim was for the people of Bombay to read it. We worked hard at distributing it, even getting vendors to sell it outside the courts.

In September 2001, when the two-year old Congress-NCP government in Maharashtra reneged on its electoral promise to get the Srikrishna Commission report implemented, we held a powerful public hearing at the KC College Mumbai. Six years later in 2007-08, I filed applications under the Right to Information Act (RTI) that exposed the government's false claims: of the thirty-one police officers indicted by the judge over eighty per cent had escaped censure or punitive action and had been promoted.

Meanwhile in Gujarat, signs were ominous and the documentation meticulous. In late 2001, on a trip to Delhi I made two crucial visits – to see Fali Nariman at the Supreme Court and to visit the National Human Rights Commission. I carried circulars and documents from the government that showed that it was conducting selective censuses of Muslims and Christians, actions that were brazenly anti-Constitutional. I had proof that top echelons of the police had issued circulars to set up a Cell at every police station to 'monitor' inter-community marriages. Again, this was unlawful. I brought dozens of hate pamphlets from all over Gujarat. My dossier had a couple of thousand pages.

Fali Nariman asked me to wait in the basement library of

the Supreme Court used by counsel. I waited in awe of where my grandfather's presence loomed. A senior court master told me a story about him as I waited. When Fali Uncle appeared, I showed him the material. I urged him to consider some public interest intervention in the Supreme Court. He advised me to keep monitoring and documenting. What I had was not enough. I was disappointed. Fali Nariman had resigned as Gujarat counsel after the attacks on Christians had increased during the first BJP-led NDA government. I next went to the office of the National Human Rights Commission, which was in Faridkot House. Justice Verma agreed to meet me. He saw the papers. I gave him his own set. He listened to what I had to say then suggested that I continue the documentation, as the material was not enough yet for the Commission to intervene.

For almost five years before the 2002 pogrom in Gujarat, I spoke at as many places as I could to warn about the worrisome signals from around the state. I pleaded with fellow activists as well as senior politicians and bureaucrats to train their lens on the state. I had absolutely no idea what form or shape the disaster would take but was eerily clear that, given the planning and build up, something ghastly, and irretrievable would happen. As late as 10 February 2002, at a meeting in Bangalore on Dalit Women's issues, I made the same point. A friend from Ahmedabad got extremely upset by what I was saying. Seventeen days later I was unfortunately and horribly proved correct.

The tenth anniversary issue of *Communalism Combat* in August 2003 was a special one and contained a fine collection of articles. It is a veritable collector's item. One particular article by a doyen of the Indian human rights movement, K. Balagopal from the Human Rights Forum Hyderabad, sums up the work of our journal,

Prediction is a demanding expression, but prescient commentary is a quality that any movement magazine can aspire to. Most do, but few achieve it.

One could not help thinking so vis-à-vis *Communalism Combat* when Gujarat 'happened'. The only other equally striking instance one could think of was Balraj Puri's commentary on Kashmir spread over the eighties, which made the rise of militancy in Kashmir seem so natural when it finally happened. Except that, in that case, the realization was not altogether unpleasant, whereas here it was something of a shock.

Today, one can read through back numbers of *Communalism Combat* and piece together the story of the sangh parivar's ascendancy in Gujarat – Almost, at any rate – the things they did along the way until they could finally manage to mobilize thousands of ordinary people to commit the most gruesome carnage India has known. If Godhra had not given them the opportunity, they would have invented one.

We certainly did require a publication devoted exclusively to the propagation, protection and advancement of secularism, plurality, communal amity, whatever you want to call it. It is arguably the most central political task today, even counting the fight against globalization. The reason, perhaps, is that perversion of the mind is more dangerous than appropriation of matter. Granted that globalization does not stop with matter, the sangh parivar's brand of poison is still a more urgent concern.

This is not the place to put forward strategies – assuming that one had any – but it is still necessary to recount the requirements that should guide strategic thinking in this area. It should be apparent that *Communalism Combat* has chosen a mix of uncompromising opposition to Hindutva and the need not to make every believing Hindu feel that he/she is an enemy of what secular minded people stand for. The same evidently goes for Muslims and Christians, too.

The anti-communal agenda does not seek the creation of more atheists and non-believers. It strives to open a dialogue with average mortals – who are almost all believers in some measure, and will remain so for ever in some measure – so that they may be encouraged to despise the hatred and the violence that are practised in their name.

There is no need to idealize religion, no need to declare grandly that 'the essence of all religions is one' (a popular but rather doubtful proposition), no need to ignore the baneful social effects of socio-religious dogmas and traditions. Without succumbing to any desire to indulge in such simplifications, one may yet hope to appeal to the positive side of religious belief in the fight against its systematic perversion.

The problem perhaps is that religious fundamentalism offers an answer to a kind of insecurity that is not always easy to handle. The reference is not to the 'heart of a heartless world' kind of insecurity. That insecurity is real, and it is equally real that religion, including the bigoted forms of it, offers solace to its victims. But that, at any rate, is an ideologically and philosophically unproblematic form of insecurity, whatever the practical difficulties of rendering the security offered by religion in such a context dispensable.

A more relevant insecurity, with regard to the genesis and spread of religious conservatism and bigotry, is the insecurity wrought by the spread of democratic aspirations. The uncertainty created by the upturning of social roles generates insecurity in more quarters than the one-dimensional analyses of social inequalities that we are habituated to would tell us. Hindutva and other fundamentalist forces have capitalized extensively on this widespread anti-democratic insecurity among the people. Even more than on the rational insecurity of unemployment, poverty, urbanization, crime, etc. That is why the if-you-don't-have-a-job-then-fight-unemployment-and-not-Muslims kind of argument will not easily succeed.

There can be no compromise here too. There can be no sanctioning of reversal of the democratization process to pull the rug of insecurity from under the feet of the success of the sangh parivar. And yet, the people who are subjects of that success cannot all be despised, a tendency not uncommon among upper caste elite secularists. Hints of an awareness of this dilemma are evident in the stands *Communalism Combat* has been taking on the problem it has posed for itself and for us. It must be brought out more openly and strategies devised to answer it. I hope that *Communalism Combat* will see more theoretical and political debate on these issues in the coming days. That would be a fitting way to continue its remarkable work.

We lost K Balagopal too early. He died in 2009, at the age of 57.

'LET HINDUS GIVE VENT'

I wiped out the huge *tikka* that used to adorn my forehead before 1992-93. The post-Babri Masjid demolition violence produced in me a sub-conscious revulsion. The mohalla-based reportage I had done brought me face to face with a certain kind of violence. Javed misses the *tikka*. Though back in some fashion now, it has simply not re-entered my repertoire often enough. Somehow, I needed to distance myself from the distasteful acts being committed in the name of my faith. Until then, loving to dress up as I did and do, the large vermillion (usually, sometimes purple and pink, *tikka*) was very much part of my overall look.

I reached Gujarat in early March 2002. I began to scour the relief camps and districts, then, returned back to Ahmedabad, exhausted. Late into the night, I would pen the alerts for the statutory bodies, the Supreme Court, the President of India, NHRC and other human rights forums. The overwhelming sense when I described things back home to Mumbai was – 'If Bombay ten years ago was bad, then Gujarat is one thousand times worse.' In the first six months, I was physically attacked five times. Twice the drivers of hired vehicles abandoned me in villages, fearful of the consequences of the journeys for them. Within days of the coverage, a resolve shaped into a dogged commitment based on these dual experiences: of having lived through Bombay 1992-1993 and now Gujarat 2002: mere documentation and advocacy and campaigning on the targeted mass crimes that exposed bitter fault-lines of bias and prejudice in our institutions of democracy and governance, would not be enough. It was time to test the criminal justice system, from several angles; can justice ever be done when mass violence happens? Can our courts restore the faith in the system? People's confidence and trust in their neighbourhoods, and even their friends, had been snatched away.

This is what I told Javed in the nightly calls I made. Since I was away alone till odd hours, there was incessant worry at home. I remember saying that now we need to move the courts and see if justice can be done, to test the system and ask whether there can be recompense. We knew that this task could not have been undertaken by us alone and that we would need a strong body of citizens committed to the rule of law to take on that task. That was how Citizens for Justice and Peace (CJP) was born. In early April, in Nandan Muluste's home, Pankaj Shankar showed us the uncut version of *In the Name of Faith*. It was a raw film that depicted all that needed to be said about the gross cruelty that was deliberately allowed free reign. Those of us in the room - Alyque Padamsee, Cyrus Guzder, Kadrisaab, Nandan Maluste, Shireesh Patel, Anil Dharker, Ghulam Peshimam, and Javed Anand - watched the film. Taizoon Khorakhiwala and his wife Edith have also been fellow travellers in our intense journey. Tears flowed freely at that screening. They turned to disbelief and anger at the extent of abdication of constitutional governance. We then resolved to action. It is no coincidence that those who were present that day were also among those who had been at the forefront of the citizen's mobilizations after the Babri demolition and Bombay pogrom in 1992-93. The understanding and connections between the two bouts of violence, both of which reflected state complicity at different levels, were there.

If our courts, politicians, bureaucrats and policemen, had punished the perpetrators of 1984, then the violence of 1992 would not have so easily happened. If the survivors of the Bombay killings of 1992-1993 had earned real reparations and justice, none in the political class, bureaucracy and police, would have so easily beaten the 2002 drum. It is this all-pervasive culture of impunity that has allowed the perpetrators of mass violence, right from Partition to the present, to go scot-free. Within India's administration and police force, too – barring a few, stray and rare exceptions – the steel frame resists accountability and transparency. It closes in like an armour of protection, freezing out and targeting even those who pursue the path of justice.[1]

Filmmaker Pankaj Shankar was to re-surface in the narrative later (2004-05), when Zahira Shaikh turned hostile for a second time in Mumbai in 2004. Among the footage he had shot in those early days in 2002 were scenes of the BEST bakery carnage the day after the incident (2 March). There was footage with Zahira recording in detail, what was her initial reaction to the carnage – what the law considers a first information report (FIR) about the crime. When Zahira tried, after November 2004, to deny that she had ever done this, the footage told its own tale. Shankar not only allowed himself to be grilled by a crude defence led by Shiv Sena's former member of parliament – Adhik Shirodkar – but refused to crack under the venomous onslaught. The judgment of the trial court has a significant section on the validity of this video testimony. It indicts the Shiv Sena counsel – Shirodkar – who spent a significant amount of the court's time during the pre-trial phase abusing my family name and me. For people like Shirodkar, it was

---

[1] In the issue of *Communalism Combat* to commemorate the fifth anniversary of the Gujarat genocide (July-August 2007), I recounted how many of the powerful bureaucrats – complicit in constitutional actions under Narendra Modi – had been carefully and quietly rehabilitated in key ministries of the United Progressive Alliance (UPA I) government. Those policemen who continue to be targeted, such as Rahul Sharma and R. B. Sreekumar, are those who refused to compromise on their stance vis-á-vis 2002. They are still being made to pay for raising the bar, testing the system, with difficult and uncomfortable questions.

the name 'Setalvad' that had pulled Thackeray to court in 1993. It had again proved to be a thorn in the flesh of the post-2002 crude and violent Hindutva project.[2]

Our nightly alerts went out to the President of India, the Chief Justice of India, the Prime Minister, the National Human Rights Commission and to other statutory bodies. They also went to thousands of citizens and journalists all over India. These alerts were invaluable first person testimonies on the extent and dimensions of the violence. The issues raised in the alerts helped dictate the legal actions that were to follow. Some of the themes that emerged out of the Gujarat carnage of 2002 were as follows:

- The post-mortem of the victims of the tragic Godhra mass arson took place in the open at the rail yard in the presence of the health minister Ashok Bhatt and thereafter, the chief minister Narendra Modi. The evidence for this became sharper as various investigations unfolded.

- The bodies of the victims arrived in Ahmedabad in a motor cavalcade. They were handed over to the Gujarat secretary of the VHP – not an organization known for its sobriety. This decision to hand them to the VHP was taken at the highest level of the state political leadership. Even P. C. Pande, then Commissioner of Police of Ahmedabad, was known to have recorded his strong displeasure at this decision.[3] It led to large mobs of angry RSS men and women joining in the daylight funeral procession on 28 February 2002. The government allowed this procession. It was an immediate provocation.

[2] Later amidst much fanfare and drama, Shirodkar's counsel got some of these remarks expunged when the appeal in the Best Bakery case was heard in Mumbai in appeal in the High Court.

[3] After 2008, Pande rose to become Director General of Police (DGP) for Gujarat. He had been silenced by lucrative promotions, first in service and then after retirement. Today he sits on the board of the Adani Group, earning a lucrative emolument.

• The state machinery did not act to arrest or detain communal criminals once Godhra had happened. There were no preventive measures taken by the government. The deliberate delay in the declaration of curfew and the use of the Army says a great deal about the interests of the government. The government, on the other hand, openly declared support for the Gujarat Bandh called on 28 February and the Bharat Bandh called on 1 March by the VHP. A strong umbilical cord binds the BJP, the VHP, the Bajrang Dal and the RSS – with the latter being the core of the Parivar.[4]

• The violence was widespread and systemic. It lasted (in its intense form) right until May 2002 when the then Prime Minister Vajpayee sent K. P. S. Gill to take charge. Things did not really settle down till August 2002, when the Chief Election Commissioner visited the state.

• The violence followed a staged pattern – similar in far-flung districts of the state. Large armed militias of ten to fifteen thousand men, many on motorbikes – following carefully directed commands – terrorized certain neighbourhoods. They used gas cylinders, white chemical powder and weapons.

• Daylight attacks lasted for hours and included acts of gendered violence unprecedented for their barbarity. This was evident in Randhikpur, Sanjeli, Eral and Fatehpur in Panchmahal/Dahod in north Gujarat, in Vadodara and Ahmedabad (Naroda Patiya and Gulberg). It was clear that subjugating a community through these attacks on girls and women was part of the pre-planned strategy. It could not have been conducted without large bands of men trained to hate Muslims and objectify their women. This is what happened in the training camps, which the tribunal had documented.[5]

---

[4] 'Preparation for Violence: Role of the BJP and Allied Organizations – the RSS, VHP BD', Concerned Citizens Tribunal Report: *Crimes Against Humanity,* Gujarat 2002 and A. G. Noorani, *The RSS and the BJP: A Division of Labour,* New Delhi: LeftWord Books, 2000.

[5] One such account of what transpired at these training camps, where hatred

- Hate-filled reports in mainstream newspapers like the *Sandesh* and also in pamphlets were recovered from all parts of the state. Some of these had been openly authored by the RSS-VHP; others were anonymous. These were open exhortations to break the law, socially boycott and even physically attack Muslims. Senior police officers, as we found during the Zakia Jafri case, urged for the prosecution of the writers of these pamphlets. Predictably the chief executive of the state, also Gujarat's chief minister and home minister, namely Narendra Modi, ignored these recommendations, despite the fact that his state intelligence chief (R. B. Sreekumar) and also another senior police officer, then SP of Bhavnagar, Rahul Sharma, had recommended – in writing – that both the newspaper *Sandesh* and the Vishwa Hindu Parishad (VHP) should be prosecuted for inciting violence against the minorities.

- State complicity came into play in the subversion of the criminal justice system. FIRs were doctored. The new FIRs diluted the crimes by clubbing criminal complaints of victims together in one magnum FIR, where the names of the accused with powerful connections disappeared. FIRs were not filed in the name of the victim complainants, who had proffered them, but in the name of police officers. Deliberately not investigating the complicity of the police officers was commonplace. The state appointed public prosecutors who owed their allegiance to the RSS and not to the Indian Constitution.

- The state showed utter callousness and absence of remorse in the way it treated the victims, who were huddled and traumatized in relief camps. They were refugees in their own land. Modi went to Becaharaji during his election campaign of 2002 and said – with venom – 'relief camps are baby making factories'. This kind of rhetoric debased the conscience of Gujarat. Star Television aired the

---

against one community was bartered through narratives against the Muslim community, has been documented in detail in the Concerned Citizens Tribunal Report, *Crimes Against Humanity*, Gujarat 2002.

tape with the obnoxious speech in September 2002, but thereafter the media has chosen, through selective amnesia, to allow public memory to easily forget. The government de-barred foreign aid to Gujarat for the camps.[6] This was even documented by the Editor's Guild of India.

• High on the success of its project, two decisions of the state government under Modi are very significant. One was to announce discriminatory amounts in compensation for the Godhra and post-Godhra victims. The second was to announce a one-man Inquiry Commission headed by retired Judge K. G. Shah, who had questionable credentials. The national public outcry, from different quarters and also by Justice J. S. Verma, former chief justice who headed the NHRC, compelled a retraction. Justice G. T. Nanavati was added as senior judge on the commission and amounts in reparation were equalized.

• Policemen who stood firm to defend the law were carefully and systematically targeted. As time wore on, and powerful perpetrators grew in political strength, those who had stood their ground began to prefer silence and invisibility. Those who subverted the law – and there were too many of them – have been rewarded.[7]

Gujarat 2002 was about impunity of the most unique and unimaginable kind. The task before us then was to legally and through advocacy puncture this abiding acceptance of the culture of impunity. This culture was visible in earlier bouts of targeted

[6] Sanjay Basak, 'TV (Star News) tapes prove Modi attacked Muslims', *Asian Age*, 15 September 2002.
[7] Many of the IAS and IPS officers who complied with the state's resolve to abdicate constitutional and legal responsibility for protecting fundamental rights of citizens, were rewarded handsomely with lucrative postings by the government in power in the state, the very same government that stood indicted, nationally and internationally for the wilful breakdown of the Constitutional machinery, between February and May 2002, in the state of Gujarat.

pogroms as well, but in this case it was at a macabre and magnified scale.

It has been our attempt – as Citizens for Justice and Peace (CJP) – over the past fifteen years to address various nuggets of this breakdown of the rule of law. CJP's memorandum of association and actions were committed to re-building confidence in the rule of law through – among other things – legal action and litigation as well as legal advocacy, confidence building measures, and mobilizations. To date, CJP has supported sixty-eight legal initiatives, petitions and interventions from the magistrate court upwards to the Supreme Court.

Our first petition was filed in the Gujarat High Court simply to ensure that the Modi government be held legally and constitutionally responsible to pay for the upkeep of relief camps in the state. It is a matter of shame that the state in Gujarat refused to open relief camps. The Vajpayee-led NDA I government provided Rs. 160 crore for relief after the pogrom. The Food and Civil Supplies Minister for Gujarat, Bharat Barot, returned that money – apart from Rs. 19 crores. He did not want to spend it on relief. Barot is on record to have led mobs and extorted money from members of the Muslim community.[8]

In March and April 2002, the atmosphere in the courts was frightening and hostile. Bands of Sangh Parivar activists – from the RSS, VHP and Bajrang Dal – would be present. They would dominate the proceedings in the High Courts and Sessions Courts. We were keen to have senior counsel Aspi Chinoy from Mumbai. He had committed to coming, but had a last minute glitch. I tried to insist that he needed to be there to, at the least, break through the terror within the courtrooms (as an outside counsel). He thought I was over-reacting. I requested him then to find counsel

---

[8] Dionne Bunsha, 'A relentless hate campaign', *Frontline*, vol. 19, issue 10, 11-24 May 2002 & 'Patterns of Violence', Concerned Citizens Tribunal.

from within Gujarat whom he had faith in for us. After a couple of hours he called back to say he would go since all those he had spoken to had expressed reluctance to argue this simple brief. What happened with Aspi the next day is something he still talks about. On a simple matter of the state accepting responsibility for providing water, milk, masalas and so on, to refugees, he, a senior lawyer, had to press and argue for five hours to obtain a favourable order. That was our first success. Suhel Tirmizi, who has been the mainstay of CJP's legal work in Gujarat, assisted Aspi. Suhel's involvement with CJP and other 2002-related cases has ensured that an upright, 'mainstream' lawyer was forever 'labelled' and professional recognition that would in the normal course – without this adventure – be his due, was denied him. This was the high cost that many in our team have had to, and have, willingly paid. Suhel, a group of lawyers and I met at a tiny hotel in Ahmedabad, trying to formulate a legal strategy even as the embers of hatred had not been doused. In 2007, this is what Suhel told me about his experience of the portals of justice, which we published in *Communalism Combat,*

I actually believed that after the first flush of activity things would pack up. So there was a great sense of satisfaction when as an advocate I experienced, in matter after matter, legal action groups like Citizens for Justice and Peace (CJP) persisting with their work even today. Even after such a long time and with many ups and downs, especially for social activists, the fight continues.

I would particularly like to mention that CJP has looked after countless victims and witnesses all over the state and undertaken legal interventions in scores of cases. And it has been there right from the start. It was in March 2002 that CJP began its legal interventions, first with its writ petition on behalf of the relief camps running in the city and state. Thereafter it has intervened in dozens of matters related to the victims and complaints of the mass carnage. There were also compensation claim cases, hate speech cases and many others.

The relief camp matter came up before the court in April 2002. The petition sought basic amenities from the state for the hapless residents of relief camps who were internally displaced refugees and to whom the state had turned a deaf ear. (Relief camps in Gujarat were *all* run privately by individuals and groups belonging to the Muslim community. The state of Gujarat did not operate a single relief camp for victims of the genocidal violence).

The court made a verbal request to the public prosecutor (PP), state of Gujarat, asking him to agree to make a voluntary statement increasing the per day expenses for each resident (from Rs. six to Rs. eight) and improving the water supply, the provision for bathrooms and so on. The atmosphere in court was especially hostile at the time. Almost every lawyer present in court was hoping, willing the court to simply dismiss the petition. On the other hand, those representing the relief camps – senior counsel, Aspi Chinoy from Mumbai, and I – expected the court to issue firm orders and directions rather than to 'request the state government to agree to oblige the poor displaced victims' by giving them the basic amenities that are their due as citizens of this country.

There was immense pressure on all of us as a team. As I, CJP Secretary, Teesta Setalvad, stood in the courtroom and as relief camp managers arrived, the place filled up not just with lawyers but also intimidatory crowds. In the Gujarat High Court sick notes from all lawyers are generally accepted as a matter of course and without much ado. On one occasion during the hearing, I was quite unwell – a result, I believe, of the constant tension, the pressures of work and the many sleepless nights. I was running a high fever and had no option but to file a sick note. So on the day the matter was to be heard I sent my junior, Anil Verma, to the court, requesting an adjournment. The court responded angrily (a sharp contrast to its amenability and courtesy towards the state of Gujarat) and passed an order stating that *all* petitioners would thereafter have to remain personally present in court each time the matter was to be heard. Now, the relief camp managers were also performing a sterling service for the community, providing food, water and shelter to victims while the whole of Gujarat was burning. But thanks to the court's attitude, the relief camp managers had to interrupt their activities and be personally present in court. In the end the state was 'obliged' to provide more bathrooms, toilets and quality food to the riot victims.

Another case that stands out was the one related to an incident in Abasana in rural Ahmedabad where six members belonging to the Muslim minority had been killed – an offence registered at the Daithroj police station. Three of the accused had approached the high court for bail. We represented the victim survivor who was the complainant and filed an affidavit by the complainant witness narrating the role of each of the accused. Some of the accused had used a sharp metal weapon (*dhariya*) to cause injuries to a victim, an injury that resulted in a fracture of the skull. The deceased victim was then thrown into a fire by other accused. In the post-mortem notes, the cause of death was shown as 'burning' although column 17 of the post-mortem report did indicate a fracture to the skull of the deceased victim.

I had opposed bail for these accused as well. However, the defence lawyer argued for bail for the accused persons who had brutally assaulted the deceased on the grounds that the skull fracture was not the cause of death. I then requested a stay on the order granting bail for four weeks so that we could approach the Supreme Court. The court referred the question to the Public Prosecutor (PP) (in itself a highly questionable practice) whereupon the Public Prosecutor advised the court that the order should not be stayed and thus my request for a stay was denied. The court then asked me if any conditions needed to be imposed on the accused. I stated that the order should constrain the accused into staying outside rural Ahmedabad until the trial was over. Once again the court referred to the Public Prosecutor who refused to accept these conditions saying that all the accused persons should not have to suffer such hardship. Ultimately, all the accused were constrained into staying outside Abasana for four to six months.

In its judgment the high court also recorded that it was the complainant who had not insisted on a reasoned order (one that provided a detailed explanation of the rationale behind its decision). However, while hearing the complainant's case for cancellation of bail, the Supreme Court took the view that the high court must record a detailed reasoned order. Following the Supreme Court judgement, the high court should have cancelled the bail granted to the accused. However, due to the long time lag, bail was not cancelled. For a substantial period of time during which the trial was being heard, the accused roamed free. It appears that during this time the witnesses had been won over by the accused persons who were allowed out on bail and they had then turned hostile. The delay in the trial forced them to bow to the influence of the accused.

There is another case related to 2002 that has been pending since December 16 that year. The petitioner, Abdul Hakim Khan, had filed a complaint at the Satellite police station, Ahmedabad, seeking registration of offences against the newspaper, *Sandesh*, under sections 153 A and 153 B of the IPC for publishing false and provocative reports on February 28 and March 1, 2002. The reports in question were extremely inflammatory and the police should themselves have registered a complaint against the newspaper concerned. Since the police did not, a private complaint was filed under Section 200 of the CrPC. The magistrate concerned dismissed the private complaint on the grounds that state government sanction was necessary for permission to prosecute. So the complainant applied to the state government seeking such sanction. As expected, the state government did not heed the representation and ultimately the complainant had to file a petition in the Gujarat High Court on December 16, 2002 when the petition was admitted and posted for 'final hearing without any returnable date'. Five years have passed and so far the matter has not been heard. It is still pending before the court and I am not sure when or if it will ever be heard. If, say, the matter were heard in 2008 or 2009, this would be six or eight years after the offence was committed. Where would the trial be then? Notwithstanding the many stumbling blocks, I still believe that if we work, as we must, with full faith and honesty, it can be a truly rewarding experience. Even so, the continuing hostility makes this a frightening exercise. There will be moments when we are disheartened. And there have been many such moments. At one stage during a crucial matter a government pleader attempted to browbeat me, saying that if I carried on like this prosecutors would be instructed to oppose me in all my regular matters as well. But I refused to give in. I have done my job with great satisfaction.

Recently we filed a petition asking that an FIR be registered against the chief minister and 62 others on charges that include criminal conspiracy, mass murder, manslaughter and intimidation (the PIL filed by Zakiya Jafri and CJP). Some lawyers telephoned me to say that my role in the proceedings, where senior policemen and bureaucrats were also accused, was a recipe for disaster. I would be making formidable enemies.

These are but cheap threats to block the sterling work being done by organizations like CJP.[9]

The close to fifteen-year long experience, tiring and tedious, within our Courts has revealed an unhappy imbalance. Courts, in

[9] M. M. Tirmizi, 'The Fight Continues', *Communalism Combat*, no. 124, July 2007.

our system of things need to play the crucial role of correcting un-Constitutional executive action. Within the Courts, however, as CJP's own experience, detailed in Suhel's own words above reveals, the State and government remain privileged, even in cases that are calling to action State functioning, behaviour and action.

Affidavits filed by officers representing government departments, based on wrong or false facts, rarely call into punitive action, the officer or the State. If an individual, mass movement or survivor, however, makes even a minor error of representation, hell often breaks loose. India is at best an electoral democracy tottering or edging often towards majoritarianism and mobocracy. In a constitutional democracy, the last word of dissent should have a legitimate place and should be respected. The rights of the voiceless and the marginalized – the victims of deep institutional communal, caste and class bias – need to be taken not just seriously, but brought on par with the resourceful defences put forward by the State that is backed by its vast administrative and monetary arsenal. Institutions such as the Judiciary, especially the higher Judiciary, exist in the Constitutional scheme to correct this imbalance, otherwise bent in all senses, towards absolute State power. This is not the case in our time. The power of the State, therefore, remains near complete.

CJP aimed to try and take up legally every aspect of the genocidal carnage, be it cases for relief camps or compensation, missing persons, accountability or the actual criminal trials. In all, we have so far fought as many as 68 cases right from the trial court up to the Supreme Court. As many as 150 convictions have been achieved (of which one hundred and thirty-seven resulted in life imprisonment at the special sessions court stage. In October 2016, the Gujarat High Court acquitted 14 of those earlier convictions in the Sardarpura case, bringing the total number of those convicted to life imprisonment to 123). The NHRC recommended that eight of the critical trails should be independently investigated.

The Superior Courts, both High Courts and the Supreme Court, are vested with the powers of original jurisdiction. Courts have exercised their inherent powers with regard to the enforcement of fundamental rights. In addition, there exists a unique power held by the courts – the *suo motu* jurisdiction. This enables the Court to intervene soon after they are cognisant of or made aware of some wrong that needs judicial intervention and correction.

This is a powerful phrase in legal parlance that can be used by the Courts to inspire faith and confidence. These are Latin phrases. *Suo motu* means 'on its own motion'. It is equivalent to the term *sua sponte* – when a lofty institution of the government *acts on its own cognisance* when there is a gross violation of fundamental rights. The term *habeas corpus* is another significant term. It refers to a writ action demanding that a person be produced in the court – literally. The phrase says – You May Have the Body.

Under *suo motu*, the Courts have taken up matters and issues on their own, when they receive a letter of complaint and when they read a media report. The power of the *suo motu* has been used once by the Supreme Court to query the defacement of the mighty Himalayas, letters to the Court have been converted into PILs by high courts and the Supreme Court. When mass crimes against sections of our own population shook the core of the Indian republic, the power of *suo motu* has not been used. I have in mind the widely-reported 1983 Nelli massacre, the extensively covered (after the first few days of paralysis and silence) 1984 Delhi riots, the 1989 Hashimpura-Meerut killings (when the bodies of those shot dead were washed upon the shores of the Yamuna, near Delhi), the 1992-93 Bombay riots and the 2002 Gujarat pogrom. Nor has the power of *suo motu* been used in the case of heinous caste crimes. A poignant question regarding the rarely exercised power of the *suo moto* intervention was put to me by Rajah Vemula – the brother of Rohith Vemula, the Dalit student whose death on 17 January 2016 has been seen as a rejection of institutional callousness and bias embodied by the Modi regime. Rohith Vemula's family and fellow students filed a case in the Hyderabad High Court against the Vice Chancellor Appa Rao Podile. It languishes in the courts. Despairingly, Rajah Vemula asked me, 'Can't the Court intervene with the power of *suo motu*?' Ashamed, and forced to answer on behalf of a system that has given us limited redress, I could not reply.

The Gujarat High Court did not – on a *suo motu* basis – take up any matter related to the 2002 violence. Never mind that two judges, one retired and one sitting of that very high court, were physically attacked. The Chief Justice of the Court is on record stating that they needed to protect themselves by moving to Muslim majority areas, as he had no faith in the law and order machinery. The letter of Justice A. N. Divecha, one of the two judges who were attacked, is a public document annexed to the report of the NHRC of 2002. The other judge was Justice M. H. Kadri. It remains a shameful reminder of the depths to where we had fallen in 2002. The Investigation records in the Zakia Jafri case show that the first attack on a Judge was within a short distance of the Gujarat High Court. It took place on the morning of 28 February 2002. No adequate protection was given to either of the judges, sitting and retired. Both, as it turned out, were Muslims.[10] This remains a serious question mark and blot on the government and administration.

The Supreme Court received regular alerts on the failures on the ground in Gujarat. Two petitions, the first by Mallika Sarabhai and the second by Citizens for Justice and Peace, were filed as early as 1 and 2 May 2002. The first time that a speaking order

---

[10] Justice Kadri died in 2014. Justice Divecha died in 2016.

emanated from this Court was, however, in July-August 2003. It was during the sensation of the Best Bakery trial. Its star witness, Zahira Shaikh, came to Mumbai. She approached us to re-open the case. She appeared before the NHRC. The trial and the events around it shook the country. One of the CJP trustees at the time asked me if I was confident of success in the Courts. Would we get the case transferred out of Gujarat and a re-trial ordered? I thought hard before replying. I answered honestly. It is rare for this provision of the law to be applied. Only once – in the 1950s – did the courts transfer a communal violence case *from one district to another*. However, I added, if ever there was a chance to forge this jurisprudence it was with this case. I got the go ahead. On 12 April 2004 I was conducting a teacher and social activist workshop at Prashant in Ahmedabad when I received a call from our lawyers. Mayhem broke loose. Aparna Bhat, normally reserved and conservative, was ecstatic. The case had been transferred to Bombay and a re-trial ordered. Senior counsel Kapil Sibal also came on the phone to congratulate me. There was jubilation all around. The group broke up. Within minutes, VHP and RSS men – Atul Vaidya and Bharat Telli – the two accused in the Gulberg trial, came physically on a motorcycle to threaten me. Sombrely we realised how real the physical threat remained. Father Cedric Prakash filed an FIR regarding the intimidation.[11]

---

[11] Media coverage was very positive at that time. In an editorial in *The Indian Express* ('Justice Triumphs', 25 February 2006), the editors wrote, 'For modern day Neros, a reminder from the court: you have to pay for your fiddling. The verdict is a ringing endorsement of the role played by sections of the media, civil society, organizations and individuals, especially Teesta Setalvad of *Communalism Combat* who, unfazed by vicious propaganda, stayed the course.' The editors of *The Telegraph* wrote in their editorial ('Just a start', 26 February 2006), 'Very few triumphs are absolutely unequivocal. It is understandable that right-thinking Indians would hail the Best Bakery convictions as a triumph of justice ... Best Bakery is only just the beginning of a process of investigation, exposure and punishment that is likely to reveal truths which could undermine some of the fundamental

One of the first major interventions we made was the establishment – by collective decision – of the Concerned Citizens Tribunal (CCT), headed by Justice V. R. Krishna Iyer. Justice P. B. Sawant, Justice Hosbet Suresh, K. G. Kannabiran, Aruna Roy, Tanika Sarkar, Ghanshyam Shah and K. G. Subramanyan formed the esteemed panel. The objective of the Tribunal was to document – with prompt and immediate effect – the testimonies of survivors, perpetrators, and officials so that we could arrive at precise conclusions and recommendations. Though such commissions do not necessarily perform cross-examinations and test the evidence as legal proceedings do, their immeasurable value lies in the immediacy of the intervention and the fact that they record with great thoroughness the intricacies of testimony and evidence. These tribunals turn the mirror on a criminal justice system that has virtually broken down due to the delays. It shows up a legal system that tilts towards the moneyed and powerful. Continued violence made us delay two scheduled hearings of the CCT. The myth, that the violence had been 'controlled within seventy-two hours', stands exposed. The exhaustive media reportage shows that this was simply not the case.

By 1 May, we were set to go. Again there were some efforts at the last moment to put off the hearings. Our friend – the actor Farooq Shaikh – nudged us to begin. Finally, the Tribunal sat from

premises of a modern secular democracy.' M. J. Akbar, then editor of *The Asian Age* and now BJP leader, wrote in his paper ('Peace of Justice', 26 February 2006), 'The important, and vital, point is that justice survived the malfeasance of the system; perhaps that is the only point. The courts were assisted by the dedication and sheer, determined obstinacy of civil society leaders like Teesta Setalvad, who refused to be defeated by the acquittal of the accused by a court in Gujarat, and went to the Supreme Court. . . .Thank God for Teesta Setalvad and the Supreme Court. And thank God for a free media too. We will see if media has the tenacity of a Teesta Setalvad or not.' Amartya Sen, the Noble Prize winner, told the media, 'I am delighted to get the news of the Best Bakery verdict and the convictions, but also of course of the complete vindication of the admirable Teesta! I am so delighted.'

1 May to 18 May – collected over eighteen thousand testimonies (written and oral), examined official witnesses and victims across the state. It was a challenging experience as a hostile government marked our every move. Vehicles hired by us to carry the judges were twice attacked in Ahmedabad. Constant surveillance on those who testified before the Tribunal was a form of intimidation. Nonetheless, the three volume report of the CCT, *Crime Against Humanity: An Inquiry into the carnage in Gujarat*, remains one of the most substantive and credible documents of the vile and vicious planning behind the spread of violence and the extent of state complicity. The opening paragraphs under the chapter on State Complicity says it all,

1. The post-Godhra carnage in Gujarat was an organized crime perpetrated by the state's chief minister and his government. The state's complicity is evident from the various acts of commission and omission of the government and its officials.

1.1. It was the chief minister who declared that the Godhra incident was pre-planned when the investigating agencies had not reached such a conclusion. Shri Modi's cabinet, notably the minister for home, Shri Gordhan Zadaphiya, reiterated strongly that Pakistani hands were behind the Godhra act. These statements were irresponsible, given the sensitivity of the situation and the anger that they generated. Once they generated a climate ripe for apportioning blame, for the acts of a few criminals, the entire Ghanchi Muslim community of Godhra was branded. This led to a feeling of justifying the systematic massacre, plunder, loot and cultural decimation of the entire Muslim community in Gujarat thereafter.

1.2. It was the chief minister who decided that the charred, unidentifiable dead bodies be taken from Godhra to Ahmedabad in a motor cavalcade. As the cavalcade headed for Ahmedabad, senior members of his party and organizations affiliated to it shouted slogans and incited mobs to retaliate. The CM's role in condoning this behaviour, and in using official machinery to propagate the unsubstantiated view that the Godhra tragedy was a sinister conspiracy, is condemnable. Thus, it was the chief minister who was primarily responsible for the spread of violence, post-Godhra, in the rest of Gujarat.[12]

It is no wonder, then, that all those associated with the effort were closely watched. The tribunal met many police officers and district collectors. The VHP-RSS also deposed before the tribunal and submitted their version, documents and videos, on the Godhra mass arson and beyond. The high point of the effort, however, was the testimony of then Minister of State for revenue Haren Pandya on 13 May 2002. His testimony was explosive and became public months later when the Tribunal's three-volume report was published. In the Tribunal's report, Pandya's identity had been withheld as he had requested anonymity. After sending the interim findings to the Gujarat government (and receiving no response), the final three-volume report was released in Ahmedabad and then in Delhi. This was in November 2002. Here is what the Tribunal said on the crucial bits of evidence it had garnered, under the indicting section called State Complicity,

1.4. Shri Modi played an active role, along with at least three cabinet colleagues, in instructing senior police personnel and civil administrators that a 'Hindu reaction was to be expected and this must not be curtailed or controlled.'[13]

---

[12] *Crime Against Humanity*, vol. II, *An Inquiry into the Carnage in Gujarat. Findings and Recommendations*. Concerned Citizens Tribunal – Gujarat 2002. Mumbai: Citizens for Peace and Justice, 2002, p. 75.

[13] Concerned Citizens Tribunal – Gujarat 2002. *Crime Against Humanity*, vol. II, p. 76.

Just before the release of the report, *Outlook* had carried an interview with Justice Hosbet Suresh, one of the tribunal members, who had indicated that a minister of the Modi government had testified that a meeting had taken place at the Chief Minister's residence on 27 February 2002. At that meeting, Narendra Modi had told the top men of his administration to allow 'people to vent their frustration and not come in the way of the Hindu backlash.' On 26 March 2003, Haren Pandya was killed and his first-hand testimony written out of the historical record.[14] State Intelligence Bureau chief, Additional Director General of Police R. B. Sreekumar's conscience register maintained between April and September 2002 records how the Chief Minister had Haren Pandya's phone tapped once it was known that a sitting minister had actually deposed before the Tribunal.

My son was only six years old and my daughter was eleven years old in 2002. For the first six months, I was away for long periods. I barely saw them through these traumatic months. In May of that year, nightmares continued for weeks as the images of the streets, the graveyards, the highways haunted my consciousness. That year, we pulled ourselves out as a family for a brief respite from the hell of hatred, and spent ten days in the Sangla valley of Himachal. A soft, sober, comforting Hinduism reigns there – soul enriching as we walked long walks in Raksham and Chitkool. Those few days away were a balm and provided some healing.

Seven years later – in 2009 – Justices P. B. Sawant and Suresh recorded their statement before A. K. Malhotra of the Special Investigative Team (SIT). They reiterated Haren Pandya's revelations. Never before in the history of human rights jurisprudence have former judges agreed with such élan to be part of an on-going investigation. Their deposition is part of the

---

[14] 'A Midnight Meeting on Feb 27 and a Murderered Minister', *Outlook*, 12 November 2007.

investigation papers in the Zakia Jafri case. They also recorded in their statement that three other officers who had knowledge of the illegal instructions given at this meeting should be examined by the SIT. The SIT chose to invalidate this crucial evidence. It is this appallingly unprofessional investigation that is being challenged by Zakia Jafri, supported by the Citizens for Justice and Peace, in the Gujarat High Court.

CJP's first significant contribution was to fully support the Tribunal and publish the report.

In October 2003, Dussehra Day, five families – survivors of the Godhra mass arson – came to CJP. They said that the RSS-VHP had completely manipulated their loss and grief. We filed an affidavit in the Supreme Court urging the transfer of the investigation and trial in the Godhra criminal trial and made a strong pitch for survivors of the Godhra train burning. When the trial court pronounced the death penalty for eleven people in 2011, Bharatbhai Panchal, a survivor whose wife had died in the arson, told the media that he did not want the death penalty for these people. 'We need this cycle of revenge to end', he said.

Friendship provided the respite from this world of pain. If the tiny office of SAHMAT, first at VP House and now on Ferozeshah Road, has been an emotional and physical adjunct of this fiercely intense journey since 2002, the home of Madhu and Rajen in Delhi has provided real succour in Delhi, almost since that date. Crisis or celebration, resting one's bones and steadying the beat of the heart, in excitement or anxiety, has been so much more soothing there. As Madhu puts it, we are Teesta's home in Delhi. Ram Rahman, his camera and eye, has been a fellow traveller, keen to pull me away to watch works of art, if nothing else to take a break from a never ending tedious and sometimes sordid, tale.

The everyday demands of an exacting legal battle, however, always pull me back. As does the all-pervasive stench of communalism, which, under the present regime, appears to have received official legitimacy. The writ of the Indian Constitution struggles to valiantly keep its space.

The grotesque violence in Gujarat in 2002 has marked me deeply. The protracted anti-minority pogrom resulted in orchestrated mass killings, public and brutal sexual violence against women and girls, the seizure and ruination of homes and property, the denial of livelihoods, as well as the desecration of religious and cultural places. This violence was foreshadowed by the systematic organization and training of cadres of youth for this violence. Individuals who belonged to organizations infiltrated positions of power with their discriminatory, non-democratic approach. This is what we had documented in *Communalism Combat* in the years before 2002.

The well-orchestrated pogrom followed the ghastly killing by burning, of fifty-nine passengers, including *kar sevaks* returning from Ayodhya, in a fire on the Sabarmati Express train on 27 February 2002. The ensuing violence, which the state police failed to contain, resulted in the death of what the state claims are nine hundred and sixty-three persons (seven hundred and four Muslims and two hundred and fifty-nine Hindus), injured thousands of people and destroyed or damaged property worth Rs. 687 crores. These numbers are too low. Our carefully calculated and reliable estimates on the basis of charge sheets filed in courts record the post-Godhra deaths at nineteen hundred and twenty-six. This does not include the two hundred and twenty-eight as yet untraced people. The damage suffered, we believe, totals Rs. 3,500 crores. If not more.

The state of Gujarat, through chief secretary Subha Rao, made a series of statements to the NHRC about destruction of homes. It admitted that the homes of 18,037 urban families (as against 13,222 until June 2002) and 11,204 families in rural areas (as against 10,025 until June 2002) had been destroyed or damaged. The widespread nature of these incidents of violence is evident from the fact that they occurred in 993 villages and 151 towns covering 284 police stations (of a total of 464 in the state) and spread over an overwhelming 153 of 182 assembly constituencies (these numbers come from the State Intelligence given to the Chief Election Commission in August 2002). Official records obtained by us through the now decade old hearings in the Zakia Jafri case reveal, how cynically the state home department, under the chief minister (who was also the home minister), wilfully misinformed the central home ministry (under L. K. Advani at the time) on the extent and spread of the violence in the state of Gujarat.

The desecration and damage of holy shrines, historic monuments, business establishments, and socio-cultural and financial institutions belonging predominantly to Muslims was another characteristic that set this orgy of violence apart from the many other anti-minority pogroms that India has witnessed in recent times (almost three hundred *dargahs* and *masjids* had been destroyed). The Gujarat High Court criticized the Gujarat government for its failure to protect these buildings. The matter is now before the Supreme Court, which has also put on record its displeasure at the arrogant intransigence of a state in refusing to re-build these cultural monuments that were destroyed due to failures of the state.[15]

Hate propaganda – in the form of anonymous pamphlets and audio-visual material – were widely distributed preceding the genocide. This material transformed entire neighbourhoods into spaces of hate. Established newspapers also used their columns for propaganda. To date, the state of Gujarat has not initiated any action against these publications. Although State Intelligence

---

[15] Teesta Setalvad, "Why Visit Religio-Cultural Sites Abroad, When We Destroy Them At Home?' *The Citizen*, 13 November 2016.

Bureau (SIB) reports, and even reports filed by senior policemen such as Rahul Sharma (SP, Bhavnagar and then DCP Crime Branch in 2002) and D. D. Tuteja (Commissioner of Police, Vadodara in 2002), strongly recommended prosecution against the offending newspapers at the time. Hate-letting by the mainstream media has gone unpunished.

In the near fifteen years since the genocidal killings, incontrovertible material evidence and chains of circumstance revealed through depositions to judicial bodies by government officials and others have thrown adequate light on the anti-minority carnage. Whether or not the violence and concomitant brutalities on the Muslim minority were the outcome of a well-designed conspiracy by the political leadership of the state is being argued and examined presently in the Zakia Jafri case before the Gujarat High Court.

On 28 February 2002, the parliamentarian Ahsan Jafri was brutally killed by mobs during the Gulberg Society incident in Ahmedabad city. Four years later, on 8 June 2006, his wife – Zakia Ahsan Jafri – sent a complaint to the then Gujarat DGP, P. C. Pande, asking that a First Information Report (FIR) be registered on his murder. The complaint was made out against Chief Minister Narendra Modi – as accused number one – and sixty-two others, including cabinet ministers and Indian Administrative Service (IAS) and IPS officials, under section 154 of the Code of Criminal Procedure (CrPC). The 119-page complaint was backed with over 2,000 pages of annexures as evidence. These were affidavits by serving police officers in Gujarat that pointed towards high-level complicity. The affidavits of former Director General of Police for Gujarat (Additional DGP in 2002) R. B. Sreekumar with their detailed annexures and the affidavits and CDs of phone call records submitted by IPS officer Rahul Sharma (first SP, Bhavnagar and then DCP, Crime Branch, Ahmedabad) became the primary sources of evidence in this case. It was in my statement before the Supreme Court appointed SIT that I requested – as co-complainant – that all state intelligence officials of the period be examined. The investigation was looking into the meeting of 27 February 2002. In my statement I listed the SIB officials who should be examined by the SIT, and later even requested that the views of officers of the Army stationed in Gujarat, the Chairperson of the NHRC – a former Chief Justice of the country, Justice Verma, the Chief Election Commissioner, James Lyndoh, and K. P. S. Gill ought to have been formerly recorded as part of this investigation. None of this was done by the SIT.

Ten months after the DGP failed to register the FIR despite a strong case being made regarding serious cognisable offences, Zakia Jafri and the CJP filed a criminal application in the Gujarat High Court. What we had asked for was a *writ of mandamus* – which essentially would order a government official to fulfil properly their responsibilities. We wanted the DGP to register the FIR and we wanted an order to transfer the case to the CBI. When the High Court rejected our plea, we approached the Supreme Court. On 3 March 2008, the Supreme Court issued a notice and on 27 April 2009, directed the SIT – already appointed – to investigate the complaint.[16] After one year, the SIT submitted its report holding that while many of the allegations in the complaint were true, they were not prosecutable. The *amicus curiae* in this case, Raju Ramachandran, begged to differ: in a sensational finding in his report dated 25 July 2011 he wrote that there was enough material to prosecute Narendra Modi.

The Supreme Court directed us to go back to the lowest rung in the criminal justice ladder. The prayer in the writ petition, pressed by us in the Special Leave Petition before the Supreme Court, was

---

[16] The SIT was appointed on 26 March 2008 to re-investigate other major 2002 carnage cases. A petition supported by the CJP spurred on this appointment.

for the simple registration of an FIR against the accused listed in the complaint. By this time, thanks to the investigations by the SIT, under the supervision of the Supreme Court, and the Amicus Curiae's report, the entire criminal complaint dated 8 June 2006 had moved way beyond the stage of the registration of the FIR. However, the ambiguity that continued even after the Supreme Court's final judgment in the first special leave petition filed by Zakia Jafri and the CJP on 12 September 2011, allowed those accused in the complaint, assisted by a compliant SIT, to poke holes in the entire process. The Magistrate's court in Ahmedabad ruled that our rights to get a copy of the investigation papers, should the SIT close the investigation, must be protected. The SIT denied Zakia Jafri and the CJP a hearing from September 2011 to February 2012. It also resisted the Supreme Court order to hand over the papers from its investigation. We approached the Supreme Court thrice to order the SIT to fulfil its obligations. Finally, between May 2012 and February 2013, we were handed over sixty-four box files of documentary evidence that ran to twenty-three thousand pages!

Since the Supreme Court had surrendered its writ of continuing mandamus and the matter had been disposed of, we were compelled to start afresh with another special leave provision. We were then given just three months by the Supreme Court to file the Protest Petition. We did so and argued the matter with zeal, dedication and commitment. On 26 December 2013, the Magistrate rejected our petition. Eight days later, after filing an FIR against Tanvir Jafri, Firoz Gulzar Pathan, Salim Sandhi, Javed Anand and myself, the Ahmedabad police (now under the control of Shivanand Jha, a close confidant of Modi) tried desperately to get us arrested and prevent the filing of the appeal. Despite these extraneous pressures – additional evidence of how state power can be abused – we filed the appeal on 15 March 2014.

This is the first time in the history of independent India that a legal action seeks to pin culpability – both criminal and administrative – on those in positions of power and responsibility when acts of mass crimes take place. Whether or not the Indian system will find the grit to take this evidence to its logical conclusion, time will tell. Already interminable delays have been the norm especially given the political situation in India since 2014.

The Raghavan-led SIT sits pretty today in a position of privilege. The chairperson and officers have been paid handsome monthly remunerations since May 2008. This money comes straight from the Gujarat Government's exchequer, out of the taxpayers' pockets essentially. Raghavan has been accused of a tardy and lazy supervision by the SIT, barely concentrating on what should have been an exacting task. He spent barely a few days every two months within Gujarat despite the weight of his responsibility. There is not even a screen of separation in this process, leading to serious questions of a conflict of interest. Responses to a Right to Information (RTI) query revealed these to be Rs 1.5 lakhs per month for Raghavan and Rs 1 lakh per month for A. K. Malhotra and the rest of the team. The closure report in the Zakia Jafri case, dated 8 February 2012, was filed not by one of these high profile, well-paid members of the SIT, but by a Gujarat-level officer, Himanshu Shukla, who signed off on the report.

The SIT was first appointed in March 2008. All prosecutorial power was invested in the SIT by the Supreme Court order of 1 May 2009. Some serious and concerned observers sharply asked me then whether the Supreme Court was not conferring too many powers on one individual, rendering the arrangement open to manipulation. As the months and years unfolded, we had to go back to the Supreme Court, first pointing out the lackadaisical investigation of the SIT, and thereafter its open hostility. These remarks by those observers were to prove prophetic. Our prayer had been (in the D. N. Pathak case) for a transfer of the investigation to the CBI and for a monitoring of the investigation by the Court. Instead, an SIT was appointed. When periodic investigation reports were submitted, we, as petitioners for the survivors were not allowed to be privy to copies: the state of Gujarat accused of deep rooted bias and complicity was allowed to read a copy of all investigation papers. This, and given the fact that the SIT did little to distance itself from the local police and its machinations, eventually made SIT function with increasing hostility to the survivors of 2002 as well as Zakia Ahsan Jafri. By the time Zakia Jafri challenged the dismissal of her protest petition through an appeal in the Gujarat High Court, supported by CJP, senior Supreme Court lawyers, appointed by the SIT were (and still are) being paid Rs. 9 lakhs per hearing in the Gujarat High Court. This is apart from the Rs. 1.5 lakhs each for every conference and apart from what the 'junior' team charges. Inexorably, the SIT has become an arm of the state of Gujarat, well heeled to defend the indefensible.

The complaint (dated 8 June 2006) sent by Zakia Jafri to the DGP pointed out in detail how the undeclared but insidious objective was to manipulate, focus and channel the Godhra incident – to create and germinate the ire of the Hindu population, facilitate a free play of their baser instincts as seen in the large-scale brutalities and thereby reap political and electoral dividends in the election year of 2002.

The chain of circumstances and the details of evidence, post-Godhra, establish that the Chief Minister, Narendra Modi, and his cabinet colleagues had conspired, planned, prepared, organized and perpetrated multifarious crimes against the Muslim minority by causing and contriving to mobilize armed anti-Muslim mobs.

The pogrom was made possible by simultaneously restraining the bureaucracy through the various instruments of punishment and reward at the government's disposal. Consequently, the officials figuring in the FIR connived with and abetted the political leadership of the state in the execution of the numerous crimes as delineated in the complaint.

The worst indictment against the state of Gujarat is however the state's unrepentant attitude towards victims of the genocide. Contrary to the claims made by the state administration in its affidavits before the Courts and its reports to the NHRC, the ground reality is in fact far from conducive for the successful rehabilitation of riot victims. There is a serious discrepancy between survivors' claims with regard to housing compensation paid and the state's unabashed efforts to brazen it out with blatant untruths. Instead, victims of the violence have been consistently intimidated into compromising with the perpetrators as a condition precedent for their safe return and rehabilitation in their pre-riot habitats. In some of the worst atrocities of the 2002 genocide, in instances of massacre where the Supreme Court has stayed judicial trials, survivors simply cannot return to their villages. Photographs taken by *Communalism Combat* illustrate that in many cases the state of their destroyed homes remains unchanged – they are in exactly the same condition as they were in 2002, on the day that tragedy struck. Not only has there been no closure, their wounds fester, their pain renewed at the hands of a callous administration. A questionable law, already existent in Gujarat, prevents the survivors of Gulberg society and Naroda Patiya massacres from selling their properties to the 'other', that is Hindus. The state and its agencies appear to be keen to maintain a ghettoized divide between communities.

In late October 2007, *Aaj Tak* broadcasted *Tehelka's* Operation Kalank. Ashish Khetan, a journalist who has over the years become a close friend, carried out this austere, path-breaking effort that requires raw courage of an exemplary kind. The sting showed tape conversations of the armed build-up of militias, it showed that Modi had given the men of RSS-VHP free reign to 'avenge' Godhra, and it showed tape conversations of police complicity as well as the appointment of prosecutors with RSS leanings. Within days of the sting, we (Zakia Jafri and the CJP) approached the Gujarat High Court to hear our petition. We wanted the Court to consider the unequivocal evidence provided by Operation Kalank. These were, essentially, extra-judicial confessions. Each aspect of the genocidal carnage that had, until then been claimed by us, through survivor accounts and documents was now being backed by confessions of the perpetrators. On 12 November, the High Court, not unexpectedly, rejected our application without reason.

I immediately moved the Supreme Court where our pleas for transfer of investigation in ten major trials were still pending. The Supreme Court asked us to come back at the appropriate stage. In March 2008, in a *suo motu* move, the NHRC in cases related to 2002, once again made history. Drawing on its powers under the Protection of Human Rights Act, Justice Rajendra Babu, through a full commission order directed that the tapes of the Operation Kalank sting operation be authenticated by the CBI. The Gujarat government objected. The NHRC held firm. Over the next ten months the CBI tested the tapes and certified them as authentic. A crucial piece of evidence related to the genocidal killings has thus been preserved for history.

Ashish, like Pankaj Shankar, made himself available to the SIT investigators. In the Godhra case, he was treated with hostility, as the SIT preferred to follow the line of investigation set by the Gujarat police. In the Naroda Patiya, Gulberg and Naroda Gam cases he recorded statements and testified. He also recorded his statement in the Zakia Jafri case. For Ashish Khetan, like me, undertaking an investigation was not just about making a sensation or hitting the headlines; it was subjecting himself to the system and its painful scrutiny to ensure that justice is done.

The nearly 2,000-page judgement in the Naroda Patiya case (29 August 2012) authored by Judge Jyotsna Yagnik does Ashish Khetan's efforts proud. In Chapter II, she relies on Khetan's sting operation and comments on its value as evidence. This is also a judgment that upholds evidence of a wider conspiracy when it convicted former minister in the Modi government – Maya Kodnani.

In total, of all the criminal trials in which the CJP has provided intrepid legal aid to the survivors, with the conviction of 11 in the Gulberg trials, a total of 137 perpetrators, have, so far, been convicted to life imprisonment. On principle, we have not argued for the death penalty. The success in these trials was due in large measure to the *writ of continuing mandamus* exercised by the Supreme Court in continuing to monitor the trials, in providing protection to 570 witness survivors and defenders like myself and in ensuring some level of accountability in the investigation.

After 2008, when the SIT was appointed, action and attention shifted from the portals of the Supreme Court to Gujarat where the SIT undertook investigations. In 2009, the special courts were set up under the monitoring eye of the Supreme Court. That is when the CJP's legal team expanded to include Yusufbhai Shaikh, S. M. Vohrasaab, Salim Shaikh, Saleem Mansuri, Altaf Jidran, Irshad Mansuri, Nasir Shaikh, Sadik Shaikh, Aslam Baig and Raju Mohammed Shaikh. Long hours and committed work, backed by our teams in the High Court and the Supreme Court, resulted in worthy legal aid during the trails. Kalpesh Shastri is also part of this effort.

By 2009, when the charge sheets were filed in these cases, the hollowness of the SIT's investigations had become apparent.

In many of the special trials, we had to petition courts for orders of further investigation under section 173(8) of the Code of Criminal Procedure. Documentary evidence had deliberately not been supplied along with the charge sheets. We approached the Supreme Court for a re-constitution of the team (December 2009). It was when the survivors refused to give up and kept exercising what they believed to be their right – given the *writ of continuing mandamus* exercised by the Supreme Court – that the relations between the investigation team and survivors became edgy and hostile. We wanted the Court to reconstitute the SIT and ensure that the investigation go back on track. Raghavan and his officers were pulled up by the Supreme Court on aspects of the investigations on a few occasions. This was especially the case when the special Public Prosecutor in the Gulberg trial – R. K. Shah – drew up a letter with severe observations about the SIT and its conduct during the Gulberg trial. This was in February 2010. Shah resigned at this point. In the end we achieved only partial success: police officers Shivanand Jha and Geeta Johri were asked to stay away from the investigations, but the anomalies in the investigations did not really get substantively corrected. This move, by the survivors and the CJP, represented by me, to push the envelope and ensure a thorough investigation invited lasting hostilities towards me from these officers and the state. I believe that this enmity provides the motive behind the false and frivolous cases filed against me. A particularly unpleasant incident was the way in which a simple letter regarding the safety of witnesses and our lawyers, written to the Office of the High Commissioner for Human Rights (OHCHR) was deliberately mis-represented by the *amicus curiae*, Harish Salve to the Supreme Court. SIT chief R. K. Raghavan prompted Salve to do so. This led the Court to make some observations on the issue. Repeated explanations by our counsel, Kamini Jaiswal, who tried to explain the context of the correspondence, were ignored. But more on this in the next chapter.

The time between 2009 and 2010 was also a very painful period for us all at Nirant personally. Our dear Atul, detected with lung cancer left us on 22 July 2010. He remained concerned for the struggle that I was so much a part of. Each time there was a Court hearing I would leave Mumbai after receiving a small chit/note with precious hand written words from him. By April-May 2010, he had grown frail. The last note and SMS I received from him was in early May 2010. He advised patience, 'You have pointed out how the SIT appointed by the Court itself has erred. It will require time and patience for the institutions to accept this, as a mistake that needs to be corrected. It will take time.' His words of caution and wisdom are missed so dearly even though a part of me feels happier that he is not around to see the degree of viciousness unleashed against me even by his colleagues at the bar. Atul's words were to prove prophetic.

Within days of Atul's passing, I had to return to the struggle. I had to release a report on female survivors, which we submitted to the UN, based on the obligations of India towards the Convention on the Elimination of all Forms of Discrimination Against Women (CEDAW).[17] By mid-August 2010, a fortnight after the loss of a beloved father and friend, I made submissions before the Shah-Nanavati-Mehta Commission, offering insights into the deep nexus between the government and the pogram, unearthed by the CJP team through the phone call record analysis and State information bureau records.[18]

It was after 2010 (September in fact) that the personal and legal attacks on me re-doubled. This had clearly got to do with our

[17] Citizens for Justice and Peace, Ahmedabad-Mumbai, *Report 2010*. For the Committee for the Elimination of Discrimination Against Women (CEDAW). *Survivors Citizens for Justice and Peace Report 2010*, Ahmedabad-Mumbai: CJP, 2010.

[18] There is more evidence through graphs and other materials that can be viewed at http://www.cjponline.org/gujaratTrials/nanavatisub/nanavatisubmission.htm.

persistence around the Zakia Jafri case. In 2010, eight years after the genocidal carnage, I had an unexpected breather in the form of an unsolicited post on my Facebook page. Himanshu Trivedi, previously a Judge in Gujarat, wrote publicly,

> Teesta Setalvad. Hats off. I have always admired you and your courage and outspokenness on these issues. I also take this opportunity to state that I am indeed pained (and I am the one who had QUIT Gujarat's Judiciary. I was a district cadre judge in Ahmedabad City Civil and Sessions Court – once a colleague of the bravest judge Ms. Jyotsna Yagnik who handed out the judgments to Babu Bajrangi and Kodnani and now lives in fear of her life) . . . because they (the State of Gujarat) wanted us (the judges and the judiciary) of Gujarat to be acting against the minority community (albeit with no written orders but DEFINITELY communicated in loud and clear messages to us). I could not be part of it as I was sworn to the Constitution of India . . .

Messages like this, when a case of serious criminal conspiracy is being investigated, should have been evidence for the SIT and even the Courts. Needless to say, just like Operation Kalank, it has been relegated to the far-edges of public memory. In a subsequent email to me, Trivedi revealed that there were many individuals who had communicated directly with members of the judiciary telling them to rule in a manner that would teach 'these people' a lesson – a reference to the Muslim minority.[19]

If justice was elusive, so was the framing of policies to help

---

[19] 'Ahmedabad Judge Quit After 2002 Violence: "I was Suffocated, Could Not Take it Anymore"', *The Citizen*, 4 August 2015, http://www.thecitizen. in/NewsDetail.aspx?Id=4637; 'Former Gujarat Judge says he quit over Government's Anti-Muslim Bias', *Siasat*, 5 August 2015, http://www.siasat. com/news/former-gujarat-judge-says-he-quit-over-governments-anti-muslim-bias-806322/.

the internally displaced persons. The plight of those internally displaced from their homes as a result of the violence is a continuing one. They remain excluded: the now near permanent abodes called Citizen's Nagar and Ekta Nagar testify to how the state and its administration as also citizens and society deal with those marginalized by such cruelty. Lands were given by community groups who have refused to transfer holdings or ownerships to the displaced survivors. This remains a source of insecurity and concern.

As far as rehabilitation is concerned, the reality is that survivors and eyewitnesses of the Sardarpura massacre cannot return to Shaikh Mohalla in their native village. They still live as refugees in Satnagar, a neighbouring district. Survivors of the Gulberg massacre cannot return to their middle class housing colony. Survivors of the Ode massacre cannot return to their village. Nearly fifteen years after the carnage, only a few victim survivors from Naroda Gaon and Patiya have returned to their locality.

At least 1,68,000 individuals were displaced as a direct result of the Gujarat genocide in 2002. A significant section reportedly left the state or have bought or rented accommodation mainly in Muslim localities across the state. An approximate 8,000 families still live in what are currently referred to as 'relief colonies' in four districts of Gujarat. Over the past five years, these habitats have become permanent places of residence for those who are too scared to return home. In the People's Union for Civil Liberties' Right to Food petition that was heard by the Supreme Court, the Court commissioner, N. C. Saxena, in 2007, has submitted a report on the pathetic living conditions of Gujarat's refugees.

The CJP and *Communalism Combat* filed a petition challenging the state of Gujarat's cavalier approach to compensation in March 2003. In October 2006, for the first time in five years, India's National Commission for Minorities also visited these 'relief colonies' following appeals by several rights groups. In 2006-07, the UPA I government increased the reparation package that the state of Gujarat had provided. We made a detailed calculation of the relief in an affidavit before the Gujarat High Court, with memorandums on similar lines, also submitted by us to the central government and NCM. It was based on these that action had been taken. But even this was not sufficient.

Close to fifteen years after independent India's worst ever state sponsored carnage directed against the Muslim minority, issues of state impunity for mass crimes, accountability to the Constitution, deliverance of justice, fair compensation and reparation, citizenship rights and an on-going climate of fear and intimidation remain.

Indian democracy's response to the Gujarat genocide has been mixed. Outrage from the media, independent citizens groups, the National Human Rights Commission and the Chief Election Commission (CEC) contrasted with an initially tardy response from the Supreme Court.[20] The subsequent, resounding defeat for the National Democratic Alliance (NDA) government in the general elections of May 2004 offered some consolation. The NDA's leading partner, the Bharatiya Janata Party (BJP), wholeheartedly supported Modi's execution of the state-sponsored carnage, while its allies covertly lent him their support, and still do. A month before the electoral results in 2004, a rare and unequivocal verdict from the Supreme Court delivered a scathing critique of Modi's regime in Gujarat when it transferred the well-publicized Best Bakery trial out of the state into neighbouring Maharashtra, undoubtedly influencing the poll's outcome. These were admirable examples of judicial corrections of unconstitutional State actions.

---

[20] *Report of the National Human Rights Commission*, 2002; Concerned Citizens Tribunal, *Crimes Against Humanity – Gujarat 2002*, 3 volumes; Human Rights Watch, *We Have No Orders to Save You*, 2003; Human Rights Watch, *Condoning Injustice*, 2003; Report on International Religious Freedom, 2003-2008; United Nation's CEDAW, 2004.

The Bilkees Bano case was also transferred to Mumbai. Both trials, despite the upheavals in the Best Bakery case, eventually resulted in convictions and the Supreme Court monitored both. In the Bilkees Bano Case, the trial for gang rape and multiple murders in Randhikpur, Dahod district, was not just subverted but involved the destruction of evidence by senior medical and police personnel.

The Chief Electoral Commission's report of August 2002 found gross constitutional lapses and faulted the government's official stance relied heavily on the bold stand taken by then ADGP Intelligence chief, R. B. Sreekumar. Elections were postponed to December 2002. This was a token postponement (Modi was ripe and ready to call them in July 2002!). The postponement appears to have been inadequate as many of the traumatized internally displaced could not in fairness exercise their franchise freely.

Despite these sharp rebukes and setbacks, the Modi government and its administration survived in office. Mere months after the carnage, in December 2002, Modi was re-elected to a second term, riding high on the genocide. A cruder version of the man that we see in public life today, Modi had begun his election campaign from Becharaji in Mehsana in north Gujarat, not far from where he was born. There he gave a speech with a hate-filled punch line - 'Relief Camps are Baby Making Factories'. For this speech, we took him to Court praying for directions that an FIR under sections 153a, 153b and 505 of the Indian Penal Code (IPC) be registered against him. The Supreme Court directed that we go to the lower courts. It was reluctant to directly intervene in both this and the Zakia Jafri case.

Gujarat after 2002 appeared to have two realities.

First, there is the shameful reality of the destruction of the Muslim community at the physical, emotional, economic, cultural and religious level. One real life image that I carried of this emotive attack was the empty restaurants in old city Ahmedabad as late as

May 2002. Proud of its cultural expansiveness and heritage that includes exquisite cuisine matched by warm hospitality, three months down, there prevailed a cowering sense of fear. Not a healthy or happy feeling to experience. This ugly reality is itself part of the overall story of a repressive state whose targets are numerous: the political dissenter, artist, women, Adivasis, and Dalits.

Second, there is the attempt by the state government, the central government, sections of the state and central bureaucracy to paint a picture of normalcy. Modi has spent huge amounts of the Gujarati taxpayer's money in staging international and national extravaganzas, before leaders of business especially, peddling the image of a vibrant and normal Gujarat.

Stung by international criticism and a silent message sent out by several international diplomatic missions, Modi has tried hard to overcome the humiliation of being India's first Chief Minister to have been denied a visa by the USA (in March 2005). The fact that the ambassadors of some western powers continued to boycott Modi until he became Prime Minister in May 2014, remained a sore point for a man whose megalomaniacal tendencies were even then evident from the way every corner of the state (between 2002-2014) were plastered with images of his face. Then school bags and biscuit packets for school children were used to drill the image of his persona into people's consciousness. Today, it is the same technique that has been amplified to the national level, as during the campaign to grab the Prime Minister's chair and thereafter, an obsessively personalized campaign continues to promote him.

To a large extent, Modi has succeeded. Captains of industry, with their own vision of 'India Shining', appeared, at least from 2007-2008 onwards, mighty impressed with the 'strong political leadership of Mr Narendra Modi'. Early that year, Ratan Tata of the Tata group, who had wept on the streets of Mumbai in empathy with Mumbai's victims of communal violence in 1992-93, had no problems sharing a dais with a politician accused of criminal conspiracy and mass murder. The Tata Nano plant shifted from West Bengal to Sanand in Gujarat in November 2008. Uttarakhand was a natural choice as several units manufacturing car parts already existed there. But the decision to move the Tata plant to Gujarat was taken and the plot at Sanand outside of Ahmedabad given at a throwaway rate, at the Gujarat taxpayer's expense, to the leader of Indian industry. After the Tatas' embrace of Modi, the Ambanis of the Reliance group, Shashi Ruia of the Essar group and Kumarmangalam Birla of the Aditya Birla group unsurprisingly joined in too, signalling corporate India's readiness to help wipe the blood off Modi's hands and help him gain respectability. The inexplicable and much publicized report of the Rajiv Gandhi Foundation calling Gujarat the 'best governed state', made public months after the UPA came to power, was at the time, one more feather in Modi's cap.

It was the same year – March 2008 – that the SIT was finally appointed by the Supreme Court though our plea for transfer of investigation had been pending since May 2002. When the government set up the special body, it set aside all the names that the survivors and the CJP suggested for the SIT. Names suggested by the counsel for Gujarat state, Mukul Rohatgi – today India's attorney general – were, without any consultation with us, agreed upon by Harish Salve, the *amicus*. When Raghavan was chosen to head the SIT he occupied a significant position on the Tata Securities Board, a position he holds today. This clear conflict of interest, can summon a sharp popular phrase in Gujarati, white washing of the investigation (*chuna laga dena*). Unfortunately this is what appears to have happened despite strenuous efforts in these cases.

'Normalization' and 'strong leadership' became terms

attributed to a vindictive administration that showed little remorse for having engineered mass crimes, that saw – and even now sees – political advantage in villages, cities and *mohallas* or neighbourhoods remaining divided by borders. This was a state that has threatened victim survivors and human rights defenders who stand up for justice with arrest and torture. Gujarat is nothing but a showpiece of unchallenged state power.

The comfort of the Indian political class with the state of affairs in Gujarat has also been reflected in the lacklustre debates on the issue in the state's assembly at the time and in Parliament, after 2002. The genocide's aftermath had not been high on the list of priorities for elected representatives who protest and force adjournments in State Assemblies and Parliament on all kinds of issues a lot of the time. It is not just the Congress party, but other partners in the UPA coalition, including the Left parties, who have also been reluctant to take the issue of punishment for mass crimes to Gujarat's streets. Or, with consistency and due diligence, invite trenchant scrutiny of the aftermath of mass crimes within the legislatures.

For human rights activists, keen to record due diligence when it comes to acknowledgment of the scale of crimes committed, the numbers of lives lost and those missing becomes crucial. The political class and structures of governance within Indian democracy have not developed any objective standards for rigour when it comes to maintenance of these records. Even figures collated by the National Crime Records Bureau (NCRB) suffer from anomalies. Specifically, when it comes to the total number of lives lost in Gujarat, post-Godhra mass arson in 2002, our figures for the dead – based on careful collating of numbers from the FIRs and charge sheets – come to 1,926. This is close to the figures cited by us, in rough estimate, during the first weeks after the genocidal massacre. These numbers far outnumber the figures placed before

Parliament by a government (NDA I) belonging to the same party that ruled the state.[21] For responsible Parliamentarians, it should surely be important to set such records straight. By failing to do so, an indicted party or government can successfully rely on inaccurate figures to truncate the impact of the violence.

Despite the change of political guard in New Delhi (2004-2014), the conduct of the central government in the courts where the struggle for justice was being vigorously fought was, in the five years since 2002, both ambivalent and equivocal. In none of the cases being fought in the Gujarat High Court or the Supreme Court, barring one exception, was the UPA government at the time as forthright as it could have been in supporting the Gujarat genocide survivor's fight for justice. With Modi sweeping to power in 2014, however, things took a qualitative and sharp downturn. The difference between a government indifferent to reparations and justice and one that is actively protecting the perpetrators, became sharp.

Since 2002, the CJP and victim survivors pleaded with the courts to transfer the investigation and trials to places where the communal atmosphere was not as charged. We relied for this on recommendations of the National Human Rights Commission. Our plea remained pending in the Supreme Court. Our advocates tried, from 2002 onwards, to push the plea. *Amicus curiae* Harish Salve initially supported our plea. But the central government remained non-committal. In the course of the repeated hearings of the major carnage cases in the Supreme Court, the Centre has been reluctant to readily accept the call for the reinvestigation by

---

[21] One of the scandalous discoveries in evidence in the course of Zakia Jafri case has been the fact that the GOI's Ministry of Home Affairs, at least on six occasions, through March and May 2002, upbraided their counterpart in Gujarat, ACS Home, Ashok Narayan, on the fact that there were discrepancies in the figures of lives lost and damages, as also extent of violence between what the DGP (read police authorities) were sending and what the government (read IAS) was offering.

the CBI in the Godhra, Gulberg, Naroda Patiya, Naroda Gaon, Ode and Sardarpura massacres. When the mass graves petition was being heard in the Gujarat High Court, the CBI counsel went so far as to actually abuse the legal action group, CJP. This was in 2006 when the matter – in utter defiance of the set and accepted procedures – came up before a different judge, not the judge who had, in December 2005 directed that the remains of the dead bodies unearthed by the survivors should be sent to the laboratory in Hyderabad, under CBI supervision. For justice to be done, procedural and substantive elements should have equal weight and importance. The lapses by the government seemed to be both procedural and substantive. These had become normal for a tardy system. The traumatized survivors of the 2002 Gujarat pogrom had to bear these lapses on top of their other problems.

When the CJP pushed the question of the mass graves before the Supreme Court, we met with one of our failures. Despite the fact that the forensic investigation had proved the survivor claims to be true, despite the fact that there had been no decent closure through performance of the last rites, a curiously unsympathetic ear was given to this matter in the highest court. With great difficulty we obtained interim orders that finally, in August 2010, eight years after the massacre, allowed a semblance of burials to take place. Our prayer for a transfer of investigation was simply turned down.

The Congress Party's stand before the Nanavati-Shah Commission of Enquiry, appointed by the Gujarat government to probe the Godhra train arson and the post-Godhra violence, was similarly ambivalent. Other political formations simply did not intervene, providing an escape route to the ruling dispensation.

Nowhere could the UPA I and II's reluctance to take a constitutional stand and position be observed more starkly than in the course of former Additional Director General of Police

(ADGP), Gujarat, R. B. Sreekumar's case before the Central Administrative Tribunal (CAT). The Indian Police Service (IPS) officer, now retired, filed a petition before CAT challenging the denial of his promotion to the post of Director General of Police (DGP), Gujarat, despite a long record of meritorious service. Sreekumar's battle was not an individual grievance but the rare and principled dissent of a serving IPS officer who refused to compromise on his principles and his oath of allegiance to the Constitution. For this he was isolated and made to suffer. Since Sreekumar was a member of the central services, the role of the Union government should have been clear. They simply had to reiterate that the grounds that the state government were using to justify an unfair denial of promotion were illegal and improper. Judicial precedents supported Sreekumar's petition. But no. Despite interventions from the top level of the UPA leadership, bureaucrats in the Union ministries even tried to smuggle in, at the last minute, an affidavit supporting the Gujarat government's untenable stand against an upright officer.

Upholding the dignity of office, former ADGP, R. B. Sreekumar spurned professional lures when he filed four affidavits before the Nanavati-Shah Commission annexing invaluable records that now form part of the public domain and historic litigation. He was made to pay by not being promoted to the post of director general of police (DGP) despite being the most appropriate candidate for the job. His personal register record indicts the chief minister and senior officials for issuing illegal instructions to the police. Sreekumar disobeyed these instructions, inviting the wrath of his political masters. The CJP was proud to associate itself with providing legal aid to a man of Sreekumar's integrity and grit. He won his case days before his retirement and retired, formally at least, as DGP.

Sloganeering at election time notwithstanding, India's so-called secular political parties have shown a reluctance and ambivalence to identify with the victim survivors' struggle for justice. After the Best Bakery retrial had commenced in Mumbai and barely a month after witness Zahira Shaikh turned hostile for the second time (on 3 November 2004), municipal elections were held in Vadodara. The Congress Party sent out a clear message when it gave an election ticket to Chandrakant Bhattu Srivastava, the cousin of a BJP member of the legislative assembly (MLA), Madhu Srivastava. The cousins had played a crucial role in attempting to subvert the struggle for justice in the Best Bakery case.

It was, initially at least, some national statutory bodies such as the NHRC and the CEC that were severely critical of the criminal negligence and even unholy collaboration of the state government and its functionaries in the perpetration of heinous crimes against minorities in 2002. These bodies have also flayed the state administration for its acts of culpable omission and commission in not actualising effective performance of various segments of the criminal justice system, not earnestly redressing the grievances of riot victims or ensuring proper and durable rehabilitation of those displaced from their pre-riot habitats. After 2002 and until now, the stance of these bodies on the follow up issues arising out of the genocidal carnage has been diluted and silenced. At best we can call ourselves a successful electoral democracy where today majoritarianism rules. Genuine democracy must embrace Constitutional values of equity and parity in governance. India remains a far cry from that.

A meeting with victim survivors on 26 April 2002 moved the then president of India, K. R. Narayanan, to tears. This was soon after SAHMAT and the CJP had organized the survivors' meet in Delhi. Three former prime ministers were also moved to tears as the survivors, still traumatized by the rawness of their ordeal, recounted the attacks. After we met President Narayanan at Rashtrapati Bhawan, he vowed to visit Gujarat. A date was nearly fixed. That visit never took place. The next President of India, A. P. J. Abdul Kalam visited Gujarat on 11 August 2002 but was prevented by a wily Modi from any direct interaction with survivors at the relief camps. The collector issued an 'order' that I should not be allowed inside the camps on the day of the visit. We cleverly subverted this: survivors insisted on my being there and smuggled me in two nights before. I was standing with women survivors clad in a *burkha* as I handed over the Tamil edition of *Communalism Combat* ('Genocide', March-April 2002) to the President. Modi was next to him.

A year after the genocide (2003), as trial after trial resulted in acquittal and the crude phenomenon of witnesses being influenced through fear and inducement received national focus, strictures flowed from the Supreme Court. It was after the Best Bakery case witness Zahira Shaikh's sensational press conference in Mumbai on 7 July 2003 seeking support from the CJP and exposing the pressures exercised on witnesses, that they were galvanized into action. The NHRC, Shaikh and the CJP filed Special Leave Petitions asking for a retrial. Finally the Supreme Court spoke out on what was transpiring in Gujarat. A series of orders and directives by former Chief Justice of India, V. N. Khare, then led to the transfer of the Best Bakery case out of Gujarat. The historic Best Bakery case verdict by Justices D. Raju and Arijit Pasiath on 12 April 2004 was yet another official ratification of the state of affairs so diligently documented by rights groups. Rarely have Indian courts spoken out so sharply and clearly on state complicity in communal violence or the blatant attempts to subvert the role of the public prosecutor.

As early as November 2002, trials in two of the many

incidents of premeditated violence had already resulted in a summary acquittal of the accused. In Pandharwada village in Panchmahal district over 40 persons were killed. In Kidiad village in Sabarkantha district, 65 persons fleeing a village in two tempos were torched to death. The NHRC, which had created history with its first report on Gujarat in 2002, failed to monitor the progress of justice consistently. This despite its own recommendations in the 2002 report that given the state's role in the violence, special courts and independently appointed public prosecutors should handle the major criminal trials. It was one step forward and many steps back for India's institutions.

Shocking exposures of likely high-level connivance revealed through telephone records and statements on oath by serving policemen kept a state government accused of mass murder constantly in the dock. Former superintendent' of police (Bhavnagar) Rahul Sharma, now retired, submitted recordings of crucial telephone conversations, of policemen and politicians, conducted between 27 February and 5 March 2002. The recordings have exposed zealous interference in police duty by major players who were also accused in the massacres at Ahmedabad and elsewhere in the state. Considering the scandalous exposures and evidence on the conspiracy behind the genocide, institutional democracy in India has so far left Modi and his co-conspirators relatively untouched. It is worth recalling the cold shoulder that even the apex court first gave legal interventions in 2002. Three critical petitions, each asking for special relief, were filed in the Supreme Court as early as in April and May 2002. One of these petitions (writ petition [criminal] No. 37-52 of 2002, *Devendrabhai Pathak and Others vs state of Gujarat*), filed by independent citizens supported by CJP, remains undecided even today. The other two petitions, filed by danseuse Mallika Sarabhai, litterateur Mahasweta Devi and others asking for relief, became out-dated after relief camps in the state were disbanded in August 2002. Despite the weight of evidence against Modi and his men, the stance of the Gujarat administration remains vindictive towards any and all who fight for justice.

The petition has made a strong pitch for the implementation of the NHRC's recommendations, asking for the major carnage cases, including Godhra, Gulberg, Naroda Gaon and Patiya, Ode and Sardarpura, to be reinvestigated independently by the CBI. After the scandal over the Best Bakery case in the Vadodara fast track courts, the NHRC and the CJP further sought that these critical trials be transferred out of the state. The stark facts put down on the affidavit by victim survivors and eyewitnesses through the CJP in the Supreme Court led the court to stay these trials on 21 November 2003. Since then there have been over two-dozen hearings. Not once did the victim survivors or the CJP seek extra time. The Court saw fit to repeatedly postpone the hearings as a result of which these major trials have been stymied. In the interim, referrals went to a Sessions Judge (Mehta) of the Delhi jurisdiction (2006) to evaluate the claims of the survivors as opposed to the state. Our legal team appeared diligently, and within months conclusions were set to be drawn. Inexplicably the *amicus curiae*, at the last moment, informed the judge that his job was not to draw conclusions, but simply to list the warring contentions. We were shocked and baffled. What was then the entire exercise about if not to reach conclusions? Through these painstaking processes, between 2003-08, repeatedly our legal team urged and pleaded for a speedy hearing and disposal. The legal team would often earn a sharp rebuke from the venerable senior counsel. Victim survivors and witnesses waited anxiously for the Supreme Court to pronounce its verdict on their simple plea: transfer of investigation and transfer of trials. Is justice delayed not itself justice denied?

The mass media, which has otherwise reported actual incidents without bias, has failed to link the genocide's aftermath with the near collapse of India's democratic institutions. As a result, the struggle against the fallout of the genocide in Gujarat and the reality of political repression and an on-going emergency in the state has been relegated to a legal battle in the courts. In 2002, the NHRC produced an exemplary report for its detailed and path-breaking recommendations. In September 2003, the NHRC had approached the Supreme Court to transfer the Best Bakery Case. But, as the years went on, the personnel at the NHRC shifted and the NHRC lost interest in pursuing critical legal challenges initiated by it.[22]

The genocide's aftermath has, apart from the issue of delayed justice, also exposed the discriminatory deliverance of justice inherent in India's criminal justice system. The conduct and practices being followed in the Gujarat courts have on occasion received sharp rebuke from the apex court. But even this has failed to correct the functioning of a tainted system.

The major perpetrators and masterminds of the post-Godhra violence were released on bail in next to no time by Gujarat's courts, especially the High Court, even though the crimes committed included barbarities like gang-rape, massacre and multiple arson. On the other hand, most of the eighty-six accused of the Godhra train arson remained in jail without bail till the verdict of the trial court in 2011. Then, the court convicted 31 (11 were given the death penalty) and 63 were acquitted.

The families of these accused, like those involved in bouts of the post-Godhra genocidal pogrom, had been reduced to penury. Included among them was a boy, Iqbal Mamdu, who is almost totally blind. Among those still imprisoned until acquittal was

[22] Only twice in its 25-year old history has the NHRC ever approached the Supreme Court: once in the Punjab Mass Cremations case and second in the Gujarat 2002 cases.

Maulana Umerji, a cleric and respected social worker, who was interned under the Prevention of Terrorism Act (POTA) a year after the incident. Umerji has a long history of social service – he collected donations from Godhra residents for victims of the Bhopal Gas tragedy and was the main person running the Godhra relief camp after the carnage in 2002. The apex court, too, remained unmoved by the bail pleas of the Godhra accused. Umerji was finally acquitted in 2011 and died a broken and grieving man months later. This discriminatory attitude of the justice system truly rankles.

In sharp contrast, Babu Bajrangi (Patel), accused number one in the Naroda Patiya carnage, roamed free, enjoying political patronage from the top man in the state. An illegal racket then run by the Navchetan group which he heads had, over the past eight or ten years, abducted many dozen Patel girls who 'dared' to marry a person outside their caste. Bajrangi escaped the long arms of the law till August 2012 when he was convicted. Bajrangi's political clout was particularly evident during the *Parzania* film controversy in 2007. A film about a Parsee family's anguished search for their missing son, Azhar, after the attack on Gulberg Society on 28 February 2002, *Parzania* was unofficially disallowed by the regime in Gujarat in early 2007. Even today there is no government order banning the film. But Gujarat has no need for such legal niceties. One word from Modi or his militia was enough to terrorize multiplex owners not to show the film. It was Bajrangi who vetted the film and declared it unfit for viewing in the state.

In December 2005, the mass grave scandal was exposed, which revealed more callousness from the Gujarat police and administration. Hurriedly dumped skeletal remains of victims of the Pandharwada massacre were recovered by victim survivors. Legal intervention brought some relief when the Gujarat High Court ordered a DNA analysis under CBI supervision. A year later, another judge of the same court rejected a plea for an overall CBI inquiry despite the fact that eight of the samples found at the scene matched the blood samples provided by surviving relatives. Ameenabehn Rasool, a victim survivor, and the CJP then filed an appeal in the Supreme Court. Finally in 2010, after several hearings, the Supreme Court rejected our plea for a transfer of the investigation. There was little empathy from the judiciary for the fact that survivors had been denied closure, the simple act of performance of the last rites of the loved ones. This finally happened after we pushed application after application in the lower court, to the police authorities and finally to the Supreme Court in August 2010. This was one of our failures. Meanwhile, victims and human rights defenders were targeted by the local police and have had to seek anticipatory bail. I was made an accused in the case in December 2010, five years after the charge sheet was filed. On 29 July 2011, I was almost arrested by a gleeful Panchmahal police at Lunawada. Sensationally, on the same day as I was scheduled to appear at the police station, the Supreme Court stayed the investigation. Tragically, despite this petition being in the Supreme Court, the remains of the loved ones were made available to relatives only in August 2010 when they finally could conduct the funeral rites and find some closure.

From 2003 till now, persistent efforts continue by the Modi (and then the Anandibehn Patel and Vijay Rupani) government, the administration and the police, to coerce and convince witnesses into turning hostile and so force the burial of their cases. Zahira Shaikh and her family were the first to succumb in November 2003, but they are not alone. Zahira Shaikh served a one-year term for perjury. The apex court, which delivered this historic judgment, stopped short of proving the involvement of those in power in Gujarat who had turned Shaikh and her family from the truth. Despite several applications to the Supreme Court by the CJP, urging that the court should order an investigation into the roles of individual politicians who were instrumental in influencing the witness and her family, the court did not do so. To date, the mystery of Zahira Shaikh's ten-day seclusion at the Silver Oak guesthouse on the Gandhinagar highway is shrouded in suspicion and secrecy. Despite the fact that this posh clubhouse was emptied of all staff for the duration of her stay, despite the fact that she was treated like a state guest by the state government and its administration, the apex court chose to leave the mystery unsolved. We all know that Zahira Shaikh committed perjury and paid for it. What we do not know are the conduits used by Modi's men and the role of cabinet colleagues, MLAs, politicians, bureaucrats, policemen, lawyers, and even a Muslim priest, in the pay-off.

Public discourse ought to deal with the role of the state as a prosecutorial agency, that is bound by the Constitution and our laws to see that the guilty are punished. To ensure that there is *independent prosecution based on a rigorous and ethical investigation,* adequate witness protection and time-bound trials are essential. The discourse today, whether in the case of caste crimes or communal crimes (see the Khairlanji case or the investigations into the Rohith Vemula institutional murder), limits itself to scant and sporadic sensations of the moment. Few are bothered by the lack of institutional accountability.

Notwithstanding all of Modi's efforts to whitewash the intricate execution of brute crimes and the veil of conspiracy behind them, his government and administration stand severely indicted for the violence of 2002 especially by police officers who have tendered accurate records of this critical period before the on-going Nanavati-Shah Commission. On the eve of the 2012 state elections, which again he won handsomely, Narendra Modi managed to convince the Nanavati-Shah-Mehta Commission to release Part 1 of its report. We challenged this action, since it goes against the grain of the Commission of Inquiry Act (1952). The conclusions in this section clearly announced that Godhra was part of a conspiracy. To date, despite it having been submitted to the government in 2014, Part II has not been tabled, as is statutorily required before the state assembly. The reasons remain a mystery.

The 2002 carnage in Gujarat was also marked by the cynical use of depressed sections, Dalits and tribals, for violence against the minorities while in most instances the dominant Brahmin and Patel castes orchestrated the carnage and watched. Those who have been arrested (and not been granted bail) are not the influential masterminds and architects of the pogrom, but foot soldiers who executed a vicious game plan. The emergence of around three hundred 'only Dalit' colonies in Ahmedabad over the past few years reveal that despite Hindutva's hyperbole and Hindu Rashtra's pan-Hindu mantra, centuries-old taboos and caste discriminations are still in place.

It has always been a battle within the mainstream media to keep alive the fall-out, memories and the legal struggles of such massacres. Until 2006-2007, thanks in some measure to statutory interventions – like the NHRC and Supreme Court in the Best Bakery and Bilkees Bano cases —the narrative, to put it crudely, was still alive and kicking. I recall the front page of *The Times of India*, on the fifth anniversary of the genocidal carnage (February-March 2007) running stories that reflected one aspect of one of our battles. The Citizens for Justice and Peace (CJP) had been tracking the missing cases and in law, seven years after, the 'missing' became in fact, 'the dead'.

It was after the December 2007 state elections, when Modi won again, that we saw a slow but complete turnaround in the media. Thus began the naturalization of the violence. There was an orchestration of voices all saying in one voice – *let it go*. There was the media reflecting the voice of top and powerful men in business. Suddenly all these narratives started coming together. It was in January 2009 when the Gujarat Vibrant Summit happened that all the corporate honchos came together and Narendra Modi's name was first brought up, at this forum, as a potential prime ministerial candidate. Mittal and Ambani mentioned his name first. Adani was almost a non-entity then.

In the midst of these corporate machinations, in March 2008, after a six-year long wait and painfully stretched out proceedings, our plea for transfer of investigation of key trials (as recommended by the NHRC) away from the Gujarat police was heard and adjudicated upon. The CJP, as petitioners, represented the survivors. Harish Salve was the *amicus curiae*. In April 2007, filing a strongly worded note related to all the trials, Salve had observed that the CD of phone call records produced by Rahul Sharma and R. B. Sreekumar's affidavits should be examined as evidence.

In the hearings between 2003-08, the Supreme Court had made harsh observations on several issues: the failure to appoint independent public prosecutors and the submission of false information on affidavits, among others. After six long years of a rigorously fought court battle, the Court decided to set up a Special Investigation Team (SIT). This was based on *our plea for transfer of investigation*. Strangely – and to our dismay, as I had mentioned already – the names suggested for the SIT were not of people who the survivor witnesses could have relied upon to be faithful. Mukul Rohatgi suggested the names, which were immediately and unquestioningly accepted by the *amicus*. Rohatgi is India's current attorney general under the Modi regime. He has always been the aggressive champion against justice seekers in the Gujarat 2002 cases. We placed our strong objections – verbally – on the record.

The next day we made these objections formal – in writing. We suggested names like Rajneesh Rai, Neeja Gotru, and Vinod Mall. These were officers known for some integrity. Unfortunately, we were not even heard. The Court suggested R. K. Raghavan's name as head of the SIT. Not soon after we learned that he was and remains to date, a Director (Securities) in the Tata group of companies. Is this a coincidence?

It has been found time and again, that the Courts, even the Supreme Court, treat petitioners or interveners who are rights advocates or witness/victim survivors on a different plane than the mighty state. When the rights advocates or witnesses initiate legal action, they are often merely given a formal role – their submissions heard by the Court. But they are not taken as seriously as the views of the State. Interventions are subtly relegated into a hierarchy. Procedural fair play is subverted and substantive shifts take place in jurisprudence. At many points in the past fifteen years, the Court has broken out of its mould. But, as the months and years grind down, the Courts revert to the 'normal'. In August-September 2004, we put an affidavit forward on discriminatory attitudes by the Gujarat Court on bail petitions. The Godhra accused remained in jail, while swift bail had been granted to most of the accused of brute reprisal killings post-Godhra. The Supreme Court pulled up the government of Gujarat and compelled it to respond. On affidavit, the government perpetuated falsehoods. At that stage, Harish Salve was so enraged he asked us, the CJP, to actually translate – from Gujarati to English – hundreds of bail orders for which he paid from his own pocket. That was in 2004.

Modi's makeover in 2007 came not only from the corporate leadership. Apco Worldwide had been hired by the Chief Minister to re-fashion his image. *Outlook* reported that the fee to this firm was $25,000 per month – not an insignificant sum for India. The US-based lobbyist firm had a fine track record: apart from a

Zionist connection it had done the job of sweetening the image of a Nigerian dictator.[23]

Between 2008-09, we had to keep up with the challenge of working with the SIT: recording of evidence, ensuring witness protection and so on. Initially things moved along and we saw some improvements in the investigation. Survivors pressed for the powerful to be named for their involvement and for investigations to include analysis of phone call records and so on. But here the SIT faltered. Raghavan's track record as SP Sriperumbudur when Rajiv Gandhi was assassinated and thereafter as director CBI does not show him up well as an investigator. We realized to our dismay that the man had limited capabilities, made worse by the polish that he displays (and misused) in his carefully penned articles in prestigious newspaper and magazines.

There is a lesson to be learned in the struggle for justice. The system that loves the *status quo* tolerates interventions up to a point, but appears to fall short of delivering radical; real or substantive justice. The system engages with the survivors and defenders in the early years, but a shakeup of the *status quo* demands an exceptional judicial mind. If survivors and defenders labour on, for decades (15 years as we have done), if we try and take it beyond the small fry offenders, somehow, the system – to keep us in check – makes us pay. And the CJP and I have been made answerable in an extremely harrowing way. Put differently; if we had been happy with the first set of successes (and convictions), and had sat pretty with those accolades and not pushed the envelope further to get to the conspirators, we too could have moved on. However, we didn't stop there. The attempt to transfer and get a re-trial of the Best Bakery case is an instance of our attempt to push the envelope. We wanted to tackle the utter impunity that allows the spectre of brute,

---

[23] 'Modi's image builders have dictators on client list', *Times of India*, 18 November 2007.

unbridled communal violence full sway, making a mockery of the Indian constitution and the rule of law. It was and is the Zakia Jafri case that began with the complaint filed in 2006. This became too much for the system to handle. It was when we pushed on in this case from 2010 onwards that the attacks on me re-doubled.

There are key bits to the Gujarat justice story that need some emphasising. The Modi-led state government was sharply pulled up by the Supreme Court, first in 2003, then in 2004 (Best Bakery transfer judgment) and more mildly in May 2009 on the issue of partisan prosecutors.[24] Did it learn a lesson? Did it find itself ashamed by this judicial reprimand? Far from it. Confident with its image of political ascendancy, it sought a unique way for further subversion. Counsel who appeared for those accused of mass killings were rewarded (albeit indirectly) by being appointed as special prosecutors at high daily rates of pay in other trials that the state was prosecuting. The Modi government, master of subversion, figured out a way to reward those fighting for the perpetrators.[25] We pointed this out repeatedly to the Supreme Court in 2010-11.

What do I mean? Lawyers who have appeared in the post-Godhra carnage special courts (under Supreme Court supervision) for the accused have simultaneously been given special assignments at high fees for the state government's other criminal trials. A list of such beneficiaries was made available by us in an affidavit. The

---

[24] Justice V. N. Khare, the then Chief Justice of Gujarat, heading a three-Judge Bench in the Supreme Court, put the Narendra Modi Government in Gujarat in the dock and made scathing observations on the State Government and the way it was handling the riot cases. Justice Khare even advised the government to follow the 'raj dharma' or quit. In an interview after his retirement Chief Justice Khare said, 'I found there was complete collusion between the accused and the prosecution in Gujarat, throwing rule of law to the winds. The Supreme Court had to step in to break the collusion to ensure protection to the victims and the witnesses.'

[25] NDTV expose, 29 March 2010.

same lawyers who appeared for the CJP's former employee, who was the source of false complaints against us, appeared for the state and are now in prominent positions in the state prosecutorial hierarchy. The Gujarat model was a masterful act of subversion of justice and use of the taxpayers' money to aid the defence of the perpetrators of violence. Raghavan took this lightly. To date, there has been no judicial reprimand. Today, the hefty monthly costs of the SIT and the lawyers the SIT engages to battle us in the Zakia Jafri case are borne by the Gujarat government and the Gujarati taxpayers' monies.

For many who believe that Gujarat is a story of investigations gone by, details slip by in the overwhelming volume of information. What are lost are documents, such as the letter from 1 June 2002 written by Vajpayee to Modi. Here, Prime Minister Vajpayee reveals his concern for the fragile communal situation in the state and reflects his doubts over whether the interests of the riot-hit had been properly looked after.[26] The letter was sent three months after the Godhra incident and the post-Godhra riots.[27] It came two months after Vajpayee's advice to Modi that as CM he must adhere to 'raj dharma' and not discriminate on the basis of caste, creed or religion. The letter, obtained through an RTI application, shows that a PM who seldom relied on detailed correspondence with CMs had thought it necessary to interfere in the affairs of Gujarat. Its tenor makes it clear that Vajpayee was concerned that not enough was being done for relief and that a sense of assurance and security was not being conveyed to those who had fled and

[26] Diptosh Majumdar, 'Atal Bihari Vajpayee's 2002 letter returns to haunt Narendra Modi', Times of India, 17 September 2011 (http://timesofindia. indiatimes.com/india/Atal-Bihari-Vajpayees-2002-letter-returns-to-haunt-Narendra-Modi/articleshow/10011704.cms).

[27] No account of the journey would be complete without a thorough, honest and to the bone de-construction of the Godhra mass arson. But given that judgment in the appeal is due, and has been pending for months, that should wait for another chronicle.

taken shelter in makeshift camps. In the letter, Vajpayee brought to the notice of Modi that there had been 'gross under-assessment of damages' to the victims' homes. 'It is possible that, for various reasons, the teams involved in work have assessed the damages on the lower side. In the interest of justice and fair play, it will be expedient to conduct test checks in selected areas. If the test checks do confirm under-assessment, the state government will reassess the damages in areas with large-scale complaints', he wrote. He even went to the extent of assuring Modi that there would be a greater flow of funds from the Centre to help meet additional expenses. Vajpayee further said, 'I have also been informed that in a large number of cases, the relatives of the dead are yet to be paid the *ex gratia* because bodies are yet to be identified and, also, applications regarding missing persons are yet to be disposed of. The inordinate delay in the disbursement of *ex gratia* payments is a matter of concern.' The then PM argued that taking DNA samples and thereby establishing identities would be a time-consuming process 'leading to further unacceptable delay.' Vajpayee also wrote to Modi on the widespread feeling of insecurity. He said, 'It is natural that the residents of the worst affected areas may be reluctant to return to their original places of residence and demand relocation in safer areas. Ideally, an atmosphere should be created whereby these people gain enough confidence to resettle at the original place of residence.' He even told the chief minister that in case relocation could not be avoided, 'particularly in worst-hit areas like Naroda Patiya in Ahmedabad and Lunawada in Panchamahal, active government support during their relocation will only protect them from unscrupulous elements.' He added, 'Needless to say that undue influence by such elements will only exacerbate the already complicated situation.' It is more than clear that the letter was penned by a PM who was dissatisfied with the state government's steps and had carefully studied the shortcomings. Vajpayee wanted to see improvements on the ground and, therefore, did what was very unlike him, interfered in the functioning of a state by offering direct advice on how to manage relief and rehabilitation. The Gujarat riots had bothered Vajpayee immensely and this letter is a proof of the anxiety he experienced for a major part of 2002. However this has escaped the public discourse related to 2002.

I continued to dig for more and more information to firm up the evidence in the Zakia Jafri case. In 2010, I learned (this time wearing my journalist and investigator cap) that the then army chief in charge of the Gujarat operations had filed a report called Operation Aman that severely indicted the Modi government. Again began another journey that is presently stuck at the Chief Information Commissioner (CIC). I gave the appearance of never wanting to give up. This persistence has cost me dearly. It has also greatly worried my family.

What has this legal struggle gained us? In terms of human rights jurisprudence, victimology is now well and truly part of Indian jurisprudence. Quite apart from the (rather historic) fact that human rights defenders (such as myself), lawyers (the CJP team) and over 570 eye witness survivors have been given state paramilitary protection since April-May 2004 is historic in itself. Besides, an amendment in 2009 to section 24(8)(2) of the Code of Criminal Procedure (CRPC) has given victim complainants the statutory right to intervene in criminal trials to assist the prosecution. This is crucial as often the prosecution rescinds from its Constitutional duty and it is left for survivors to plod on. As precedents, this is a lasting contribution to Indian human rights jurisprudence just as the over two-dozen orders (trial courts to Supreme Court) on witness protection are.

The Zakia Jafri case could well prove to be path breaking in another area: for the collating and collection of evidence. Over

23,000 pages of state intelligence records, police control room and fire brigade records all to be enablers to proving – through documentary evidence – administrative lapses, even complicity in the events of 2002.

Our system of jurisprudence is adversarial. Many rights are afforded to the accused. The prosecution lies in the hands of the State. While defence counsels are paid high fees, public prosecutors are not just ill paid but often come from lower down in the integrity and capability pecking order. All these reforms need to be effected and built upon to ensure that the courtroom is a level playing field not an uneven, almost fixed match. In that journey, the collective efforts to provide justice to the survivors of 2002, spearheaded by the CJP, helped flag or showcase these everyday, routine lacunae. The next step will be to ensure institutionalized radical change.

It was during the day-to-day hearings of the Best Bakery re-trial in Mumbai that several nitty gritties of the system – including its hopeless inequities – were brought home to me. I would attend the hearings almost every day, sitting and taking copious notes. Adhik Shirodkar led the defence. Each day my name and my families' would be abused by him in open Court. Showering choice abuses, playing to the gallery, Shirodkar would turn around for appreciation and applause from his supporters who had gathered at the courtroom in Mazgaon court. I watched in disbelief as he did this again and again in a crass bid to gain public attention and worse – to influence the course of public justice. It was through these proceedings that the crucial issue of the physical presence and solidarity of comrades during the trial hearings became a real need. Day after day, from 2004 to February 2006, staunch feminists, lawyers, Dalits and minority rights activists, sat with us – Sharayu Yadav (a young lawyer colleague) and myself – as we faced the court.

The gruelling sittings showcased a little-talked about but

absolute, non-negotiable entity – namely, the importance of the temperament and integrity of the judge. As witness after witness in a criminal trial are brought before the court, the role of the defence in our system allows the procedure to break down and wear down a witness. Often this means allowing intimidation, even browbeating. For men, women even children in the box the process can be excruciating, paralysing, and intimidating. The judges play a key role here.

The work of being a Judge is not just about knowledge about the law but deliverance of justice. In cases of mass crimes – on the lines of caste and communal – it is also about compassion and seeing the wider picture. It was fortuitous that on at least two occasions, in the special court set up by the Supreme Court for the 2002 cases, the Judges who presided displayed innate understanding and knowledge of the law guided by compassion. One was in the re-trial in the Best Bakery case when the star witness turned hostile for the second time and the drama unfolded day after day, in and out of court. Unflappable, Judge Abhay Thipsay steered the hearings, ensuring that the poor bakery worker who was appearing for the first time in this trial felt confident enough to depose. The second time was during the hearings of the Naroda Patiya trial, the most grisly and ghastly incident of violence. The charge sheet says 96 persons were killed; we claim 124. It is rare that the narrative of brute gender violence returns during trial. This and more happened as the trial unfolded and the verdict was pronounced on 29 August 2012. As much as the verdict, the process was cathartic and therapeutic for the eye witness survivors, a vast majority of them women who had seen the most unimaginable crimes being heaped on their own. The judge, a woman, Judge Jyotsna Yagnik, protected her witnesses with dignity and firmness, showing that justice must not only be done but be seen to be done. The near 2,000 page verdict is a study in reasoned argument. The conduct of the proceedings was a real life experience of faith being redeemed through the judicial process.

I have spoken in this book about Suhel Tirmizi. No account of this journey would be complete without mentioning some of the other lawyers. Mihir Desai, a devout fellow traveller like none other, committed to any and every legal challenge related to 2002. High Court or Supreme Court, Magistrate's Court or trial court, he performs his task with rare capabilities and grace. Gujarat 2002 was for him, as for many of us, something that needed to be resisted and corrected in a fundamental way. I met Aparna Bhat through Mihir in 2003 during the Best Bakery challenge in the Supreme Court. We are close friends now. Temperamentally though we differ in approach, chalk and cheese as it were, but not in our convictions. But never has a working relationship been more meaningful, possibly because of this variance in perspective. Ramesh Pukhrambam, also from Delhi and our very own Kamini Jaiswal, redoubtable, committed and stoic. On many an occasion – not least by the rather obnoxious behaviour of Ram Jethmalani before the Court, she has firmly stood her ground. On principle. Sanjay Parikh, along with many before, like M. S. Ganesh, have been co-architects of the Zakia Jafri challenge, a historic legal initiative. Sanjayji, with his innumerable human rights interventions in the Supreme Court, has brought a rare rights perspective into our battle. There are so many more that I can mention and some I will: Navroz Seervai, Aspi Chinoy and, of course, Kapil Sibal. Kipal's commitment to the fundamental values of the Indian republic runs deep. Others I shall remember another day.

I would not like an account about Gujarat 2002 to become about me. But given the circumstances I thought it worthy to reproduce the statement made by Justice J. S. Verma, former Chief Justice of India. These words are from his written speech while awarding me the Vigil India Award in 2004. Here is Justice Verma, at the ceremony,

What has Teesta Setalvad done? She has performed in full measure her fundamental duties as a citizen and if every one of us were to follow suit there would be no Gujarat and there would be no hell. . . . So I must congratulate Vigil India Movement for conferring this honour on her. She rightly deserved it. I think it would be unfair on my part if I would not make a brief mention of her role in Gujarat, which I directly saw.

When I went around in Shah Alam camp, I couldn't stay and talk to everyone, because it is not physically possible to have talked to ten thousand people. Once the government officials realized what I had in mind they were trying their best to see that I interact with as few people as possible, but Teesta was the one who was finding out and pointing out to me the areas which I needed to see, the persons I needed to talk to, because in spite of my best efforts I was surrounded by so many who were trying to frustrate all my attempts.

At one stage she told me: 'Please come'. Many of you may have seen the photograph of one boy to whom I was talking. I didn't realize then, till I saw the photograph later in the media, that this was a 10- year-old boy whose entire family had been wiped out, who was an eyewitness to that massacre. Now she told me: 'You must talk to this boy!' When I went and talked to that boy, I came away with the feeling, after talking to him, that if this boy doesn't become a terrorist it is God's Grace. It is no contribution of the government or any authority to prevent him from becoming a terrorist. If you see that carnage in front of your eyes, your family being wiped, that is one of the many things. Of course I can't divulge all what I told Narendra Modi but this is one of the things I told him, I said: 'I don't know how to look at it. If this boy does not become a terrorist it will be in spite of you and not because of you. Because it will be some other force which will guide him in the right direction.'

Then she told me that there were groups of women who wanted to talk to me, and of course in private. She was there with me and she brought some of them who talked to me, I can tell you I never felt more ashamed in my life, I could not lift my eyes hearing them narrating what had happened to them. The only thing I could tell them was: 'You don't have to be ashamed; all of us need to be ashamed, that such a thing happened to you.'

Teesta's car was attacked. I realized by the time I was in Godhra what great trouble she was likely to be in. I instructed my officers to ensure that her car was safe and she does not travel in my company.

I told Narendra Modi the next day: 'I don't need any more evidence now, what happened to me, or rather what did not happen to me and what could have happened, what more evidence do I need? If you say that nothing happened, it is only to save yourself, but I wish something had happened to me at least this madness would have stopped.' Now, in that madness she moved unescorted, undeterred all the time. So my anxiety when I came back from Godhra was for her protection. But she went and returned, and of course whatever I could do, within the limits of my power and my powers were more, not the direct powers which I wielded, but the fear which the authority had of me, of being one person who would say anything to anyone. Now, you see, she represented that category, but a lot needs to be done. What is more important is, there should be no Ayodhya and no Gujarat again that is what you must commit it to be and this award if it helps to promote that public consciousness in that direction, which I am sure it will seeing the galaxy of ladies and gentlemen who are here, committed to the cause, but everyone of us has to give this message to many more and it is that ripple effect.

Let us have more Teesta Setalvads, let us have more people committed to the cause. Then only the creed of secularism and the unity in diversity for which we are known for, for which we are peculiar, the world over will survive.

From the time that the CJP was set up, we intervened in various issues outside the 2002 Gujarat pogrom. When the 2005 floods in Mumbai devastated the city, we were involved. We suspended all other commitments to get involved in relief and rehabilitation in areas as far off as Chiplun and Kalyan. In 2006 when the bomb blasts in Mumbai's trains took place, then again when the Ahmedabad blasts took place and the 26 November ghastly terror attack took place, the CJP and its trustees chipped in for months. The CJP raised monies to run two ambulances in the city that still run. Be it mob terror or bomb terror, we have tried, as citizens to intervene with conscience.

In March 2006, on the eve of the final judgement in the second Best Bakery case (filed by me after Zahira Shaikh turned hostile for a second time in November 2004), Banaras experienced the tremors of hatred. Bombs were set of at the popularly visited Sankat Mochan temple on a Tuesday evening, an important day for the worship of Hanuman, the Monkey God. Veer Bhadra Mishra, a priest and a hydraulic engineer, was the Mahant of the Sankat Mochan temple. He did as Maulana Umerji had done in Godhra town in December 1984, drawing the strength of the people to help the survivors of the Bhopal Gas tragedy. Veer Bhadra Mishra held the wolves of hatred at bay.[28]

Mishra embraced Mufti Batin and the Bishop of Banaras. He shut the doors of the Sankat Mochan to Vinay Katiyar of the Bajrang Dal as well as to BJP leaders L. K. Advani and Murli Manohar Joshi. Kashi sent out a strong message of brotherhood, not allowing this town, crucial to the Hindu faith, to follow the Godhra-Gujarat trajectory. I wrote some words on the Mahant and the Mufti. The title of my essay is 'Two Sides of the Same Beautiful Coin'. It reads,

Two months apart, 13 January and 13 March 2013 we lost two

---

[28] http://sabrang.com/cc/archive/2006/mar06/index.html;
https://www.sabrangindia.in/ann/kashi-shows-us-way

visionary religious men. On the earlier date, a Sunday evening, Maulana Umerji from Godhra passed away. He who ran the Godhra Relief Camp in 2002 where survivors from Panchmahal, Dahod and other districts took shelter and drew succour is a symbol of Courage, Resistance and Faith. He was made a specific and vicious target by a man and an administration that has built its development plank on the humiliation and subjugation of Muslims.

From 2003-2011 he has to spend in jail, seriously ill and heartbroken the victim of a vindictive government who invoked POTA to incarcerate him *without any substantive proof,* simply because he had extended a courageous helping hand to his community women, girls boys and men. Finally he was 'honourably acquitted' when the final judgement was delivered in February 2011. No bail was granted to him even after he approached the Supreme Court. Other accused of the Godhra mass arson (Muslims) were similarly refused bail while eighty per cent of those accused of the post Godhra reprisal massacres were given bail within six months to a year. Hence my *Salaams* to sisters from Naroda Patiya who deposed without fear or favour while Kodnani and Bajrangi roamed free in their areas without bail, even as the trial progressed, for years.

Two months later, last week, we lost another man. Before he could light the lamp for the daily evening *aarti* at the Sankat Mochan mandir last Wednesday evening, 13 March 2013, Dr. Veer Bhadra Mishra – seer and scientist – breathed his last. The *mahant*, whose modest abode was at the legendary Tulsighat of Benaras, succumbed to lung congestion at 75. A post-graduate from the Benares Hindu University, Dr. Mishra was also a hydraulic engineer by profession using all his scientific knowledge and spiritual strength to urge cynical governments to get his beloved Ganga *mai* re-born in her life-sustaining image.

Gifted with two critical faculties, as he put it, he had come to become the voice for a clean and re-born Ganga. 'There is a necessary interface between the two, a committed heart and a rationally trained mind', he shared in a candid conversation with me in 2006 after his beloved temple and city had been ripped with the violence of twin bombings. 'Today men of science have gradually begun to accept that there is a world beyond the mere physical. I have been saying for over 25 years that the fish in the Ganga are dying, soon we human beings living on its banks will follow. I have been working on the issue of purification of fresh water bodies with Ganga as the symbol. The Ganga catchment area provides sustenance to 40 crore human lives, Domestic sewage and industrial pollution contributes to 95 per cent of the pollution and this can be stopped.' He never lost a public opportunity to raise this issue.

It was in the aftermath of the vicious violence however, that his deep conviction met another kind of challenge when he rose to the highest demands of all faiths when he called the peace. Seven years ago to a week, on 7 March 2006, a week before the festival of Holi could be celebrated, twin bomb blasts rocked the mystical city on the banks of the Ganges and sent resounding shock waves throughout the country. A total of 23 persons were killed, 21 of them worshippers within the precincts of the Sankat Mochan temple, a temple devoted to Lord Hanuman and to whom the devout offer special prayers on Tuesdays and Saturdays. The calculated acts of violence were aimed beyond the lives that they took, the ultimate provocation. Located on the banks of the holy Ganges, Kashi, is the pilgrimage centre for the devout and central to Hindu scriptures and religiosity, Hindustani music and poetry. Deep grief and legitimate outrage could have spilled into spiraling violence.

Instead, drawing deep from the spirituality and mysticism that has woven itself around Kashi, devotees responded by continuing their *darshan* before Lord Hanuman within 40 minutes of the tragedy, close to the spot where blood had been spilt hours earlier. Temple *mahant*, Dr. Veer Bhadra Mishra, led the devout, in his calm way, refusing to let this blow tarnish the temple's tradition of inclusiveness and tolerance. Best efforts of politico-religious figures to gain entry were thwarted. Adversity, says the cliché draws out the best or the worst in us. The mahant's call for calm and peace made the tide turn, nationally. By the next morning, residents of the city – Hindus, Muslims, Sikhs and Christians – demonstrated, in peaceful outrage against the acts of terror. Burkha-clad women, traders and Muslim clergy were not only visible in their protest and grief but could also be seen offering prayers at the temple. Any outsider could have mistaken Tulsi ghat for a Muslim neighbourhood.

Maulana Umerji carried the same vision, commitment, inclusion and sagacity. I remember the several occasions I met him before and after he was unfairly and vindictively jailed in 2003. Not only did he give courage and succor to children, women, men devastated by a perpetrated attack on them in 2002, including the indomitable Bilkees Bano. He had run the Godhra Relief Camp from Panchmahals and Dahod the two worst affected districts after Ahmedabad, that housed the raped, maimed and dishoused for six-eight months, in 2002. He had, in 1984 when the ghastly gas leak of the poisonous Methyl Icocynate gas spread over Bhopal claining over 3,000 lives raised relief for his fellow citizens. Yet our system, we, you and I, denied him dignified treatment and even the Courts, including our Supreme Court did not grant him bail when there was no proof against him. The government of his state used money power and resources in the Courts to present a scary picture of the Godhra accused – many of whom finally got acquitted in February 2011– and denied them a freedom that the law and the Constitution gives all citizens. Umerjisaab died a broken man, he would sob in jail quietly when visitors met him and the only sad vindication was the thousands who thronged to pay last respects that Sunday – 13 January 2013.

This week as we mourn the loss of two visionary men, men of faith, who did not fail their secular duty of compassion, justice and truth, we need to re-double our efforts to ensure that our system returns to the fundamental principles of Constitutional Governance, fair play and non discrimination. It would be our best tribute to them.

Amen.

CJP had invited Mahant Veer Bhadra Mishra to Mumbai after the train blasts in 2006. Along with a Mufti from Punjab they issued strong declarations against hate-driven violence, mob terror and bomb terror.[29] That is what it means to be a citizen. To be active, to be aware, to insist that the state operate based on the letter and spirit of the constitution.

[29] http://cjponline.org/muftifatwa.htm

BEING THEIR TARGET

I had a premonition on 24 July 2015, the day of the hearing before the Central Bureau of Investigation (CBI) court in Mumbai. I could see the stakes clearly: the might of the State and the hatred directed towards me. I was in the dock. I could go to jail, where the incarceration would have been in the hands of the foot-soldiers of a hate-driven administration. Anticipatory bail seemed improbable given the attitude of the CBI and the courts.

The past ten days had been tense. The CBI conducted ignominious, clumsy and vindictive raids against me, both at my home and office, on 14 and 15 July. This agency is directly under the command of the Prime Minister's office. It seemed motivated to harass me, to intimidate me into silence. The raids had drawn national and international media attention. The media wondered about the motives behind the raid. Was this to do with the Zakia Jafri criminal revision? Zakia Jafri had filed her appeal against the rejection of her protest petition (26 December 2014) in disagreement with the investigating agency – the SIT. Filed on 15 March 2014, that petition was to be heard by the Gujarat High Court on 4 and 5 August.[1] Weeks before that hearing, the

---

[1] The battle was fought zealously on social media as well, where journalist friends were made and alliances were forged. Here is what Amir Rizvi, a dear friend with the most crazy sense of humour, wrote on Facebook on 24 July 2015, 'From the 27th of this month final arguments in the Zakia Jafri case will begin. The new FIR by the CBI (directly under the PMO) needs to be seen in that light!!! "CBI books Teesta Setalvad and her husband for 'illegal' foreign aid" [Note: Teesta Setalvad is the first and only person in India who has sent 117 killers to jail, including the closest friends of Modi. On 27th of

State threw its might at me. Was this a coincidence or was this an attempt by the government to intimidate the persistent quest for justice into silence?

What was I being charged with? The accusations dripped with vindictiveness. Earlier it had been a criminal case by the Gujarat police. Now it was accusations of violations of the Foreign Contribution Regulation Act (FCRA) by the Government. In both cases, for the first time both Javed and I were being drawn into the web of State intimidation. Earlier in four false criminal cases filed against me since 2004, I had been the sole target. We had turned over twenty five thousand pages of documents to the investigating agency in the first case (January 2014-April 2015) and when we had whiffs of the second one, had written to the CBI (30 June 2015) offering full cooperation. There was nothing to hide. The Government that denied a CBI investigation in the Vyapam scam case, decided to prosecute me with alacrity.

I don't wear the feeling of being a victim on my sleeve. That is not my character. But I did feel as I went into the courtroom that morning that the State's vindictiveness towards me was venal. I was a target of this government, which was hell bent on my incarceration at any cost. I did not share this premonition with anyone. The CBI had insisted on our presence in the courtroom. This is a requirement in the Maharashtra courts. The hearing went on interminably. The afternoon drew towards evening. I was sure that the Judge would reject our bail application and send us, with little time to appeal, to a police lock up.

Our lawyers were fully prepared to rush down the street to make a quick appeal at the High Court. But this was Friday and the day was almost over. When the Judge finally rejected my appeal, I broke convention, walked to the front of the bench and addressed

---

this month, final arguments in the Zakia Jafri case will begin. Modi is the prime accused in this case].'

the Court. 'M'Lord, I do hope that you know what you have done. Being a judicial decision, I respect it. But by taking this view, with the full knowledge of the vendetta directed against me, you have endangered the life of my family and myself.'

What followed was a tense and chilling blur.

Friends and comrades – activist journalists, activists from the far left and from the Communist Party of India (Marxist) – had stood with us in the court. I knew they were there. I got immense strength from them.

We moved swiftly to the High Court for a stay on the CBI Court's order. Television cameras played out the drama. There was barely-veiled and gleeful vindictiveness in their voyeurism. No one was sure of the outcome. These were difficult hours. Finally, just before the Bombay High Court concluded its work for the day, the Judge hearing the matter stayed the order and granted us protection. It was an immeasurable relief.

*   *   *   *   *

The Government has – almost obsessively – sought to cut me down to size. In 2004, I was accused of kidnapping and tutoring witnesses. The accusations of Zahira Shaikh became the spear. By 2010-11, the accusations changed to 'submitting false affidavits before the Courts'. By 2014, it was 'financial embezzlement', in which both Javed and I were implicated (including Tanvirbhai Jafri, Firoz Pathan and Salim Sandhi – all victim survivors and eye-witnesses in the case). By 2016, we had become a threat to 'national security'. The ostensible reason was a consultancy with Ford Foundation, entered into after taking full legal advice between 2004 and 2009. It is ironic that the Modi regime wanted to 'book us for offences' that allegedly took place five years before 2016! Spokespersons of the ruling dispensation – possibly in a cheap bid to scare us off – have said in June of 2016 on commercial national television (Zee News) that they'd get us one way or another.

The edge of intimidation and violence should not be ignored. My car was stoned in Gujarat on 22 March 2002. In September 2010, a car tried to run me down on the premises of the old High Court buildings, where the Gulberg, Naroda Patiya and Gaam trials were being heard. In the mid-2000s, powerful accused politicians Babu Bajrangi Patel and Maya Kodnani (former minister and elected MLA of the BJP) burned effigies of me at Holi. They have done all they could to whip up hostile sentiments of the mob against me.

In Ahmedabad, within the courts, senior advocates have been known to hurl threats, such as 'We will ensure that she flees the country, never to return'! This was shouted by a senior lawyer with a known RSS background, who has enjoyed influential posts in the UPA II government. He enjoys a lucrative and influential practice even today in the national capital after the change of guard at the Centre. The Shiv Sena mouthpiece *Saamna* has reviled me long before social media appeared to take over the job. When the Best Bakery case was transferred from Gujarat to Mumbai, the Shiv Sena felt it had to take charge on its turf. Some of this goes back to the days after 1992-93, when we had called for accountability based on Justice B. N. Srikrishna's Report on the violence in Bombay. The Shiv Sena – as the rest of the supremacist right – does not easily forget.

I remember one such abusive call in the aftermath of the Gujarat carnage. My phone rang. It came from a landline. The gentleman tried to engage me in conversation for forty-five minutes. I kept my calm. That was itself an act of liberation. He hurled provocative gendered sexual abuse at me over the telephone. My colleagues in the office were aghast, upset, embarrassed, and worried. I somehow felt it was crucial not to be the one who gives in. He was the aggressor, the *agent provocateur*, pushed into actions that were small as they were demeaning. Finally, in sheer frustration, it was he who disconnected the call. This was of course not the only call. They came like waves from the sea, looking furious but simply water pushed along by the political currents.

That kind of abuse came from all quarters. I was in the Supreme Court in December 2004 to answer allegations made by Zahira Sheikh. I was sentimental, going to visit the Bar Library where M. C. Setalvad's majestic portrait hung. I wanted Dada to give me courage before facing the single-minded hate within the court. I sought succour and security. Within the Court, after hearings began, senior advocate P. N. Lekhi sought me out and hurled horrific gendered and communal language at me. His daughter-in-law – Meenakshi Lekhi – also an advocate – has now taken this abuse to even more vicious levels, first in the media and now in government. P. N. Lekhi made crude allusions to my marriage by *nikaah* (an offence it would seem!). I was upset by his language, but more so by the senior counsel who appeared for me. He was a relative of my father. I had expected him to stand up to P. N. Lekhi's barrage. I remember thinking, 'he has known me since my birth. He knows I was married by a civil ceremony. He attended the party at Juhu after our marriage. Why did he not more firmly and aggressively counter the viciousness of Lekhi?' I have lived, and learned, now through hardened personal experience, that this is what proto-fascists (RSS) do; they paralyse even seemingly good people into silence. They insidiously penetrate institutions of democracy – wedded to inclusive and non-discriminatory governance under the Indian Constitution – with a deeply embedded majoritarian psyche.

That day in December 2004, I won my plea. The Court allowed my application and directed that an independent investigation into the allegations be conducted by the registrar general of the Supreme Court, B. M. Gupta. It was neither the only time nor the first time that I came out of court, watery-eyed, bludgeoned as it were by the personal viciousness and vitriol directed at me. I expected the portals of the Supreme Court to be firmly resistant to, or against such outright vilification. Repeatedly since, and especially after 2010, members of the legal profession have been garnered to head the rapacious vanguard against me, because our struggle for accountability has been a legal one. Many of these men have abandoned all morality and ethics as they have shamelessly mouthed lies perpetrated by an indicted, insecure and vindictive state in Court. The portals of justice await redemption from such lies.

Matters got so bad that the Chief Justice of the Supreme Court was drawn into an attack against me. In 2008, the Malayalam weekly *Mathrubhumi* published an article by me. I had written this when the third of the three under-trials in the Godhra mass arson case had died a pathetic death, after being refused bail, despite repeated attempts. The Chief Justice K. G. Balakrishnan read it and was deeply angry. In open court, the Chief Justice chastised me. This was during the bail hearings for the Godhra arson case. Before the lawyers of the accused could make their arguments, the Chief Justice asked if the lawyers who were appearing for the accused were in any way connected to me. The bench, he said, would not like to hear any petitions that were in any way linked to her. 'Who is this Teesta Setalvad? Is she a spokesperson of these persons or petitioners? There is one article that appeared. If she is representing these persons [Godhra accused], we do not wish to hear them.' Senior and esteemed members of the Bar were silent when this question was raised. The Speaker of the Lok Sabha – Somnath Chatterjee – and others wrote an open letter to the Chief Justice in my defence.[2]

---

[2] Venkitesh Ramakrishnan, 'Speaker expresses surprise over CJI's reported stand on hearing Teesta Setalvad', *The Hindu*, 25 February 2008. The Speaker observed, 'I do not konw of any procedure known to law or the Constitution

What had I written that had been so enraging to the Chief Justice of the Supreme Court? These were the opening paragraphs,

Come February-March 2008, six years after post-independent India's worst ever-communal carnage, victims, perpetrators and masterminds not only roam free but have now obtained redoubled electoral legitimacy. In the year 2002 itself, those accused who were politically powerful in caste and monetary terms obtained easy bail from Gujarat's courts. (Citizens for Justice and Peace, CJP, has placed a tabulation of over 600 bail orders on record at the Supreme Court demonstrating this and *Tehelka*'s 'Operation Kalank' has some further evidence in this regard.) In sharp contrast, six years down, 84 persons accused of the Godhra coach fire – most of whom are innocent, having been picked up on the basis of cooked up police witnesses, and one, a boy, is near 100 per cent blind! – still rot in Gujarat's jails years after the incident.

The fact that many of them are ill, one is blind; the fact that their families have been reduced to penury and indignity while the main accused and masterminds of the post-Godhra carnages not only roam free, but rule Gujarat by action and word, raises the niggling, troublesome question once again. Discriminatory justice. Can a discriminatory system of justice be viable in principle, given what our Constitution espouses? What does this reality mean in practical terms, given that today we also face the challenge of another kind of terror, internationally supported bomb terror? Can such a blatantly discriminatory scheme of dispensation of criminal justice win the faith of each and every citizen, particularly a community that is at the receiving end of such a system?

Bail is a natural and normal remedy for any accused according to our system of criminal jurisprudence. Even draconian laws, anti-

---

that would allow this [denial of a hearing before a court of law]. You can dismiss something on merit. You can refuse to admit a petition. But you cannot say that you would not hear X and Y.'

terror laws that have questionable provisions on bail, simply *do not* allow for sustained and continued detention of persons in this fashion. How then can Indian democracy, booming in its growth rate, shining with the glitter of development, explain away the dark crevices of sustained institutionalized torture and prejudice?

In *Communalism Combat* in March 2008, we published the article and also an open letter from various people and organizations that defended us before the Chief Justice of the Supreme Court,

It is with deep concern that we read about the remarks passed by yourself in open court on February 19, 2008 against human rights activist, Ms. Teesta Setalvad. Not only Ms Teesta Setalvad but thousands of others all over the country, including the undersigned, have been extremely disturbed and anguished by the inordinate delay in dealing with the cases of victims of the Gujarat genocide pending in the Supreme Court. You may be aware that the issue of court delay has also been raised in Parliament, in the National Integration Council, and other fora. In this context, to single out for public criticism Teesta Setalvad, a citizen who has crusaded tirelessly for the rights of victims both inside and outside the court at great personal cost, may tend to send a wrong message.

Sir, in a democracy every wing of the state, including the judiciary, needs to have a healthy and robust attitude towards critiques which are not motivated in any sense of the word. Are such remarks, especially without giving an opportunity to a committed activist to be heard, befitting of the highest court in the land? The task of ensuring judicial accountability and sensitivity at the highest levels is a heavy responsibility which ultimately rests on the shoulders of the honourable chief justice. Since the Supreme Court is the final arbiter, we request that this issue may be examined in the proper context and we hope for your intervention to ensure that the faith that people have reposed in the judicial system may be vindicated and upheld.

This letter was signed by people such as Brinda Karat, Vrinda Grover, Urvashi Butalia and the leadership of All India Democratic Women's Association, National Federation of Indian Women, YMCA, Joint Women's Program and Muslim Women's Forum.

In April 2009, Dhananjay Mahapatra – the ever-present legal reporter with the *Times of India* – had, on being fed news by powerful men from the opposition BJP, falsely reported the 'news' of 'Teesta and CJP concocting statements and tutoring witnesses.' Pulled up by the Supreme Court at the next date of the hearing (April 2009), the newspaper had to apologise and carry its clarification prominently. The reason for mentioning this example is to indicate how even responsible publications of the mainstream media fell prey to the relentless falsification campaign against us led by powerful powerbrokers in the BJP.[3] The Supreme Court had expressed anguish at the selective leak of a portion of the SIT report. Those present in the Court had seen how Arun Jaitley, the Rajya Sabha member of the BJP and Mukul Rohatgi, now India's Attorney General, had worked with sections of the media.

Soon after we filed an application in the Supreme Court in 2009 for a re-constitution of the SIT, the attacks became ferocious and more marked. By 2010, all manner of arsenal were garnered by a nasty State headed by a man who has vendetta and insecurity as his abiding credo. These attacks tried to discredit and malign our thankless struggle and crusade. The media joined in. It was never very good at following due process. This was evident in the way the

---

[3] Dhananjay Mahapatra, 'NGOs, Teesta spiced up Gujarat riot incidents: SIT', *Times of India*, 14 April 2009; Shivam Vij, 'About Warped Minds', *Kafila*, 19 April 2009; 'Whoever leaked post-Godhra SIT report betrayed trust of court, says Supreme Court', *Times of India*, 22 April 2009; 'SC anguished over leak of SIT report to media', *Indian Express*, 22 April 2009.

media covered the 2002 carnage. It is even true when it became a collaborator with the attacks on me. And truer still when it joined the corporate honchos to sell the 'wonders of the Gujarat model' for the rehabilitation of Modi. The media did not merely report the attacks on me. They participated in them.[4] I reproduce below a press release issued by the CJP in this period,

One of the interesting fallouts of the battle for justice and reparation for the victim survivors of the Gujarat carnage of 2002 has been the blatant attempts by stooges for the state government like its counsel in the Supreme Court and others to deliberately defame those human rights defenders and organizations who have stuck it out for the past eight years and assisted eye-witnesses depose, without fear or favour to ensure that justice is done. We have consistently been victim of this vicious defamation drive. Few of those who told these stories in 2002-03 have however come to the rescue.

Woefully, unmindful of the kind of articles carried by their own publications during the traumatic period of 2002, mainstream Indian newspapers and even the hysterical news anchors of our 'national' television channels have echoed the vilification drive launched by the Gujarat state, never once looking back, over their shoulder into their own archives where correspondent after correspondent had used space telling these very horror stories.

A prime example of this abdication of media responsibility is the case of Kauserbano, a victim of murder at Naroda Patia, accounts of eye witnesses at the time describing how a bloodthirsty mob slit open her womb (carrying a foetus almost nine months old), swirled it on a sword before burning mother and child alive. Not only did *The Times of India* and *The Indian Express* apart from the *Statesman* and *The Deccan Herald* extensively report the narrative in

[4] Manoj Mitta, 'Is SC seeking to shore up SIT's lost credibility?' *Times of India*, 28 May 2010.

print, but Women's Visiting teams including one headed by former chairperson of the National Commission of Women Syeda Hamid spoke, and wrote of it extensively. Feminists from Mumbai including lawyer Flavia Agnes assisted women record their affidavits before the official Nanavati Shah Commission and Kauserbano's sad tale was a significant part of the narrative.

Now, today when the doctor who did the post mortem denies that such a murderous attack took place before the burning, do not one and all who told this story in those days after 2002 owe something to the memory of Kauserbano? Why are they all silent?

In May 2010, a Gujarati periodical went after me with special venom. Kamini Jaiswal, senior lawyer in the Supreme Court, was so outraged by the article that she responded to it at great length. Her response was called 'How Intellectuals Sell their Souls'. It was written in Gujarati. Here is the article in translation,

It is vacation time in the Supreme Court. Most of the lawyers and honourable Judges are either out of town on a holiday or perhaps are tending to personal and social engagements. The pressure that a lawyer practising in the Supreme Court undergoes is by now a well-known phenomenon. It was on one such day last week that I received a call from an acquaintance in Gujarat. The state holds a special place in my heart. Apart from having many close friends, I obtained my postgraduate degree in Law from MS University, Vadodara.

The call however disturbed the even tempo of last Sunday as my interlocutor informed me about a piece written by one Gunvant Shah in the Sunday supplement of the Gujarati daily, *Divya Bhaskar*. The caller was himself confused since Gunvant Shah is a well-known and well-respected literary figure in the state normally known for his balanced writing. He read out certain portions of the article and since there was a mention about Teesta Setalvad, whom I represent in the Supreme Court of India, it became imperative to write this article in response.

A bare reading of the article entitled *Karmsheel Juttu Bole Ke?* ("Does a sincere worker tell a lie?") refers to Setalvad's father Atul Setalvad and calls him a man of principle. It then proceeds to cite instances, which according to the author establish that Setalvad under the grab of being a sincere worker has been telling lies.

It is first important to go back into the family history of Teesta as Gunvant Shah has already referred to her father. Very few people may now remember that she is the great granddaughter of Sir Chimanlal Setalvad, an eminent advocate in the Bombay High Court during the British Raj. Such was the eminence of Sir Setalvad that in the aftermath of the Jallianwala Bagh massacre and the atrocities committed during the imposition of martial law in the then undivided Punjab, he was made a member of the Disorders Inquiry Committee which was appointed by the British Government to go into the causes of the disturbances.

It is to the fullest credit of Sir Setalvad and another Indian member, Sardar Sahibzada Sultan Ahmed Khan, Bar-at-Law, Member for Appeals, Gwalior State, that they had the courage to record a dissenting note to the findings with regard to the Jallianwala Bagh massacre and the imposition of Martial Law in Punjab.

Sir Setalvad's son, that is Teesta's grandfather, retired as a senior counsel in the Supreme Court of India after being the first Attorney General of Independent India. If it was the intention of Gunvant Shah to establish that though sired by a principled father Teesta did not uphold the same values, he should now fully realize that the family values of this lady are far deeper and beyond any horizons than Gunvant Shah could have ever imagined.

The communal colour of the article becomes apparent when he makes it a point to say that she is married to Javed Anand and lest readers may mistake the Anand surname as a Hindu one, he makes it clear by suffixing '*Begum*' to Teesta's name. In a cleverer manner, he refers to Javed's own article published in the *Indian Express* (16 March 2010) to make the point that within the Muslim community Teesta is referred to as a '*mujahid*'.

Gunvant Shah is a respectable name in the Gujarati literary scene. He is the author of many seminal works, which are well regarded and well read. Without any doubt he must realize that honesty is of two types and that intellectual honesty is by far the most important and superior to any other form of honesty which can be measured in rupees and/ or paise. Therefore can Gunvant Shah honestly say that in citing the above example it was not his intention to convey that it is because Teesta married a Muslim that she is espousing the case of the victims of communal riots, one of the most horrific that ever happened in India after 1947? Does he realize that Teesta neither changed her name to adopt a Muslim name nor converted to Islam?

The dishonesty of the author may have been intentional or unintentional. I would like to presume it was the latter, else how could he cite the example of Kausarbanu, a pregnant woman whose belly was torn upon by a sword during the riots and about whom relying on the evidence recorded by the SIT, Gunvant Shah proceeds to call Teesta a liar. I say that Shah has made this statement by mistake because he perhaps does not know the SIT on whose credibility he lays such a store by, stands discredited in the eyes of the apex court to the extent that two Additional Director Generals of Police of the SIT, namely Shivanand Jha and Geeta Johri have been directed to stay out of the same. The latter has already been exposed for her deliberate failure in the investigation of Sohrabuddin case now being investigated by the CBI. The second point Gunvant Shah has completely forgotten is the *Tehelka* expose, which was telecast in the last quarter of 2007 where the perpetrator himself has admitted to the crime on camera.

I do not write in defence of Teesta, she can more than take care of herself. This response is actually a call to all law-abiding citizens to sit up and take notice of what is happening in the state of Gujarat. If public-spirited citizens and votaries of civil society are to justify their existence in this country, they need to expose as vigorously as possible, and preferably outside the judicial forum, intentional misuse of state power to suppress crimes of serious nature. Let the citizens ask why the state sent the chief secretary, home secretary and the DGP to meet the director, CBI with regard to the criminal investigation of the Sohrabuddin case as reported by several newspapers, to convey to the chief of the Central agency that following the orders of the Supreme Court, according to these worthies, is going against the public opinion in Gujarat.

This is an unprecedented move never heard of before. A former DGP of Gujarat is already in the dock for obstructing justice. This is an investigation ordered by the Supreme Court after three years of deliberation. The state itself arrested 14 police officers of Gujarat and Rajasthan. When the CBI arrested one more police officer, Abhay Chudasma, DCP (Crime), there is an immediate uproar that it is going against sentiments of the people of Gujarat. Is it not for the governor of the state to take notice of the fact that the affairs of the government of Gujarat are conducted under rules framed as per Article 166 of the Constitution of India and therefore, by what administrative or constitutional propriety and under whose instructions or with whose connivance did the chief secretary, home secretary and the DGP proceed to Delhi to meet the CBI director?

*   *   *   *   *

On 11 August 2015, the Bombay High Court granted us anticipatory bail. The court gave us a speaking order, which made specific observations about the freedom of speech. 'Holding views that are against *a government* does not amount to be *against the nation*'. This was in response to half-baked arguments made by the CBI counsel on the activities of Sabrang Communications, which it said was a 'threat to national security'. There is nothing anti-national about being critical of the actions of a government.

The Gujarat state apparatus did all it could to bury the narrative of its omissions and commissions in 2002. This attempt intensified during the Best Bakery case in Mumbai in 2004-05. It only increased when the SIT was finally appointed and operated from 2008 onwards, to date. It was a dreary time. I had to protect myself and at the same time keep the spirits of the survivors up.

Dalit and Adivasi groups and mass organizations took me to their bosom when this attack was unleashed. At meeting after meeting in Mumbai, Kerala, Chhattisgarh, Wardha and elsewhere they came out in my support when the Gujarat State unleashed its venom. I was struck by this show of solidarity. I asked friends and leaders, closely what lay behind their understanding: why was it necessary to lend this support? How did the struggle for justice for 2002 matter in the overall scheme of things, for them? Their response was grounded and sobering. If a malevolent state gets away with this obviously motivated attack on you, our defences also get breached. It means that it could as easily, or more easily get at us. It is the sheer depth of this kind of learning that has helped me to grow and mature politically.

The struggle for justice has become multiple things. It is to speak truth to power regardless of the consequences. It is to fight the good fight even when others tire. It is to relentlessly pursue, gather and cull through evidence while protecting my own back. The entire process has been exhausting. I have to look over my shoulder at every turn. I know that my mobile phone is tapped, my emails are being tracked. The police and other agencies of an increasingly desperate government are on my back. To battle the perverted demon that lurks behind narrow religious-based nationalism, that justifies well-choreographed mutilation and killing, let alone rape, is to lay yourself open both literally and figuratively to all means and manner of attack. It is to make yourself vulnerable and threatened.

Stamina and inner force remain my strength. From 2004 onwards, I was determined not to allow my work to suffer – whether it was the legal aid work, the work with education in our schools, or my journalistic and academic writing. This meant making potentially exhausting demands on my mind and body. My heels dug into the ground. I have kept going.

My work with KHOJ – working with children to develop educational curricula – is a source of great restorative energy and strength.[5] My team at Sabrang, CJP and KHOJ are my closest allies in all that we do. Arguably the years since 2014 have been the most challenging and this redoubtable team — in Mumbai and Ahmedabad, has stood firmly by our side, never wavering. To each one of them – Santosh, Irfan, Alice, Surekha, Pradeep, Dada, Shankar, Rafiqbhai – words can never be enough. My homemakers, who keep the sanity in our abode by the sea, Geeta, darling Harshit and Aji – with my daughter and sister as close supervisors, there is no room for feeling alone.

Close friends in information technology persuaded me to ensure that *Communalism Combat* (dormant since 2012) be re-launched online. Thanks to this huge support from a body of professionals who still man our site and keep it secure, thanks to the hand holding of Prabir Purkayastha, *sabrangindia.in* was

[5] www.khojedu.net: KHOJ is about you and about me. Are all people the same? Do we even know what all these types mean?How are we different from others? And how are we the same? KHOJ means to search, to discover, to explore.And this is what we plan to do.Search within for the questions we long to ask, never mind if we do not have the answers.Explore without for the thoughts and feelings of people around us.To get to know more. About Ourselves. Our Families. The Neighbourhood. Our City. The Country. Our world.

launched on Constitution Day, 26 November 2015. With its increasing readership, this is the surest sign of resistance against repression and intimidation. It is a sign of the investment of our people in freedom and inquiry.

The sheer pressure has – fortunately – made dear, dear friends of some very precious people. Amongst them are my lawyers. I cannot name many of these friends, since they are placed in sensitive places. Their story will have to wait for another, calmer occasion. My lawyers have been on call 24x7 – emergencies, anxieties, precautionary measures, and letters to authorities, from one crisis to the next. It has been the zealous and meticulous documentation of my legal team that has kept us safe. The demands I have made on them are far beyond the realm of what is 'normal' and acceptable. At every stage they have come up on top. Here they are: Suhel Tirmizi in Ahmedabad, Mihir Desai, Aspi Chinoy, Navroz Seervai in Mumbai as well as Aparna Bhat, Kamini Jaiswal, Ramesh Pukhrambam in Delhi. Not to mention Sanjay Parikh and Kapil Sibal. When the fire heated up in 2016, Aparna wrote the following in a Facebook post, 'Sharing this (a post by someone else) with a footnote from me. In my 14 years of representing her (Teesta) she has not asked me to do or endorse anything illegal. She has always helped people in need. She has respected professional support and has supported the victims with a tenacity few of us can boast of. I am proud to be her lawyer though my own contribution as a lawyer has been negligible.' It is this self-effacement of the support that makes it so very precious. This is the level of generosity and humility in the legal team. Always encouraging, always in solidarity, never mind that many of them may just believe that I might have pushed the envelope a trite too far!

Through all these years, a redoubtable and committed group of counsel, not necessarily backed by family name and fame, have stood their ground, firm in their belief in our integrity and commitment. That itself has been redemption. It is the harsh challenges that life has thrown that show people's worth and mettle. Outstanding women and men from the legal profession have stood with and behind us – sheet anchors, even as hoary winds have blown our way.

Apart from lawyers, many bureaucrats and politicians have surprised me with their support. Around the time that the SIT began to probe the Zakia Jafri case, a former Chief Minister of Gujarat, Sureshbhai Mehta – number two in Modi's cabinet – contacted me. He is sworn to the Constitutional framework. Although we may differ on the finer points of politics, his commitment to the Indian Constitutional framework is deep and he has defended me against the attacks. R. B. Sreekumar, that rare breed of policeman who is sworn to his integrity with a superb sense of humour, has also not wavered. We have taken many a ride together across Gujarat, attending trials and visiting camps and villages were survivors live.

My old acquaintance Dilip D' Souza, who has been a friend of the family since childhood, never fails to repeat the same question, now three or four times over the past three decades: 'How do you cope with the hatred and the bile?' 'Simpliciter', as my Atul would have bluntly said.[6] 'You don't *cope* with it. You *cannot* cope with it. You simply learn how to deal with it and yes, even live with it.' These people – my comrades and friends – have given the organizations we represent free space to carry on our activities, and have done so since 1993. I have always believed that if we did not have this, the deep claws of vendetta would have squeezed our work out of relevance, and us out of existence. Yes, I have learnt to live with the bile. But it does not define me.

Rukmini Sen has been a friend found through this struggle for

---

[6] Simpliciter comes from the world of the law, mainly Scots Law. It means simply or without qualification.

sanity, and justice. She has been unwavering in her support, and her deep understanding. Our close association has fostered not just a friendship, but opened areas of collaborative work and growth, through interventions in the electronic media and the Internet. Post-2014, her presence has enabled an embattled existence to ease up, build another kind of resistance and a wonderful friendship to grow. Muniza Khan is another. Her home in Banaras is another home away from home.

Groups, individuals and movements who have deep respect and solidarity for our work invite me to come and speak – one day in Banaras, the next in Trivandrum, the next in Warangal. During my travels, I get lots of looks of recognition thanks to the devil that is television. Some looks are guarded, many open and friendly and some, downright warm, affectionate and effusive. So my answer to Dilip and all those concerned souls is that you deal with the venom and hatred being flung at you – bile that is generated through well-heeled and politically organized trolls. You engulf yourself and cocoon yourself with love, affection and admiration of so many millions of Indians who believe as you do in the republic and its values. Do they outnumber the trolls and outweigh the insidious venom? It is hard to say. Only time will tell.

There are some people who believe that they will get me in the end. There is one elderly gent, who claims to be based in the United Kingdom, who phones Javed with devilish regularity, 'Your wife's fate is to *chakki pisaon* [grind at the mill] in prison. Watch out and beware.'

*   *   *   *   *

The verdict of the Gulberg massacre case was delivered on 2 June 2016. It was a disappointing verdict. In 2002, sixty-nine people were killed in the Gulberg Society, while thirty-one others went missing. This was the second largest massacre of the Gujarat pogrom. When the verdict was announced in the Gulberg case, most families of victims were deeply hurt and disappointed. Tanvir Jafri, son of Ahsan Jafri, said, 'The Gulberg society is not *chai ki lari* (tea stall), which can be burnt by one person. It is a very big society. Fifteen-twenty bungalows were there. Ten flats were also there with 400-500 people staying there. Twenty-four people cannot burn the whole society, loot, kill, burn large numbers of people in such a brutal manner for over twelve hours.' He added, 'It looks a little odd. Thirty-six people have been acquitted. We will decide on whether to go for further appeal or not.'

The single largest massacre was at Naroda Patiya, where – according to the charge sheet – ninety-six people were killed, although our figures are one hundred and twenty-four killed. The judgment in the Naroda Patiya case was delivered on 29 August 2012. Thirty-two people, including a former minister, were convicted. In the Gulberg case, eleven people received a life sentence. A VHP leader – Atul Vaidya – was sent to prison for seven years. This was a low sentence for the kind of atrocities that they conducted at Gulberg.

While I was deeply disappointed in the verdict from the Gulberg trial, I could not help but notice how the media seemed to report the verdict without caring to explore the reasons for survivors' despair with the verdict. While recording the 'reactions' of the survivors to the judgement, they did not make a slightly more insightful effort to understand why the victims were so disappointed that there was no discussion in the court about the criminal conspiracy. I was glad of one thing though. The verdict had brought the Gulberg case and the narrative of the carnage back centre stage. This is not how it had been since 2014.

In his oral observations as he pronounced judgment in the case, special judge P. B. Desai said in open court that he had not accepted the idea of a wider conspiracy behind the Gulberg massacre, an argument that had been made rigorously since the start of the trial by advocates for the witness survivors. This aspect of the investigation was doggedly resisted by SIT investigators and prosecutors. The SIT prosecutor R. C. Kodekar did not make a case for conspiracy at all. Yet, in his reaction to the media on 2 June, SIT chief Raghavan said that the 'judge did not buy the prosecution's conspiracy theory, but it was not because the evidence pointing to a conspiracy was weak. Possibly, in the eyes of the judge, it was not convincing enough to sustain a conviction.' Was this evidence actually weak? Or was it consciously not pressed by the SIT in its arguments before the trial concluded? The reasoning in the judgment provided on 17 June 2016 provided the answers.

On pages 778 and 779 of the 1345 page judgment, the special judge writes, 'No material has been considered even *prima facie* worthwhile to arraign such special police officer and Government officials and politicians in power as accused in a number of proceedings including the present proceedings and in my opinion, therefore, it would be unsafe and improper to even have a further discussion on this aspect. The controversy, in my opinion, has been laid to rest and is required to be given its due burial.'

Here lies the tale behind the weak and disappointing verdict. The Supreme Court appointed SIT assigned with the worthy task of both investigating and prosecuting these trials, simply did not press hard enough to establish the charge of criminal conspiracy, never mind the availability of sustainable evidence.

In our desire to ensure that the SIT probe deepened and improved, senior counsel Mihir Desai argued for the arraignment of four officers: Commissioner P. C. Pande, Joint Commissioner M. K. Tandon, then DCP P. B. Gondia and Abhay Chudasama as accused in the Gulberg case under section 319 of the Code of Criminal Procedure. This was in January 2010. I first filed affidavits in the Supreme Court on 1 December 2009. Since then I have approached the courts on a number of occasions. These affidavits have been backed by documentary evidence procured through repeated applications in the Gulberg society massacre trial. We revealed that the SIT has deliberately or consciously failed to investigate key aspects of documentary evidence from the documentary records procured after the trial began (the SIT had not placed these on record with the charge sheet). What were these documents? They were charts showing arms and ammunition available with policemen stationed on duty (including the rounds of bullets they did not fire). They were records of the Fire Brigade register in Ahmedabad. They were the Police Control Room Records (PCR). They were the analysis of the CD of phone call records first presented before the Nanavati-Shah Commission by then DCP Crime Branch (March-July 2002) in 2004. These were the voluminous records that needed to be investigated.

These phone call records placed before the Court have assumed the status of a 'hot potato' that few want to touch or peel. They point to wider knowledge of the massacres executed in broad daylight. An analysis of the CDs made available by former IPS officer, then DCP Crime, Rahul Sharma reveal a total of 15 calls that day received and made by Pande with different officials from the then chief ministers office. The first telephonic exchange began as early as 11:14 a.m. Of a total of 302 calls received and made on his mobile by Pande on 28 February, he spoke several times to his boss, DGP Chakravarthi and 8 times to Joint Commissioner of Police, Shivanand Jha. Pande called DCP Gondia (responsible for the jurisdictions of Naroda and Gulberg) only twice, that too after the worst was over (15:16:12 hours and 15:54:39 hours). Despite the proximity of the commissioner's office and despite the fact that PI K. G. Erda was in constant and regular touch with his higher-ups, curfew was not declared in the Meghaninagar area till as late as 12.54 p.m., an act that is inexplicable. This delay demonstrates violations of standard operating procedure by the officials of the ranks of police commissioner and additional police commissioner.

Our advocates for the witnesses have argued (and at least four eyewitnesses from Gulberg have testified to this) that the high-level conspiracy behind Gulberg went beyond the bestiality of the mob attack. Tandon's role, callous and calculated, included the destruction of evidence. Around 5:30 p.m. on the evening of the bestial attack, when the survivors were being rescued by a police van, two survivors pleaded to be allowed to take the bodies of their near and dear ones who had been raped and killed with them. 'You look after yourself, we'll take care of the dead', Tandon had reportedly told them. The panchnamas of the site reveal how the embers were allowed to burn, undoused at Gulberg society for three days after the attack, ensuring that any forensic evidence behind the killings was properly destroyed. When survivors buried the charred remains of their loved ones at the Kalandari Masjid Kabrastan on 3 March 2002, these bodies had been reduced to ashes. There is little deliberation on this destruction of evidence in the judgment.

This and more nuggets of substantive circumstantial and documentary evidence appear to have been overlooked in a judgment that shows no appreciation or empathy for the 69 lives so brutally lost to the fires of a hate-driven politics. Testimonies of witnesses who broke down in court as they recounted the horrors of their ordeal find a similar, callous disregard by the judge.

Judge P. B. Desai often observes that the SIT investigation made a weak argument on the charge of conspiracy. This left the advocates of the witnesses to argue the case for conspiracy. This shows that the SIT's investigation into the Gulberg affairs was less than serious.

Part of the goal here seems to be to undermine the very idea of a criminal conspiracy in the Gujarat carnage. On 29 August 2012, the verdict in the Naroda Patiya case upheld the possibility of a wider conspiracy. It lauded Ashish Khetan's sting operation as corroborative evidence (his tapes were examined and found to be genuine by the CBI following an Order of the National Human Rights Commission in 2008). If, in the Gulberg trial the SIT and its prosecutor had argued, as evidence demanded, for charges of criminal conspiracy to be upheld, it would have made arguments for Zakia Jafri in the High Court that much easier. The Zakia Jafri case is pending in the Gujarat High Court. Even here the SIT refused to investigate the demands of criminal conspiracy into the three hundred incidents that took place across the state. The Gulberg massacre case relates to one incident in 2002, in which sixty-nine people were killed. The Zakia Jafri case, on the other hand, relates to three hundred incidents across Gujarat. It would pin down the criminal culpability of the administration in the violence. The Zakia Jafri case is at the pre-prosecution stage. The 2 June verdict in the Gulberg case is among the last of those 2002 riot trials being monitored by the Supreme Court. By avoiding any admission of pre-planning and conspiracy in the Gulberg massacre case (especially after the special sessions judge hearing the Naroda Patiya case had made strong findings on criminal conspiracy), the motivation is clearly to weaken the wider claims of state-wide criminal conspiracy being made in the Zakia Jafri case.

An unfortunate hostility by SIT towards victim survivors and witnesses was observed as trials wore on. This hostility was even directed against us on more than one occasion. At the moment when the interim report of the Amicus Curaie, Raju Ramachandran was impacting on the hearings of the Supreme Court (January 2011), Chairman SIT, R. K. Raghavan's intervention via senior counsel and amicus (in other cases) Harish Salve to push the Supreme Court to 'reprimand' me for communicating with the Office of the High Commissioner for Human Rights (OHCHR) on the issue of the safety of our lawyers, is a stark example. The letter I had written was to the Office of the High Commissioner for Human Rights (OHCHR) at the United Nations. India is a signatory of the treaty that governs the treaties that provide OHCHR with its mandate. It is therefore perfectly acceptable for a citizen or organization to interact with the OHCHR. 'We can't allow foreign interference in our affairs and we can't approve it', said justices D. K. Jain. P. Sathasivam and Aftab Alam. They argued that my letters to the OHCHR constituted interference. 'We don't appreciate letters being sent to a foreign country', said the judges. The OHCHR is based in Geneva, Switzerland. So the judges were correct that the letters went to a 'foreign country'. But India is party to the OHCHR and is frequently – including now – a member of the United Nations Human Rights Council. In other words, the letters by us (Citizens for Justice and Peace) were not sent to a 'foreign country' per se, but to a UN body that India acknowledges has a role to play in questions of human rights.

It is an unfortunate fallout of the robust struggle for justice that human rights defenders have had such comments passed against them by the court. I believe we have the right to continued engagement with the courts within India, while exercising our rights to report in fairness of the progress of the trials. Our institutions remain trapped in an unfortunate double-standard: while corporations and financial institutions 'collaborate' and 'influence' all manner of public policy (including by senior IAS, IPS, Intelligence officials being actually employed and on the payroll of powerful Indian and international corporations), activists and organizations struggling for Constitutional governance and the rule of law are often singled out for judicial reprimand and criticism.

✻   ✻   ✻   ✻   ✻

Since 2014, I had been battling heavy fire from Ahmedabad. In January of that year, the Ahmedabad police registered a First Information Report against my husband and myself. They alleged that I had cheated the residents of Gulberg Society of money collected in 2008 by Sabrang Trust and Citizens for Justice and Peace. The intention of the State through its police and collaborators was to make people forget about the 2002 Gulberg killings and began to see Gulberg through the prism of this fabricated case – namely as if the entire Gulberg case was not about the cold-blooded massacre of 69 people in broad daylight, an attack that included mass rape and arson, but that it was about the embezzlement of funds. The idea for a 'museum of resistance' was a collective idea born through conversations with survivors between 2007 and 2012 to keep the collective memory of resistance alive. The call for donations explained our idea,

> For nearly six years now, more than a hundred thousand survivors of independent India's state-sponsored carnage in the western Indian state of Gujarat have been denied dignified acknowledgement of, or reparation for, the magnitude of indignity and violence they suffered. With the BJP's recent electoral victory in the state, the pain and humiliation of the victim survivors has been further exacerbated. A quiet yet dignified and firm resistance to this state callousness and impunity lies at the heart of this idea of resistance.

We had raised small amounts of money towards that end. The process of fund-raising was transparent.

The FIR lodged against us was registered in response to a nine-month old complaint by some relatives and residents of the Gulberg Society, not from the office bearers of the cooperative housing society. The complaint was made on forged letterhead against which official society members have lodged a criminal complaint. This false complaint was registered in March 2013. We responded in detail to the complaint between March and May of 2013. We made declarations about the nature of our accounts and the nature of the donations we had received, as well as how we had utilised the money. The Ahmedabad Police's Crime Branch did nothing about the complaint for about nine months. They simply did not take our considered responses seriously.

Then, they suddenly registered an FIR against us. This came days after Zakia Jafri and I had announced our decision to challenge the lower court's order in the Gujarat High Court, asking that charges be framed against the then Chief Minister Narendra Modi. An old complaint that was clearly frivolous was brought out of a drawer and used for political purposes. The Crime Branch of the Gujarat Police acted with extraordinary zeal. Shivanand Jha, who was Commissioner of Police, was removed by the SIT in May 2010, at our behest on behalf of victim survivors, when the investigations were found to be faltering. He was Modi's blue-eyed boy. Jha is now in the Gujarat State Intelligence having 'served' as Commissioner of Police, Ahmedabad, for over three years. He has done well, along with other former Gujarat IPS officers with dubious records such as Keshav Kumar and A. K. Sharma.

The FIR claimed that donations were asked for and received by both Sabrang and the CJP. But this is an elementary error. It was only Sabrang that solicited money. The CJP works mainly to give legal aid to riot victims, whereas Sabrang is the general trust to work on communal harmony. On an illegal seizure notice personal bank accounts of Javed and myself as well as CJP and Sabrang's accounts have been frozen since January 2014. This illegal action by the police and even the banks shows a crude desire to paralyse our functioning while defaming us and maligning us in public. That there is no evidence for CJP's involvement shows how shoddy has been the investigation into this case.

At the time of the proposed memorial, there were no papers and no transaction between CJP, the Sabrang Trust or the residents of Gulberg Society. This shows that there is no evidence of fraud. What is cheating? You can say it is cheating if I have taken money from you or property from you. Neither has happened. There is no evidence here to amount to that. In fact, the original complaint about the cheating against us was not filed by representatives of the Society, but – as I have mentioned – had been typed by a few members on a forged letterhead, not the official one of the society. The authorized representatives of the society released an affidavit on 13 March 2013 to categorically deny that they had any conflict with us or our NGOs. They wrote,

> We state that the NGO has already authorized the society to sell the property last year and therefore there cannot be any grievance against the NGO as the society has not parted with any part of the land. Moreover, the donors don't feel cheated and therefore the signatories, who have not parted with a single pie, have no locus to file any such complaint against the NGO.

At the time the memorial was proposed, there were no takers for the flats in the Gulberg Society, which is in a Hindu-dominated area in the main city of Ahmedabad. Sabrang Trust proposed to raise money through donations to purchase the properties from residents at market rates, if it were able to raise the funds. Residents in turn promised not to sell their property until Sabrang was able to raise enough funds. By 2012 it was clear that land prices had gone up by four times, so we would have needed an amount which was now impossible to collect through individual donations.

Sabrang then informed Gulberg Society about the decision, which the Society accepted. At the end of 2012, the Society passed a resolution stating that owners could sell their property to people of any religion or race, as was the case since the society was built in 1963. This resolution was rendered void a little over half a year later, when the Gujarat government dredged up an old law that prevents citizens of a community from selling their property to people outside the community. The Gujarat Prohibition of Transfer of Immovable Property and Provision for Protection of Tenants from Premises in Disturbed Areas Act of 1986 was meant to protect people fleeing their homes from communal violence from making a hasty decision of disposing of their property and later regretting it. Around 40 per cent of Ahmedabad is covered by this act. In August 2013, eight months after the Gulberg Society resolution to sell their property to whomever residents pleased, and four months after Zakia Jafri filed her first case against the SIT's closure report, the Gujarat government suddenly extended the application of the law to, among other places, the Gulberg Society and Naroda Patiya. Gulberg and Naroda Patiya are two pockets in completely Hindu-dominated areas, which means they are obviously not going to be able to sell to their own community. Muslims don't want to live in the Hindu areas for the fear of risking their lives in a possible future pogrom. The law is illegal and it violates the right to own and sell property. The government has tied the hands of the residents, and in doing so, has forced them onto their knees. Their case is still pending in the court. This law and its use in Gujarat ought to have been a matter of independent investigation by the media in this country.

I have alleged openly that the fabricated case and application of an unconstitutional law have been engineered by a hostile state to try and push the survivors of Gulberg Society to the wall, in the hope that maybe one or two of them in desperation might bend to the will of the State and turn hostile even in their own criminal trial.

One of the main charges in the FIR is that the two organizations collected funds from foreign donors for the memorial and that these donations had been denied to the residents. This is inherently false as the work of the trusts involved a set of activities related to legal interventions and advocacy and communal harmony, advocacy and documentation, with the proposal for the memorial only as an aspect of a proposed project of the Sabrang Trust if enough donations had been collected. None of the donors to either Trusts have had any complaints with the manner or fashion in which the donated funds were used. No legal exchange of land or promises were ever made between us and the survivors. The memorial/museum was simply an aspiration that did not materialise.

The FIR was systematically conflated by false affidavits filed by the Gujarat Police Crime Branch. Figures and allegations varied: that the foreign donations Sabrang Trust received between 10 April 2007 and 20 February 2014, amounting to Rs. 2.62 crores, and that these were intended for the memorial. It also said that Citizens for Justice and Peace received foreign donations of Rs. 1.31 crores, also for the memorial. Both claims are false. In a 41-page public affidavit, we have shown excerpts from our accounts to prove that the total amount raised for the museum did not exceed Rs. 4.6 lakhs, only Rs. 50,000 of which came from foreign donors. Sabrang Trust received only Rs. 1.33 crore in total foreign funds during this period, the bulk of which went towards Awareness, Documentation and Peace Building. Citizens for Justice and Peace received Rs. 1.15 crores. The Ahmedabad crime branch manipulated our bank statements to arrive at the figures of Rs. 2.62 crores and Rs. 1.31 crores.

Looking over the evidence of the attack on me, Mridula Chari wrote,

The noise around the Gulberg museum case makes better copy than the tedious process of repeated appeals in courts, but the timeline of the controversy created around the memorial intertwines closely with that of Zakia Jafri's petition against the SIT report. On February 8, 2006, Jafri filed a 119-page charge sheet alleging that Gujarat's state machinery was involved in the riots. It took two years and a Supreme Court order for the complaint to be recognized. The court ordered certain cases to be reopened and investigated by a Special Investigative Team comprising five officers, some of whom were replaced over the years.

The SIT filed a closure report in 2012, but failed to share its findings with the complainants. The Supreme Court had to step in again and ordered them to file the report with a local court, which the SIT did only in February 2013. The closure report, which the defenders of Narendra Modi interpret as a clean chit for the Chief Minister, merely says that despite the evidence gathered by the SIT, which is documented in its voluminous report, there is not enough to merit a case against him.

But Raju Ramachandran, an *amicus curiae* appointed by the Supreme Court to independently assist the Court, disagreed, saying that the evidence against Modi was too significant to be judged at a pre-trial stage. In a parallel track, the first complaint about the Gulberg Society memorial was filed in March 2013, a month before Jafri and Setalvad filed their protest petition in April, and in August that year, the Gujarat government extended the Disturbed Areas Act to Gulberg Society.

'Narendra Modi is very upset with [Teesta Setalvad] because she is going after him', said Kingshuk Nag, author of a biography on the Gujarat chief minister. 'She is a hard-core Gujarati, and though she grew up in Bombay, she is from a highly regarded family. A lot of other people have not been as active as she has. She has been proactive in doing relief and rehabilitation work with victims, women and following up with Modi. Therefore he is taking advantage of the fact that she is in charge of these large organizations.'

While the merits of the Gulberg Museum case will be decided in court [our application for bail and de-freezing of accounts are now pending before the Supreme Court], this is not the first time that Setalvad and Citizens for Justice and Peace have been targeted by the Gujarat government. In the years after 2002, as it became clear that Citizens for Justice and Peace was going to continue to support riot survivors in their fight for legal justice, the Gujarat police filed FIR after FIR against me. Many of these have been stayed with the higher courts finding the claims in the criminal cases spurious.

The Gujarat government has had very little to do with any of the convictions in the 2002 pogrom cases. Of the cases pursued by the Gujarat government, only five per cent resulted in conviction. Of the cases pursued by the SIT or moved to courts in the neighbouring Maharashtra state, the conviction rate has been 39 per cent.[7]

In Mridula Chari's report, Ashok Mallik, a journalist with the BJP, said 'It is a fair argument that Setalvad is obsessed with a political battle against Modi. It is valid to say that he was the chief minister and he failed to control the riots. But to confuse a valid political case against him, with a legal case is a weak point.'

I dismiss this criticism. If it was the case that there was no material against Modi, then I think the Supreme Court of this country would not have ordered an investigation by the SIT. The fact that the SIT report could not find conclusive evidence, but the *amicus curiae* appointed by the court read the evidence differently, is obviously something the critics chose to deliberately ignore. The charges are against not just Narendra Modi but policemen and administrators in positions of power and responsibility. The

---

[7] Mridula Chari, 'The real story behind the corruption charges against activist Teesta Setalvad', *Scroll*, 21 March 2014.

case seeks to build a chain of command responsibility around the complete breakdown of governance and rule of law in the state of Gujarat in 2002; and does so meticulously, piece by piece, through evidence-gathering through state intelligence records, police control room records, phone call records and other evidence. R. B. Sreekumar, who was Gujarat's chief of intelligence in the months directly after the riots and who submitted a 200-page affidavit listing the circumstantial evidence against Modi, also disagrees with the idea that targeting Modi is unnecessary. 'Narendra Modi's plan is to keep the complicity level as low as possible, so that it doesn't reach him', he said.

In *First Post*, G. Pramod Kumar notes the Gujarat Police's 'overt enthusiasm' to arrest Javed and myself.[8] This eagerness followed the Gujarat High Court's rejection of a plea for anticipatory bail in the 'curious' embezzlement case. It proved, he wrote, 'the perception that the BJP government was on a hot pursuit of the activist.' The Gujarat Police rushed to arrest me from my home in Mumbai. They did not pause. What was not noted in all this, as Pramod Kumar suggests, was the 'deviousness in the police's insistence of custodial interrogation of the couple for alleged diversion of funds collected by her NGO to convert Gulberg Society in Ahmedabad, where 69 people were killed in the 2002 riots, into a museum.' We had been accused of transferring around 36 lakhs from Sabrang and CJP to clear our credit card bills and transfering large sums of money to our personal accounts. These allegations are utterly baseless. The credit card expenses falsely named as spent from trust funds were spent by us from our personal earnings and accounts. Since trusts cannot get credit cards in their names, we were each authorized to spend for the 'activities of the trusts', funds that were duly cleared by the board of trustees. Only those monies spent on travel, legal

---

[8] G. Pramod Kumar, 'Teesta Setalvad is being framed by the Gujarat government but why is there no outrage?' *First Post*, 19 February 2015.

aid and related expenditures as legitimate activities of the trusts were reclaimed by us.

By deliberately conflating the two sets of expenses – those for which we claimed re-imbursements and those we did not – the Gujarat Police, with the might of the powers that be behind them, falsely said that our personal expenses, which had been paid from our own income and included payments for wine, groceries and hair saloon, had been charged to the Trusts. The police viciously conflated my personal expenses charged to my card for wine, groceries and books with the official uses. This was done to damage my reputation. Journalists, many of them at least initially, unused by now to read and decipher legal documents themselves preferred to reproduce the bile of the State. For the record, for the period under discussion of nine years between 2004 and 2013, the average monthly honorarium for me was about Rs 39,000 per month and Rs 29,000 per month for Javed. Many of the journalists, editors and especially television anchors who unethically covered the allegations as incontrovertible fact today earn significantly higher remunerations backed as these channels are by the corporate sector!

Ravi Shankar, in the *New Indian Express*, known to be close to the RSS eco-ideologue S. Gurumurthy, even compared these allegations to those made against R. K. Pachauri – a man who had been accused by many of having sexually harassed them.[9] Shankar found no need to do any research. He did not talk to the secretary and the chairman of the Gulberg Housing Society, who had said that the twelve members who filed the complaint did not speak in an official capacity. Nor did he suggest that the twelve complainants had misused office stationary. He did not say that the complaint lay dormant till it became useful for the government. None of this

[9] Ravi Shankar, 'Out with the Dirty', *Indian Express*, 23 August 2015 and 'Beware the Pedestals of Infamy', *New Indian Express*, 26 July 2015.

appears in his two articles. It seems as if Ravi Shankar as many journalists on Times Now and Zee News, echoed the version of the Gujarat Police.[10]

Senior advocate Indira Jaisingh expressed her anger at these allegations of abuse of funds. 'As for the proverbial wine and visits to the beauty parlour, apart from the fact that they sustain the myth of the "five-star" activists, I must remind the courts that they hold their own legal aid meetings spending money meant for the poor in seven-star hotels. There is a record of a protest as regards this lodged by no less a person than a former judge of the Chennai High Court. Will they be swayed by such allegations now to refuse Teesta bail? This is not to admit on my part that money was so spent, but rather to expose the hollow legal nature of the reasons to oppose bail. It is nobody's case that there should be no investigation into the alleged misuse of funds, rather that the investigation be free and fair.'

'One cannot clearly miss the police targeting Setalvad,' wrote journalist Pramod Kumar, 'but what makes one more worried about their motive is their track record in foisting spurious cases against her.' He notes that in 2012 the Supreme Court slammed the state for initiating a probe for 'illegal exhumation' of the 2002 riot victims. The court said, 'This is a hundred per cent spurious case to victimize the petitioner', namely me. 'This type of case does no credit to the state of Gujarat in any way', said the Court. *It was a*

---

[10] *Pioneer*, edited by Rajya Sabha Member of the BJP, Chandan Mitra, has between 2010-14 been at the forefront of the vilification campaign and on three occasions we have served them notices for their spurious headlines and coverage, almost always with a large photograph. The reason I have relegated *Pioneer's* conduct to a footnote is because *Pioneer* has not functioned as an independent newspaper; *Indian Express*, otherwise a fine example of journalism, also succumbed on occasion to an onslaught from the powers that be. *The Hindu*, too, often failed to maintain a professional distance in its assessment of the SIT, perhaps becuase R. K. Raghavan is a regular columnist.

powerful judgment and should have been provided as context when the attack against me came over the credit card expenditure. A year after the Court had made that remark, the Gujarat Police used the charge of embezzlement to come after me. This was despite the fact that the office bearers of the Gulberg Society said that they had no complaint against me.

Why did the Gujarat Police come to Mumbai to arrest me? Pramod Kumar makes the case better than I could,

> The police's dogged pursuit brings us to the question of who Setalvad is. She is an exceptional character in India's human rights campaigns. She is the principal reason for getting justice, although partial, to the victims of the 2002 communal riots in Gujarat. For the first time in India, 117 perpetrators of communal violence, including a minister in the then Modi state cabinet, had been convicted. Had it not been for her and other rights activists, the victims would be gagged to submission. She is also the biggest obstacle to Modi's image management efforts.
>
> Obviously, Setalvad is a marked person because she is refusing to give up, along with Zakia Jafri, the complainant in the Gulberg Society massacre case, against the Gujarat state government and the then chief minister Narendra Modi although a Special Investigation Team had found no prosecutable evidence against him. Setalvad and her supporters, point to the dissenting notes by the Supreme Court appointed *amicus curiae* Raju Ramachandran, who had said that the evidence against Modi was significant.

Our victimization is 'too evident' to ignore, as Kumar and some seasoned activists and journalists could also see. And it hadn't started recently. In 2004-05, I was accused of pressuring Zahira Sheikh to give evidence against the government in the Best Bakery Case. The Supreme Court had later absolved me and sent

Zahira Sheikh to jail for a year. 'This is a classic example of a case where evidence were tampered with and witnesses won over', the court had then said.

On 14 July 2015, exactly a year before the Gulberg massacre verdict and more importantly a month before the hearing of the petition of the Zakia Jafri case, the CBI raided our home. This was exactly a week after the Union Home Ministry transferred an on-going investigation into our finances to the CBI.

Why has the government persisted in going after me? It was to stop me from pursing justice for the victims. As also to send a sinister message down the line. A brief recap of the timeline is instructive.

In April 2004 the Best Bakery Case is transferred and a re-trial ordered. On 3 November 2004, Zahira Shaikh turns hostile for the second time. This is after five eye-witness survivors – not previously examined by the trial court at Vadodara – have deposed and identified the accused. This was also the day before Zahira Shaikh was scheduled to depose before the re-trial court in Mumbai. Within three days, I move the Supreme Court for an Investigation into the allegations. An Inquiry under the Registrar General B. M. Gupta is ordered on 10 December 2004 and the report – that exonerates CJP and myself – is tabled before the Supreme Court in late August 2005. I have to seek anticipatory bail for the first time.

From December 2009, we persist in getting the SIT reconstituted and pursue the flimsy investigation by the SIT in the Zakia Jafri case before the Supreme Court. I appear before the Amicus Curiae after 20 January 2010. In September 2010, CJP submits explosive documentary evidence, including phone-call records of powerful perpetrators. The attacks against us become systematic and re-doubled.

Between December 2010 and February 2011, I had to

seek anticipatory bail twice. This means I had by then sought anticipatory bail three times. While in 2004, Zahira Shaikh had been manipulated by the state against us, come 2010 and a former employee was used as a means of attack. We now had to not only strive hard to meticulously build cases for the legal rights of the survivors of 2002, but spend time and energy on our own legal defence. We still pursued the Zakia Jafri case doggedly. By end July 2011, Raju Ramachandran, the amicus curaiae, in his report to the Supreme Court, clearly opines that there is evidence to prosecute the chief minister. The final order is delivered on 12 September 2011, preserving Zakia Jafri's right to pursue the criminal trial.

In April 2013, Zakia Ahsan Jafri, assisted by CJP, filed her Protest Petition. This is close to seven years after she had first proferred the criminal complaint against the chief minister and 61 others alleging criminal conspiracy, to the Director General of Police (DGP) on 8 June 2006. The filing of a Protest Petition is one allowed under the law when a complainant (this time also a survivor) fundamentally disagrees with the investigating agency. In this case, Zakia Jafri did not agree with the direction taken by the SIT led by Raghavan. His final report in the case came on 8 February 2012. It took Zakia Jafri and CJP over a year to access the investigation papers and reports of A. K. Malhotra (SIT member) filed before the Supreme Court. After arguments through most of year 2013, the Magistrate rejected the Protest Petition (26 December 2013). Within eight days, the son of Zakia Jafri, two other survivors of the Gulberg massacre and two trustees of CJP (Javed and myself) were falsely implicated in a criminal case by the Gujarat police. All attempts were made to prevent filing of the Criminal Revision Application (CRA) in the Gujarat High Court. This is required to be done within three months of the Order. Despite all the pressures, the CRA was filed in March 2014. For a year, official translations were undertaken of all documents. Just as the appeal was to be heard (August 2015), the CBI's onslaught on me began. The timing of the attacks is instructive. They come each time the case for criminal conspiracy moves forward.

The attacks on me and on Sabrang as well as CJP were all attempts to take away the focus from Zakia Jafri's petition and the victims of Gujarat. This was not the first time we were being defamed and I know this will not be the last. The strategy of the powerful perpetrator is mostly the same. Create an opponent in the enemy team. Buy off someone who seems close to us, has worked for us or someone we have worked with. Secondly, change the faces of the fight. Gently bring out the main perpetrator of violations. Let it no more be the fight between the victims of Gujarat and the rioters. Let the news become that I – who am giving legal aid – have cheated the victims. It might not change anything for the victims in the higher courts but it does change public perception towards us. The whole strategy is fascinating. It is both Machiavellian and Goebellsian.

Sabrang collected a total of Rs. 4.6 lakhs for the museum; it is still lying dormant in the trusts' accounts even as a bunch of frenzied men and women garner unsubstantiated lies to simply vilify us in the public domain.

Meanwhile the hearings in the Zakia Jafri case remain stalled. Hearings began on 3 and 4 August 2015. They continued for three more sessions in August before the SIT asked for adjournments. On the eve of the dates in March (10 and 11) set for commencement of the arguments, the SIT again asked for an adjournment. They said that the counsel was sick. The Gujarat High Court said that arguments would recommence on 6 and 7 April 2016. We have been since on hold, awaiting patiently our turn to make arguments against both the dismissal of the Protest Petition and the demand for transfer of investigation away from the much-discredited SIT.

Julio Ribeiro formerly of the Indian police wrote that the 'caged parrot' that sings to its master's tune 'is at it again'. He meant the CBI. It is an indictment coming from a man who was awarded the Padma Bhushan for his service to the police.

*   *   *   *   *

The media has been appalling in reporting the Gulberg massacre case and the Zakia Jafri petition. Since 2006, when the criminal complaint was sought to be filed, till date, there hasn't really been a sober and considered discussion on national television about what the case seeks to do. For a few brief hours, around 15 April 2013, after the Protest Petition was filed, a few channels projected the wealth of evidence that had been unearthed. To be lost again, in the deliberate and calculated slander campaign that was to follow.

My experience in going on Arnab Goswami's show on *Times Now* is indicative of the very poor situation in the media, especially the electronic media. Meenakshi Lekhi, whose father-in-law had insulted me in the Supreme Court in 2004, is of course with the BJP. She suggested on the show that Zakia Jafri, the co-complainant in the Gulberg case, had withdrawn her complaint. I refuted this and said that Meenakshi Lekhi was uttering a falsehood. I added that the Supreme Court has in fact treated Zakia Jafri's complaint as a First Information Report and has asked that either a charge sheet or a closure report be filed. I urged the anchor Arnab Goswami not to allow factual inaccuracies to go unchallenged. He breezily turned to Meenakshi Lekhi and asked her to respond to me. There was no attempt to ask her to stay with the facts. I am not sure if a journalist of Goswami's seniority was simply unaware of the facts or he simply didn't want to state the facts. It is hard to believe that he did not know that Zakia Jafri had not changed any of her statements in the courts (perjury). Or that he was not aware that the BJP's elected MLA Madhu Srivastava refused to cooperate with the Supreme Court investigation and give his voice sample to prove that he was not the person who openly claimed to have 'induced' Zahira Shaikh to have changed her version in Court. It was harder to believe that he didn't know that Supreme Court had taken cognizance of Zakia Jafri's complaint as an FIR. Seeing that the moderator lacked the integrity and intelligence to call spade a spade I walked out of the show.

Believing in the law and due process as I do, it has taken me a while to process that some lawyers just blatantly lie. Meenakshi Lekhi mentioned Zahira Sheikh on the show. As an Editor of *Times Now* and as an anchor of a Prime Time show, Goswami – who consistently displays his unprofessional bias by loading his newshour 'panels' to twist the tale – had also completely shirked his commitment to facts. Who in this country among senior journalists and editors – and who run 'shows' on 'law and legal jurisprudence' – would not know that Zahira had been put behind bars for a year by the Supreme Court for perjury? This was a historic judgment where for the first time a victim was put behind bars. It was also a strong message from the Supreme Court that lies will not be tolerated. Yet Goswami allowed his 'newshour' to continue as he has often done, with no respect for the truth, or facts. And allowed his 'favourite' Lekhi to spin lies on television.

But Arnab Goswami was not alone. The full spectrum of the press seemed eager to sensationalize the Gujarat Police's version of events and to ignore the facts. Or else the press seemed keen to please the Prime Minister.

Most powerful has been the open letter from Zakia Appa posted on Facebook, as abuse was sought to be heaped upon me and this post by her daughter Nishrin:

Betiyon ki baat niklegi to mere Abba ki baat aayegi . . .
Gujarat ki baat niklegi to Ahsan Jafri ki baat aayegi . . .
aur justice ke liye ladne ki baat aaygi to M.C. Setalvad, India's
first Attorney General ki grand daughter Teesta Setalvad ki baat
aayegi . . .
aur baat nikalegi toh phir dur talak jaayegi . . .

When the self-obsessed Narendra Modi had told the nation to 'post selfies' with their daughters as a tribute to the girl child, Nishrin had posted hers, with Ahsansaab, massacred brutally in Ahmedabad, on 28 February 2002.

*   *   *   *   *

I'm not always sure what motivates me to keep at it. Indira Jaisingh, an old friend and comrade in arms, says that my parents named me after 'a river in Bangladesh which flows fearlessly across borders'. There is also a clearer motivation. Soon after the 1992 riots, at a public meeting in Mumbai, many of us human rights activists, including Indira and I had agreed that if we had fought for justice against the perpetrators of the 1984 killings in Delhi, then the violence of 1992-93 might not have happened. It was the culture of impunity that had to be punctured. If after 1992-93 the findings of the Justice Srikrishna Commission had been accepted, and if the courts had convicted all the killers – including the instigators at the highest level – then 2002 might not have happened. During my struggle for bail, Indira Jaisingh remembered this discussion. 'It is this understanding that compels her to continue with the fight against the killers of the 2002 carnage. What we are witnessing is the power of the state and its terrorising arm, the CBI, to mount a raid on Teesta's home and office to prove that she misused foreign funds versus the power of the courts to hold power to account.

Who will win this battle? It is the courts of this country that are on trial, not Teesta.' My challenge is to fight the culture of impunity. That is what I have been motivated to do.

This long and dreary battle continues and when justice sometimes comes. it redeems our faith. One such moment was on 12 April 2004. It was the Supreme Court judgment in the Best Bakery case. The court said,

> When the ghastly killings take place in the land of Mahatma Gandhi, it raised a very pertinent question as to whether some people have become so bankrupt in their ideology that they have deviated from everything which was so dear to him. When large number(s) of people including innocent and helpless children and women are killed in a diabolic manner, it brings disgrace to the entire society. Criminals have no religion. No religion teaches violence and cruelty-based religion is no religion at all, but a mere cloak to usurp power by fanning ill feeling and playing on feelings aroused thereby. The golden thread passing through every religion is love and compassion. The fanatics who spread violence in the name of religion are worse than terrorists and more dangerous than an alien enemy.

A fortnight later the same bench of the Supreme Court also struck down the Gujarat High Court judgement calling both senior counsel Mihir Desai and me 'anti-national'. What was our offence? Assisting Zahira Shaikh to speak and record the truth in an affidavit before the Supreme Court. The brazen defiance of the Judge whose judgement was overturned became evident in 2016 when he delivered a speech calling the Supreme Court's judgement as act of 'judicial terrorism'.[11] When the CJP had, in 2003, decided to approach the Supreme Court for redressal after the star witness

---

[11] 'Former Gujarat HC judge questions independence of judiciary, talks of "judicial terrorism"', *The Indian Express*, 10 October 2016.

in the case Zahira Shaikh approached us, it was K. J. Sethna, brother to the judge and a senior criminal lawyer, who had given us sound legal advice. This had been confirmed by senior counsel Ram Jethmalani too, who until about 2006 at least chose to be on 'this side'. By 2009, he had become a firm supporter of Narendra Modi, even appearing for some powerful accused against us in the Supreme Court. His son displayed particular degrees of unprofessionalism in leading a campaign of animus against us.

As this book goes to print I was asked for a singular honour: to deliver the K.G. Kannabiran Memorial lecture in Madurai. Ending on a personal note, I quoted from a powerful piece this rare human being, human rights advocate and jurist had written for us in the April-May 2004 issue of *Communalism Combat,* after the historic verdict of the Supreme Court in the Best Bakery Case. Titled, 'A Question of Justice', Kannabiran severely reprimanded our Courts as only a person of his experience and understanding could do.

What happened in Gujarat in March 2002, what happened in Mumbai in January 1993, and to members of the Sikh community in 1984 are genocidal trends and courts, as enforcers of International Covenants, ought to have taken serious note of these blatant transgressions of human rights and devised jurisprudential and procedural tools to deal with this situation. 'A magniloquent attack on lawlessness is hardly a substitute for doing justice to the wronged. A court which innovatively protected propertied interests by devising the concepts of prospective over ruling and basic structure could have devised a concept for disqualifying a chief minister or other ministers as having been constructively responsible for the carnage by redefining a writ of quo warranto for meeting these situations. If the chief minister Modi had been disqualified on the principle of constructive responsibility, Rule of Law would not have become the fugitive that it has become now. Bal Thackaray's Mumbai is not going to be any different. Seeing Rule of Law fleeing like a fugitive could invite private justice and the terrorist may say, 'I shall repay.'

Another critical aspect, where we come in, both individually and as Citizens for Justice and Peace, was how the apex court has dealt with the issue of rights' activists and groups intervening actively to be with the victims and to see their fight through. The Gujarat High Court had seen fit to pass scathing remarks against us. Even on this, the Supreme Court ruling has created a judicial precedent. By not simply expunging the remarks but doing so actively with stern observations on the baseless observations by the High Court, the judgment lends credibility and strength to legal interventions by human rights defenders in the future,

The High Court appears to have miserably failed to maintain the required judicial balance and sobriety in making unwarranted references to personalities and their legitimate moves before the competent courts – the highest court of the nation, despite knowing fully well that it could not deal with such aspects or matters. Irresponsible allegations, suggestions and challenges may be made by parties . . . But such besmirching tactics, meant as innuendoes or serving as surrogacy ought not to be made or allowed to be made, to become part of solemn judgments, of at any rate by high courts, which are created as courts of record as well. Decency, decorum and judicial discipline should never be made casualties by adopting such intemperate attitudes of judicial obstinacy.

By ordering the historic transfer of this trial outside Gujarat to Maharashtra, the highest court has deliberated upon and accepted the arguments being made for decades – that were amplified a thousand times in the case of the Gujarat genocide – that such incidents underline the need for the system to operationalize areas and mechanisms of neutrality to avoid subversion of the process of fair investigation and justice, in short, due process of law. This judicial acknowledgment needs to be expanded to ensure institutional memory through reform. Be it Muzaffarnagar of 2013 or Assam of 2011 – if similar judicial standards are applied as happened during the intrepid Gujarat 2002 struggle for justice, will not justice become a more realisable norm? The unfortunate instances of communal violence that in the past decade-and-a-half have taken the distinct character of pogroms against religious minorities – Muslims and Christians – reveal distinct patterns and similarities. These were evident in full-blown measure in the Gujarat genocide. The first is the months of insidious preparation by outfits committed to the politics of hatred and division. They initially use hate-speech and hate writing to vilify and demonize a particular section, here a religious minority, and create a climate conducive to violent crimes against the demonized section. This technique, which has been well-honed, and also proven by over two dozen commissions of inquiry after every bout of communal violence, has, after the Gujarat genocide, acquired even more vicious dimensions. Documented cases of such a bias guiding or rather affecting the conduct of the police are now legion. Those of justice being delivered are rare and few. Preparations for communal carnage are not now restricted to hate pamphlets and speeches though these form a vital ingredient to cooking up such a hate-filled atmosphere. As I personally experienced and witnessed in Gujarat, preparations are now taking the form of full-fledged training camps of young men and women, where violence is projected as the sole means to self-empowerment and weapons are openly distributed, unchallenged by wings of the state and the law and order machinery. The potent drug that intoxicates these camps is hate anecdotes against communities wherein history is interwoven with current day politics and with the demonization made legitimate.

The system on its own does not intervene to deliver justice, condemn discrimination and slaughter; it has to be pushed to do so. It has been rare that our system has delivered in the case of communal carnage and crime. The pogrom against Sikhs in 1984 in the nation's capital or the post-demolition pogrom targeting Muslims in Mumbai have escaped judicial condemnation and correction. If the victims of earlier bouts of communal violence or pogroms did not have the satisfaction of a resounding judicial verdict in their favour, it doesn't speak well of the role of the police and the state and the existing legal and justice system. Our Constitution, then, remains on paper. Rarely do our courts initiate *suo motu* action on issues of mass homicide and rights atrocities.

It was only after the country experienced Zahira Sheikh's sensational testimony in a press conference organized by Citizens for Justice and Peace, Mumbai that the true import of the situation in Gujarat became real and was addressed by the courts.

What became transparent before the Supreme Court was not simply that a huge human tragedy had befallen Gujarat in 2002. The tragedy was compounded by an unrepentant administration and executive that two years later was without guilt or remorse. All police officers who had functioned without fear or favour, and they were many, are today side-lined in Gujarat. The vindictiveness of Modi and his men against Rahul Sharma, Rajnish Rai, Satish Verma and R. B. Sreekumar continues to this day, an all out effort to even deny honest officers their pension. The state, meant to rule by the Constitution is being used – and abused – to target those engaged in risky truth telling and documentation of a kind that is rare in post-Independence India. The role of the public prosecutor has been truly subverted by the state, with persons with distinct allegiance to the outfits who perpetrated the hatred and violence against the minorities being asked to represent the state! The struggle for justice has meant meticulously documenting all this before the courts so that any claim that we made was backed by irrefutable facts.

In September 2003 the then Chief Justice of India, V. N. Khare, had sharply chastised the Gujarat government for not only its failure to protect lives and property but for its open collusion in the subversion of the justice process. He had subpoenaed evidence in the now famous Best Bakery case. In 2004, Modi said of Khare, 'He can't distinguish between *khare* (just) and *khote* (unjust), but I would not like to make any statement against him.'[12] This was only one of two times that Modi heaped insults on Khare. The judge's remarks were occasioned by the state's abysmal failure to offer cogent explanations for the hasty completion of the Best Bakery trial (in a matter of a few weeks!) and the failure to protect evidence or to ensure that all witnesses had appeared for the prosecution, which led to speedy acquittals. It was possibly the first time ever in the history of independent India that the higher judiciary had spoken, and spoken sharply, in a case of mass communal violence. (The apex court then decided to monitor the government's appeal in the case and subsequently, in an indictment of the Gujarat high court which had dismissed the appeal, ordered retrial and transfer of the case to Mumbai, Maharashtra.). The indignities heaped on the Gujarat state apparatus included the cross-examination in open court of the two most senior civil servants in Gujarat at the time – its chief secretary, P. K. Lahiri, and director general of police, K. Chakravarti.

Two months after Khare's sharp remarks, the first ever conviction in a 2002 carnage case came from a court in Nadiad in Kheda district. On 24 November 2003 Judge C. K. Rane sentenced 12 persons to life imprisonment and three to two years' rigorous imprisonment. Forty-eight persons were acquitted. The crime: the brutal massacre of 14 Muslims at Ghodasar and Jinger

---

[12] 'Justice Khare's Remarks Irk Gujarat CM', *Times of India*, 3 May 2004.

villages in Kheda on 3 March 2002. Six years later, six convicts had jumped parole and the Gujarat state apparatus claimed inability to track them down. About a year earlier, in October 2002, two other carnage cases, Pandharwada, where about 25 Muslims were killed (the unofficial figure is higher), and Kidiad, where 61 Muslims had been chased and burnt alive in two tempos, saw complete acquittals. In both cases, senior elected representatives and functionaries of the ruling dispensation were accused; in both cases, the story behind the acquittals was similar to that in the Best Bakery fast track trial in Vadodara in May 2003 – witnesses had been made to turn hostile.

In February 2006 the Best Bakery retrial judgment of Judge A. M. Thipsay finally convicted nine persons (if the Gujarat police are to be believed, seven of the accused are still absconding!). On 30 October 2007 eight persons who were accused of rape and murder in Eral, Panchmahal, were sentenced for life, while 29 were acquitted. They were part of a mob that had brutalized, raped and then killed seven Muslims. In January 2008, in the Bilkees Bano case, also transferred to Mumbai, Judge U. D. Salvi sentenced 11 to life imprisonment. The case involved the brutal gang rape of Bilkees and the slaughter of her three-year-old daughter Saleha, during an incident in which 14 Muslims had been massacred. Though a constable was convicted for destruction of evidence, government functionaries, including doctors, escaped the arm of the law and senior policemen who had orchestrated the subversion of the case were let off by the court.

It is in this overall context that the 9 November 2011 verdict in the Sardarpura massacre case – which convicted 31 persons, all of them landed Patels responsible for assaulting defenceless agricultural labourers who had toiled in their fields for generations – must be viewed and assessed. Until then, this was the highest number of convictions ever recorded in a case of targeted communal violence in independent India. It is a tribute to the grit and courage of the 33 survivor witnesses, displaced from their homes, who testified in court, identified the accused despite threats and inducements and ensured that justice was delivered. That the case was one among those monitored by the Supreme Court, whose directives had ensured effective witness protection, enabled the impossible to happen. That the judge cleared Citizens for Justice and Peace and its secretary of malicious and motivated charges of tutoring witnesses was another landmark. None of this would have been possible without the energetic and committed CJP team, especially its lawyers in Gujarat. Advocates Yusuf Shaikh, Aslam Baig and Sameer Mansuri assiduously participated in an onerous process. In October 2016, the High Court pronounced its verdict on the appeal, acquitting 14 of the 31 convicted and confirming the convictions of 17 powerful accused. The next round of our legal interventions will now begin, appealing this verdict in the Supreme Court!

Remember that Gujarat 2002 was about 300 ghastly incidents in 19 of the state's 25 districts. Evidence was led through witnesses who testified about significant preparations by politicians and leaders of the Bajrang Dal who enjoyed state patronage and protection. Witnesses also sought to lead evidence on *Tehelka*'s courageous sting 'Operation Kalank' which revealed specific and relevant aspects concerning arms and ammunition being brought into Mehsana (the district in which Sardarpura is located) prior to the Godhra killings on 27 February 2002. At witnesses' insistence, the SIT did record the statement of *Tehelka*'s correspondent Ashish Khetan but they did not call him as a witness. Why? Though former director general of police R. B. Sreekumar's affidavits, with annexed reports of the State Intelligence Bureau, corroborated some of this evidence, the SIT was reluctant to probe this aspect further.

Sharp and aggressive in its approach to the Godhra train burning tragedy, the SIT and its prosecutor had not only bought the Gujarat police's shaky and shady version of conspiracy but had argued for the death penalty, which was imposed on 11 of the 31 accused. In the Sardarpura case, witnesses, being opposed to retributive justice, did not argue for the death penalty at all. And thus a niggling question remains: do we view the incidents of Godhra and post-Godhra as qualitatively and quantitatively different kinds of crimes? This is a tough one, which the Indian system would do well to answer.

While the above-mentioned verdicts stand out, individually and collectively, so far as criminal jurisprudence in the context of communal violence is concerned, the Naroda Patiya judgement is especially significant for more than one reason. In the other Gujarat verdicts, those convicted were mere 'foot soldiers'. But included among those given life sentences in the Naroda Patiya case are Babu Bajrangi and Dr. Maya Kodnani. Babu Bajrangi was a leader of the Bajrang Dal who enjoyed the patronage of top-level politicians in Gujarat. Dr. Kodnani, a BJP MLA in 2002, was elevated by Chief minister Narendra Modi to the rank of minister after the 2007 assembly elections in Gujarat. Judge Jyotsna Yagnik's verdict holds Dr. Kodnani guilty of criminal conspiracy, names her as the 'kingpin' behind the crimes committed in Naroda Patiya on 28 February 2002, describing the incident as a 'cancer for our cherished constitutional value of secularism', and awards her a stringent 28-year jail term.

It may be recalled that Dr. Kodnani is one of those named in the complaint of Zakia Jafri wherein she has accused Modi and 61 others, including top BJP politicians, bureaucrats and police officers, of 'criminal conspiracy to commit mass murder'. Thus

Judge Yagnik's ruling may well have implications for the case against Modi and others that is still before the courts. It was also a verdict where the narrative of gender violence returned, irrevocably to the legal jurisprudence, a rare tribute to the proceedings before the Judge.

* * * * *

If the constructed narrative to justify targeted crimes in 1992 and 2002 related to 'retaliation against violence (of the victim)' or 'who cast the first stone', three other narratives have since then been built upon these, brick by brick.

'Love Jihad', 'Ghar Vapsi' and now 'Gau Raksha' are the new slogans of the storm troopers of the extreme right: their targets are girls and women who express autonomy in forging relationships, Dalits, Christians and Muslims who are accused of 'converting away' from the main faith, and culture and food choice as vegetarianism is sought to be imposed.

All these terms are terminologies circulated to justify mass, targeted violence. They are also being used to test democratic institutions, especially Indian Courts, and actually bully them into accepting, as valid, a majoritarian and discriminatory governance and discourse. Slowly and surely what we are witnessing is a re-fashioning of the Indian Republic.

Where, then, will the resistance emerge?

What happens after the tale of mass violence is first told? Survivor's stories, narratives of neighbourhoods, all need not just re-telling but re-building. What happens to those who have been used as foot-soldiers, fed on tales of enemy othering and hate, even as the chief architects fast ascend the pyramid of state power?

These are some of the questions that have lingered on, seeking resolution through further action, maybe of an even more intense and all-encompassing kind. For lasting peace, and harmony, an edifice of justice must exist or be created. But do the paths of the peace-maker, the harbinger of harmony need to be distant or parallel from those who seek justice? Can they not, through concerted action, merge?

From November 2011 to February 2012, despite being the centre of vicious attack, we planned the tenth memorial of the Gujarat carnage, differently. We drew in young students of schools and colleges as well as reached out to the media and filmmakers who had in some way been part of the journey. For a week before, we worked, cajoling and persuading workers at the Ahmedabad Municipal Corporation to help spruce up the society. When I say 'we', it was a large collective effort, of activists, academics, students, photographers, writers and artists.

It was all to culminate in a one day memorial at the Gulberg society, where in the open, Shubha Mudgal would render songs of resistance, and healing. For months, we toiled within the society and the neighbourhood that had seen such blood letting and hatred. Deserted homes showcased narratives, banners with powerful words in Gujarati and English, proclaimed the tale. As night drew in and Shubha climbed on to the roof of Kasim Mansuri's home that was set as the dramatic, open-air stage with Aneesh Pradhan and Sudhir Patwardhan beside her, the strains of trial runs of the *tanpoora* and *tabla* filled the air. For an hour and a quarter soon after that, the voice of Shubha Mudgal, honed through the annual, January 1 performances at SAHMAT since 1990, rang through the neighbourhood. We had kept one of the side gates open; many 'others' from the neighbourhood crept in. Neighbourhood wedding processions quietened themselves for an hour, in what we believe, was a silent homage. Over one thousand survivors and friends from all over Gujarat, Mumbai and Delhi shared those precious moments and the journey. It seemed to throw open a pathway to the future.

For Zakia Appa, Salimbhai, Sairabehn, Kasimbhai, Tanveerbhai, Nishrin, their precious Gulberg society had, for some moments that day, become once again that dream bouquet of Indian pluralism that Ahsansaab had dreamt of.

There are a couple of favourite stories of mine that I share when I speak to young people, cajoling them to join the good fight, spare those precious few hours of every day to battle the politics of hate and deepen values of solidarity, equality and non-discrimination. One related to Khan *chacha* from Dharavi who, despite losing his elder son in December 1992 refused to divulge the identity of the assailants to his younger son. 'I want the cycle of killing to stop', was his simple rationale. Or Vimlabai Khavnekar, mother of Shiv Sena Shakha pramukh from Kurla who confronted the mob led by her son, Bharat Khavnekar and prevented it from marauding and butchering Muslim residents of a building located in an 'all Hindu street' (on the midnight of 7 December 1992). Can we build an India with footsoldiers of peace, harmony and justice in every mohalla and street? Can we reclaim this public space as our own? A space that belongs to the Constitutionally created Indian republic?

A battle rages for the heart and soul of India out there and in our homes, and we do not know yet, who shall win. It needs to be fought on the streets, within our homes and classrooms armed with arsenal from history, culture, poetry, music, literature – both everyday lived reality and a committed politics.

But when in the Naroda Patiya of Ahmedabad – on 27 July 2016 – Dalits marched silently with candle lights quietly proclaiming 'Dalit Muslim unity', survivors who had wept and fought, deposed in court and even won, received a powerful message: of an attempt to apologize for the brutalization of 2002.[13]

Maybe that then is one way into the future. Mass organization and mobilization on the path of reparation for crimes, affirmative action to ensure social justice, paved with attempts, at least, of a genuine reconciliation: based on the non-negotiable, equality and non-discrimination. Against the divisive politics of hate.

---

[13] https://www.sabrangindia.in/article/dalit-revolt-hindutva%E2%80%99s-successful-laboratory-gujarat

ACKNOWLEDGEMENTS

I now know what many women and men have meant when they said and wrote, how difficult it is to write about oneself. Myself.

For a chronicler, through journalism, law, history or social studies, trained through learning and hard experience to communicate ideas, beliefs, facts to be told by my publishers and friends that these Memoirs must be written, that they would serve a larger purpose, was difficult. I did not make my publishers sit easy. I have troubled them at every turn and they have borne this with grace and affection. Vijay Prashad and Sudhanva Deshpande, truly, this effort would not, could not, have come together without your patience and expertise. Thank You.

From almost the moment I began, until I finished, the writing of this book has been dogged by consistent and continued persecutions that not just continue but take newer and more vicious forms. 2017 is unlikely to be different, as vengeance appears to be the guiding star of the present regime. The CBI, directly under the Prime Minister's office, with senior officers from Gujarat ensconced there, has decided to charge sheet us on false claims of 'FCRA violations' when real monetary breaches of the same law (FCR Act) by trusts run by the former Gujarat Chief Minister, Anandibehn Patel and her daughter's trusts have, according to finding by RTI activists, been simply ignored with the Ministry of Home Affairs declaring that 'case is closed'. The media appears to have turned its eye away from this story, too. I face the possibility of yet another false criminal case (if 'leaked' newspaper reports are to be believed), this time for generating 'hatred' through my writings in training manuals for teachers and young learners. If the regime goes ahead with this, it will be the eighth false criminal case, this time lodged with the full weight of the government in power at the centre.

Overwhelming? Sometimes. Defeating, no. I remind myself, as I dig deep into reserves of mind and heart, as I realize as time wears on that it is indeed a lonesome battle, that there are other activists-journalists, battling as worthy a cause, in the far reaches of Odisha, Jharkand and Chhatisgarh, who have as many as 12 or 18 or 30 criminal cases filed against them by an increasingly rapacious state. Not only am I not the only one; there are others who are far, far worse off, facing even more serious charges. Solidarity is the need of the hour, the ability to re-enforce each other's worth, work and struggles, mandatory. The utter unaccountability of state agencies, law enforcement, intelligence and others is the single greatest threat to the quality of Indian democracy, a fact that our Courts still have to substantively respond to. Deep breaths and this constant reminder, helps me carry on.

The founding trustees of Citizens for Justice and Peace (CJP) and Sabrang trust deserve special mention here. CJP's founder president was Vijay Tendulkar. Living his entire life in Vile Parle, an icon among the rich world of Marathi theatre, the haunting spectre of divisive politics and communalism ate at him, from the 1990s right until the horrors of the Gujarat genocidal carnage burst upon us. I.M. Kadri and Alyque Padamsee, Cyrus Guzder, Anil Dharker, Nandan Maluste and Cedric Prakash, Javed Anand the work that CJP has accomplished would not have been possible without the exacting standards of accountability and transparency set by the board that matched the substantive and uphill task that CJP has taken upon itself. Ravi Kulkarni, Nakul Mehta and my very own baby sister, Amili Setalvad have been fellow and sagacious travellers in this arduous journey.

Though the *Memoirs* mention this at some length, some things bear repetition here. It is rare and lucky to have your lawyers, in the legal battle for human dignities and freedoms, also become close and trusted friends, the wider community that provides both succour and strength. So it has been with me. Mihir Desai, Aspi Chinoy, Aparna Bhat, Navroz Seervai, Suhel Tirmizi, Kamini Jaiswal, Sanjay Parikh, Ramesh Pukhrambam, not to mention Mihir's entire team be it Vijay Hiremath, Vinamra, Chetan, Anand. The going would not have been so much fun without you! Linked to this vast community is a growing chain of generous supporters, unshaken by the vicious bile unleashed against us, because of whom we have been able to doggedly continue. Their names are just too many to list.

As time flew by, and almost before I even knew it, two little precious babies have all grown up with minds and hearts and souls of their own: each with very different ways of showing this, yet so similar in their caring and sensitivity. For Tamara and Jibran a Ma's special love and regret for the family times lost to a near-obsession and passion, battling the fires of hate. Sorry. And thank you, for simply being you.

Mumbai
1 January 2017

TEESTA SETALVAD
is a journalist, educationist and activist.

Setalvad has worked with several Indian publications since 1983.
In 1993, she launched and co-edited *Communalism Combat* along
with colleague and husband, Javed Anand. This has been re-born
as an online portal, sabrangindia.in, since November 2015.

Trained in the law, Setalvad was convenor of the
Concerned Citizens Tribunal – Crimes Against Humanity,
headed by justices Krishna Iyer, P.B. Sawant and Hosbet Suresh.
The Tribunal included several eminent academicians and activists
and conducted an investigation into the genocidal carnage in
Gujarat in 2002.

Since April 2002, along with concerned citizens of Mumbai, she
set up Citizens for Justice and Peace (CJP), a civil rights group
to give quality and sustained legal aid to victims of mass crimes.
Setalvad is also an educationist working on issues related to
pluralism and democratic values in the curriculum especially
related to the teaching of history and social studies.

Setalvad has received national and international recognition
for her work.